CW00665702

THE RECIPE FOR HAPPINESS

JANE LOVERING

Boldwood

First published in Great Britain in 2023 by Boldwood Books Ltd.

Copyright © Jane Lovering, 2023

Cover Design by Debbie Clement Design

Cover Photography: Shutterstock

The moral right of Jane Lovering to be identified as the author of this work has been asserted in accordance with the Copyright, Designs and Patents Act 1988.

All rights reserved. No part of this book may be reproduced in any form or by any electronic or mechanical means, including information storage and retrieval systems, without written permission from the author, except for the use of brief quotations in a book review.

This book is a work of fiction and, except in the case of historical fact, any resemblance to actual persons, living or dead, is purely coincidental.

Every effort has been made to obtain the necessary permissions with reference to copyright material, both illustrative and quoted. We apologise for any omissions in this respect and will be pleased to make the appropriate acknowledgements in any future edition.

A CIP catalogue record for this book is available from the British Library.

Paperback ISBN 978-1-80415-252-2

Large Print ISBN 978-1-80415-253-9

Hardback ISBN 978-1-80415-251-5

Ebook ISBN 978-1-80415-254-6

Kindle ISBN 978-1-80415-255-3

Audio CD ISBN 978-1-80415-246-1

MP3 CD ISBN 978-1-80415-247-8

Digital audio download ISBN 978-1-80415-250-8

Boldwood Books Ltd
23 Bowerdean Street
London SW6 3TN
www.boldwoodbooks.com

This book is dedicated to the Kirkbymoorside Brass Band, who are absolutely real, very much deserve the accolades and awards they have won, and very much don't deserve the terrible things I have done to them in this book. It is also dedicated to my children, Tom, Vienna, Fern, Will and Addie, and their partners Zoe, Heather, Ryan, Emily and Sam. Love you all, guys.

PROLOGUE
YORKSHIRE DATING

Please complete all fields to help you have the best chance of finding a compatible match:

Name: Seren James

Age: 32

Height: 1.7 metres

Medium
Body Type: Select One From Box Above:

Divorced, living alone
Status: Select One From Box Above

Hobbies/Interests:

Tell us a bit about you!
I work as a cook at a daycare centre for senior citizens and also as a

housekeeper for the site, so I live above the job. And I'm looking for a friend/relationship with a man.

* * *

Three months later

From: YorkshireDating@toodleoo.com
To: SerenJames@yoyoboy.com
Hi, Seren!
We note that you've been a member for three months now and not had a single match from your chosen partner group! We've had a look through your profile and think you'd probably have a little more success if you put in a bit more about you! We've deleted, as requested, those less-than-satisfactory approaches (sorry about those, there's always a few and it's very hard to weed them out), but, in order for you to find your Perfect Match, we think you should consider filling in a few of your hobbies and interests – the things you do on a Saturday, the places you like to go, how you spend your spare time, that kind of thing.
Basically, make yourself sound a bit more interesting and we are sure that the dates will just flood in!
If you haven't matched with one person before 1 August, we will terminate your membership.
Yours
Richard, Sue, Bev and Amanda; the team behind YORKSHIRE DATING.

I held my phone up to Gregor, who had inadvisably, and somewhat drunkenly, asked about my love life. He and my brother, Andrew, had been the ones who'd got me signed up to Yorkshire Dating. Glowing with the success of their own relationship, which had now reached married status, they'd seen fit to decide that a single girl in possession of hair, teeth and half a brain must be in want of a boyfriend.

They were wrong. I mean, obviously not in the hair, teeth and brain department, I'd definitely got all those. But wanting a partner? Not so much.

'The dating agency is throwing me out. Even *they* can't find me anyone. Apart from those men who've sent me unsolicited pictures of what I have to assume were their willies. The pictures are usually so shaky-handed and out of focus that it's sometimes hard to know whether they photographed their genitals or their lunch.' I waggled the screen in front of Gregor as the wedding after-party continued around us at full volume.

'But they are right!' He swayed a bit. Those cocktails were *potent* and probably responsible for my oversharing. 'You must tell them all about you! Otherwise they cannot see the full glory that is Seren!' Gregor drained another glass of very pink alcohol. I'd steered clear of the punch because the stuff looked like it might glow in the dark. 'Andrew! You come tell your sister she must put all about her life!'

Andrew loomed over the back of the sofa. 'He's right, Seren, love,' he said, holding aloft a glass of something that looked as though it should register on the Geiger scale. 'You need to fill the form in properly. Greg, come over here, I've been telling Ernst about your latest design...'

I went to stand in the hallway. Around me, music played and couples danced, Andrew anxiously hovered to prevent food getting mashed into the carpet and nobody bothered about me and my email. It was the first time I'd ever been nagged by a commercial company. 'Make yourself sound a bit more interesting.' Huh. I *was* interesting! I'd just been having a down day when I'd filled in that form, and having Andrew and Gregor hanging over me, peering at everything I wrote, had been decidedly off-putting. Especially when I'd put 'medium' in the build/body type box, and Andrew had sucked his teeth and made wobbly head motions. But then, he was my brother, so winding me up was practically *his* hobby.

There were loads of things I could have put in the 'hobbies' box. There was... well. I quite liked walking. Outside, place to place, looking at views, rather than just perambulating up and down a corridor, obviously. Yes, walking. And... books? I liked books. Some of them. When I got time to read. Which wasn't often, now I came to think of it. I didn't have time for much walking either, except round the kitchen.

To be honest, my job left me so little time for hobbies that I didn't see how I was going to manage to fit a boyfriend in either. I narrowed my eyes at Andrew and Gregor, laughing, arms draped over one another's shoulders. I was fine as I was. My lack of anything approaching a life didn't bother me.

Odile, one of Greg's coworkers at the design agency, flopped against the wall next to me and fanned herself. 'Phew. Hot in here.'

'Mmmm.'

'You don't look like you're enjoying yourself much, Seren. What's up? Your brother's finally married, we can stop with all the planning and the lists and the stuff about the flowers and the cake – pressure's off! Let's party!'

'Mmm.'

Odile shrugged and whirled away off into the throng again. The high-ceilinged room was full of the smell of the very expensive floral arrangements. It was like being hit around the nose by a perfume manufacturer, and the white walls, dotted with choice pieces of artwork, led to the impression that I was existing inside an advertisement.

Everyone seemed happy. Everyone was drinking and chatting and dancing. Except me. Me and my email, telling me that I was such a loser that even a paid-for dating site was willing to drop me. I was probably dragging their statistics down.

Hobbies and interests? Who had time for hobbies and interests? Surely everyone got up, went to work and then came home to collapse onto a sofa and stare bleakly into space until it was time for bed. Didn't they?

I looked around me at the shrieking throng. This was the unfortunate thing, well, unfortunate for me, anyway. All Andrew and Gregor's friends looked like the kind of people who went to see Orson Welles retrospectives at weekends. Who wandered around art galleries and picked up 'choice pieces' from up-and-coming new artists for their homes. Who were taking classes in blacksmithing or burlesque dancing or, I dunno, rare frog breeding. In short, they all looked like people who had lives. Rich, fulfilling, activity-filled lives. And, in consequence, not one of them looked short of a partner.

But then, I tried to reassure myself, this is a wedding. Of course they've all brought partners. Who goes to a wedding alone?

And, over on the other side of the room, my reflection in a mirror that wouldn't have looked out of place at Versailles stared back at me and said, '*You* do.'

1

Two weeks later, once everyone had got the alcohol out of their systems and Andrew and Gregor were back from their honeymoon (ten days in Cancun), I was round at their flat again. For dinner this time, just the three of us.

'I have been thinking,' Gregor announced. He was big, and Polish, and every pronouncement sounded as though he were about to launch into an operatic aria. 'That we must find you a pastime.'

'*Little* bit patronising, love.' Andrew came in bearing something that looked home-cooked, although my professional eye spotted the slightly too regular sides, which meant he'd tipped it out of the Marks & Spencer container it had come in. 'Seren is quite capable of finding her own hobbies. Er. If she wants any,' he added, catching my glare.

'But she will be fired from her dating app.' Greg, not one whit abashed, tucked his napkin into his collar and picked up his knife and fork in happy anticipation. 'He's adorable,' Andrew always said about his husband, 'but a complete philistine.' But, since Greg always called Andrew something so totally Polish that neither of us could pick out any words, we let this go.

'I don't mind, honestly.' It was just nice to be sitting here in their immaculate Georgian house in York, with the original window shutters and the sweeping staircase that made me feel as though I should come down it in a ballgown doing high kicks. 'I don't really want anyone, Greg, honestly.'

'I have been thinking.' Greg helped himself to shepherd's pie. The two of them lived the life of art gallery owners; stylish and cutting edge, but they ate like a pair of pub landlords on their day off. 'You need a hobby.'

'No, I don't.' Definitely one of Marks' finest, I thought, staring at the meat and potato concoction in front of me. Slightly too much potato, that would be a budgetary choice, and I wouldn't have made the gravy quite so thick. But then, I pondered, turning over my serving with a fork, I cooked for people who complained about the texture and colour of everything I made.

'And I think you should come along to my evenings.' Gregor finished his pronouncement by ladling up a forkful of mash and smacking his lips with anticipatory relish.

'Oh, God, no.' Andrew covered his eyes. 'Please, love, don't subject Seren to your group!'

'And why not?' Greg eyeballed my brother across the immaculately set table. I mean, only these two would use antique china and hallmarked silver to serve a supermarket ready meal. I quietly envied them. Oh, not for their coupledom, which seemed to consist of discussions about work, interspersed with meals of incredible homogeneity. More for their sheer reckless style, where nothing mattered enough to be kept 'for best'.

I had a whole wardrobe of clothes and a dresser of china I was keeping 'for best'. There was dust on the handles of both.

'Because – well, it's Dungeons & Dragons, isn't it?' Andrew

lifted appealing eyes to me across the Regency table. 'Seren isn't interested in playing games with your Band of Brothers.'

His certainty annoyed me. All right, he was my older brother, but he seemed to think that my life was so stereotypically 'single woman' that he was only one step away from passing me knitting patterns and *Hetty Wainthropp Investigates* DVDs.

'I might be.' I helped myself to the food. It was just nice to be able to eat something I hadn't had to cook, even if Messrs Marks & Spencer had squeezed most of the flavour out of something I could have made both sing *and* dance. 'When's your next session?'

SEREN'S ABSOLUTE ULTIMATE COTTAGE PIE

Honestly the best thing ever, and it mostly looks after itself after the initial prep, so it's great for meals where you don't want to, or can't, be in the kitchen all day.

Take some minced beef. You can use Quorn too, apparently. I haven't tested that so don't quote me, but for vegetarians it's worth a shot. How much you need depends on how many you are feeding, so I won't bother with quantities. Fry it off in a saucepan with a little oil and some chopped onion, garlic, mushrooms and any other bits of veg that are lurking in the bottom of the fridge and looking a bit wrinkly and like they want using up. Once the mince is brown and looking 'mincey' tip the whole lot into a slow cooker. Yes, you really need a slow cooker for this one, the oven just doesn't do the job, plus then you can cook it overnight if you need it for lunch. Slow, gentle cooking is the real secret here.

To your mince-and-awful-veg, add a cup of red wine, a tin of chopped tomatoes, one of those Stock Pot things (beef is good, or veg if you are using Quorn or it's all that you've got in the cupboard) and a sprinkle of gravy granules. Basically, you can shove in anything that isn't too heavy on the liquid. The slow cooker doesn't allow evaporation, so if you use too much liquid, your results will be very sloppy – this doesn't really matter, you can always pour off some liquid at the end and use it as a sauce on something else later. Give it all a good stir, turn the slow cooker on to low, and leave for at least seven hours. Overnight, as I said, is good, because then it's ready for lunch time, but if you're serving in the evening you can leave it on all day. Slow cookers are made for this sort of thing – it won't burn the house down or use a fortune in electricity.

When you need to think about assembling your cottage pie, turn off the slow cooker. Make some mash (don't waste cheesy mash on this, just ordinary mash will do). Pour the mince into an ovenproof dish (now is the time to drain off any excess liquid if it's a bit runny) and dollop on the mash. Do not forget to fluff the potato so you get crispy bits! Now put your dish into a hottish oven (about 200 degrees C, but, to be honest, it doesn't matter too much) until the top of the potato looks brown and the mince is hot right through.

2

'Custard was a bit lumpy today,' Joe commented. It was Monday and I was back at work, at what we sometimes referred to as 'Day Care' – the drop-in centre for the elderly where I cooked, cleaned, helped with some basic tasks and played more Scrabble than any human should ever have to.

'It was not,' I responded, mildly. 'And Qwerty isn't a word, Joe.'

'Bloody is. It's the name of a keyboard.' Joe, who was ninety and would use his age to give himself an advantage in anything, shifted in his chair. 'I should know, I only bought one the other day.'

'Then it's a trade name and disallowed.' I hunted for the dictionary – battered and abused and, I suspected, with several 'rude' pages removed.

We were busy today. An increasing number of what we had to call our 'service users' were coming in the morning and staying all day now, when we'd originally been conceived of as a lunch club. More older people were moving in with family, or having family move in with them, and as costs rose many of those families now comprised two working parents and children who were at school or college all day. Fewer of the maiden aunts, the widowed sisters and the housewives who would previously have provided company to the less than sprightly. So our 'customers' were increasingly being left alone all day, and choosing to come here rather than sit by themselves in home, library or coffee shop. For a monthly fee we provided heat, company and food. And also, someone to listen to them.

Behind Joe and me, the room was full of bustle. Lena and Margaret were knitting side by side, looking companionable but in actual fact deep into competitive grandchildren territory. John was shuffling his way down to the TV, using his frame to batter all comers out of the way. Tom and Grace, whom we had long suspected of conducting a flirtation, were sitting together on the donated sofa sorting through a pile of – also donated – books, and Will was showing Jim, our newest member, around the room with particular attention being paid to the aircraft photographs on the wall. Will *really* liked aeroplanes.

'Couple of new people to introduce today, Seren.' Holly, the senior manager, who ran the charity, came into the room. Everywhere Holly went, she bustled. She could make herself look busy just walking down the street. She always seemed to have arms and legs going like pistons as though every step she took were a matter of life and death, and she made carrying a box from one end of the room to another feel like the most important job in the world. Her husband was a small, pale man who looked as though he didn't get enough sleep, and we rarely saw him. He probably used Holly's working hours to lie very quietly in a darkened room.

'I've already met Jim,' I said, putting 'wand' down underneath the disputed 'Qwerty'. It really wasn't worth arguing with Joe. He'd hit you around the head with the fact that he was ninety until you gave in.

'No, other new ones.' Holly rotated, presumably in search of the newcomers, giving every centimetre of movement the same degree of importance as a lighthouse beaming its searchlight out to sea to protect mariners. 'Mimi and Ned. Where *are* they?'

'I'm over here.' A muffled voice came from behind a pile of cushions being transported from the store cupboard under the stairs by a selection of arms and legs that presumably belonged to either Mimi or Ned.

'Oh, so you are.' Holly continued to save lives at sea. 'And Mimi?'

'I left her over there.' The cushion pile dipped, indicating the far corner, where I could now see a lady sitting, alone. She looked to be in her early eighties, immaculately dressed but in a circle of quiet and solitude, which was unusual in our crowded little location. Usually, newcomers would be swiftly descended upon and drained of details of housing situation and grandchildren within seconds. Lena and Margaret were like life-experience vampires.

Well, that narrowed it down to the cushion-carrier being Ned, anyway.

'Ned's just joined us.' Holly went on, now stooping to pick bits of lint off the carpet. Keeping these rooms clean and tidy was my job, and part of the reason I got to live in the flat upstairs. Holly could make Mrs Hinch feel as though she weren't doing a thorough enough job. 'He's going to be driving the pick-up bus that collects some of our members from home.'

I had no idea why she was telling me this, as though I had no idea what the 'pick-up bus' was, and perhaps suspected that it was for more nefarious purposes.

'He's also going to assist with general medical needs and jobs about the place,' Holly went on, then lowered her voice slightly. 'He's salaried.'

Those of us who were paid to be here occupied a slightly higher tier in the minds of our customers than the volunteers who came and went. I think they liked the fact that we were constant and they gained comfort from knowing that familiar faces would be here, as the floating population of volunteers could change almost from day to day. Given Joe, John's shuffly processes, Lena and Margaret's grandchild obsessions and Will's peculiarities regarding aviation, nobody could really blame them. A lot of volunteers thought the job would be sitting around chatting about the old days to people with ill-fitting dentures, when really it was like managing a school playground whose occupants were allowed to smoke and watch 18-rated films.

Since Ned was still currently just a pile of upholstery, I couldn't comment.

'Can you go and talk to Mimi?' Holly continued to act as though the carpet were a haven for filth, picking at it as if the pattern personally offended her. 'She's very quiet and I'm worried she might be lonely. She's coming in from a cottage up on the high moor, her people made the arrangements.'

'Her people' would be the family Mimi lived with. A surprising number of families treated us as though we were synonymous with DPD and would 'make arrangements' for elderly relations to be picked up and taken back to their homes like parcels.

'I can try.' I stood up.

'You're only going cos you're losing,' Joe remarked, putting 'dimity' on my D from 'wand'.

'I'll take over,' the pile of cushions said, and wobbled their way to the table, while I went across the room to where Mimi sat, hands in her lap and eyes turned to the window.

'Hello,' I said brightly. 'Have you been introduced to everyone?'

Mimi continued to sit. She wore immaculate make-up and her hair was carefully coiffed into soft waves, as though she'd taken a good deal of care over her appearance to come here. The hands resting in her lap were twisted and misshapen with arthritis and there was a stick propped beside her chair.

'It can be a bit overwhelming at first when everyone seems to know everyone else. But you soon get used to it. We're a very friendly lot,' I continued, although Mimi did nothing but turn her head slightly away and shift her hands under her skirt.

'Would you like me to fetch you a magazine? Or a puzzle?' I sounded a bit desperate now. I was fairly certain Mimi could hear, despite her resolute refusal to look at my face. Maybe she was recently bereaved and not yet ready for thrusting into the throng. Some of the families of our customers seemed to believe that the best cure for the death of a spouse was for their elderly relative to immediately get out of the house, as though death were an infectious disease. I could only try to imagine what it must be like to lose the companion of half a century and then be expected to re-enter busy society. To shrug off the death of someone so close; parcel them up and dispose of them like a week-old bouquet.

'I'll fetch you a cup of tea.' This was my final gambit. Normally, even with the most reticent of service users, that would bring a wan smile, an acknowledgement that the British answer to everything was a good cup of tea. From Mimi, though, it brought nothing. Her pale, composed face with its sapphire-blue eyes continued impassive.

'We're having music,' Will declared to me as I crossed the room again in search of the teapot, which was ever present, circling the throng like an eager dog. 'It says here.'

He tapped his stick on a wall poster that announced that the Kirkbymoorside Brass Band would be playing in the car park next month. Tea and cake would be served and there would be stalls selling produce. It was another of Holly's 'fundraising initiatives'. I had to hand it to her. She was very big on things like 'involving the community' and 'integrations', but she was even bigger on making sure there was enough money to pay our wages and keep this place ticking over. Her ceaseless energy and incessant need for 'incentives' might be incredibly wearing, but it kept us financially afloat and made sure there were enough funds for big dinners and an annual trip to Fountains Abbey.

'She didn't speak to me either.' A man I'd never seen before was suddenly at my elbow. He had the look of someone built out of fuse wire, all lean and crackling with energy. I wondered if Holly had a load of rechargeable people in her understairs cupboard, with the hoover and lawn mower. 'Sorry,' he continued, holding out a hand. 'I'm Ned. I was behind the cushions earlier.'

'Oh.' I was surprised by his apparent youth. Well, 'youth', he was probably about the same age as me, early thirties, although his dark hair was flecked with grey and there were lines on his face that made his age impossible to guess. 'Welcome on board.' I shook his hand. 'You soon get used to it.'

'Er,' he said. 'Yes.' He was exactly my height, so when he looked at me we were eye to eye and there was an expression hidden within the depths of his hazel gaze that made me wonder. 'Anyway. As I said, Mimi didn't speak all the way down in the bus. I picked her up at Farndale. High in the moors,' he added, pointing behind him in the vague direction, as though I, born and raised in North Yorkshire, might be uncertain as to their precise location. 'It's very remote,' he finished, as though it were my fault.

'They still talk up there though,' I said. 'It's not all hand signals and whistling.'

'Sorry?'

'I doubt the remoteness is the cause of Mimi not speaking.' I looked over again at the lady, still sitting erect on the chair, head slightly averted from the noise and kerfuffle of the room. 'She seems – lonely,' I added, aware that I shouldn't ascribe emotions and intentions to those who didn't want to communicate them to me. Plenty of our people had grown up in a time where feelings were not talked about.

'Well, we can't make her socialise. She may warm up a bit when she gets more used to things.' Ned gave me a grin. 'I'll leave you to the tea you promised her. I ought to get back to Scrabble. Joe's just having "thinking time".'

'He's got a dictionary on his phone,' I said. 'Watch him like a hawk.'

Another sudden grin from the surprising Ned. 'Thanks. I will do.'

I wandered into the kitchen to make more tea and, while the kettle boiled, I leaned against the lovely scrubbed-pine table and stared out of the window. Maybe I could put 'Scrabble' down as a hobby on the dating app? No, it made me sound as though I never went outside. The car park, with the minibus blocking my view of the town, gave me no inspiration. 'Making tea' wasn't a goer either, even though it was how I spent a lot of my time when I wasn't playing Scrabble.

The dishwasher thrummed into its rinse cycle behind me. What *did* I do with my spare time? Did I even have any spare time? This was the problem when you lived over the shop, so to speak. Even when you weren't at work, you were at work, and I'd often potter downstairs after everyone had gone home, to straighten cushions and blankets, change the odd dried floral arrangement and generally enjoy the peace of the place.

'Pottering' wasn't a hobby either, unless you were over seventy. I wanted to make myself sound go-getting and a catch for the right man and so far all I'd got was a knowledge of all the two-letter words in the dictionary, a winning way with fifty varieties of tea and a cupboard full of crocheted throws. Yeah. I was a real guy magnet. As long as the guy in question was a permanently hydrated anagram fetishist with a love of blanket stitch. Which was not what I was looking for.

Unfortunately, since I didn't really know what I *was* looking for, and doubted that Tom Hiddleston had any interest in handicrafts or word puzzles, I was floundering.

3

So I really only had myself to blame, I thought, sitting later that week around Andrew and Gregor's table again, now stripped of its snowy linen and instead covered in a green cloth and a large board.

Gregor, 'Dungeon Master', which sounded a lot more excitingly S & M than it turned out to be, was at the head of the table. Bent close around me were seven men. They'd been introduced, but they had all blurred into single syllables like Jed, and Seb, and a background wash of logo'd T-shirts and tattoos. There was quite a lot of hair too, some beards with metal woven amongst the growth, and more flopping locks than I'd ever seen outside a cheerleader convention. Apparently, 'the boys', as Greg fondly referred to them, operated as a heavy-metal cover band when they weren't playing Dungeons & Dragons. I wanted to take them aside and have a word about stereotyping, but they were all over six feet tall and mostly built of leather, so I didn't dare.

I pulled my chair back slightly so someone could 'roll for damage', whatever that was. I half expected them to get down on the floor and try to batter themselves against the Victorian bureau, but they didn't.

What on earth was I doing?

'Your turn, Seren,' Greg announced and the entire group looked at me expectantly. 'Your character needs to make a decision. Go on through the enchanted wood or go into town to try to find the magician.'

Seven lots of hair whipped in my direction as we all bent low around the board. 'We shouldn't head into the wood,' muttered the one who I thought was called Nate. 'We need the magician.'

'But if he's not in the town, he may be in the wood,' another one whispered to me. He had a name with slightly more syllables, but a T-shirt so embellished with skulls and rivets that I hadn't been concentrating when he'd been introduced. I'd been wondering how he got it through the washing machine.

'Just roll and see what happens,' Gregor suggested.

I rolled and my chaotic neutral wood nymph character was enabled to do something, which made all the men gasp and mutter various solutions to me, most of which I obediently carried out, without having the slightest idea what was going on.

I was tired. It had been a busy day. I'd overcooked the banana bread and there had been rumblings of dissent during afternoon tea. What I'd really wanted to do with my evening was sit up in my little flat with a magazine telling me how wonderful my life could be if I wore more make-up and went on city breaks, and then go to bed.

And yet, here I was. Even though the first five minutes of play had promptly demonstrated that Dungeons & Dragons – filled to the brim with eligible men though it might be – was not going to be my new hobby of choice.

'So, you going to take this up, then, Seren?' The generously bearded face of Seb, who'd apparently been in my war party, which should give us a level of closeness if only I knew what a war party was, grinned at me as we shoved the board away into its corner. 'It's great, eh?'

'It's a bit confusing,' I said honestly.

'To start with, yeah, but you soon get into it.' Ulrich clapped me on the shoulder. 'You did good.' The rest of the men nodded and asserted that, yes, apparently I had done good. It was like being approved of by the Foo Fighters.

'Next time you can build your own character.' Jed nodded. 'It's better if you do it yourself.'

Andrew, hovering anxiously over the table with an armful of white linen, nodded vigorously and gave me a look, which I asked him about as soon as the door had closed behind the last leather gauntlet and motorcycle boot.

'What was that for?' I began helping him to reset the table.

'What?'

But I'd known my brother all his life, minus the first eight years before I'd been born. He was tall, blond and tidy and we looked as though we came from two different families. '*You* know. That look.'

Andrew gave a huge sigh and sat down on the antique chair. He conspicuously checked around the room for Gregor, but he was downstairs, showing the boys out. 'You're letting things happen again, Seren,' he said, on another sigh. 'And don't pretend you don't know what I'm talking about. We've had this conversation before.'

Then he stood up and began smoothing the tablecloth over the highly polished surface of the table, murmuring soothing words to it about its desecration at the hands of the gamers. Andrew tended to have control issues, which, again, made it appear we came from very different stock.

'I'm not,' I said, but without much conviction because he was right, but him being my elder brother meant that I had to negate everything he said, from force of habit.

'You want to meet someone special, but you don't do anything about making it happen – you only joined that dating site because Greg and I pushed you into it. You didn't want to come here and play that stupid game...' He looked around quickly in case Greg had come into the room unheard. Andrew didn't understand his husband's desire to be surrounded by battle elves, mages and sorcerers, but he endured it. 'You want a hobby or some interests, but you don't want to actually go and get any.'

The cloth was neatened and straightened and he put the vase of flowers back in the middle, carefully centred on its mat.

'I'm busy,' I said, and the note of defence was so loud that it pinged off the mirror. 'I don't have time to wander about getting hobbies and stuff.'

'Well then, how the hell do you *think* you're going to meet anyone to date, then?' Andrew stood back, tweaked the floral arrangement, then nodded, satisfied. 'Unless you're going to start on the octogenarians you work with, you *need* to get out! You need to put yourself about and actually *do* things! I know you feel all lovely and safe in that tiny flat with work downstairs, so you don't even need to go outside unless you have to – and, I have to say, the lack of exercise is beginning to tell, love, you need to start Pilates or something – but safety isn't going to find you a partner, is it?'

Gregor could be heard now, rattling back up the stairs amid a flourish of Polish. Andrew widened his eyes at me, an unsaid reproach, and we dropped the subject.

But I thought about it on my drive home. The winding lanes between my brother's immaculate flat in York and my place on the edge of the small town were most conducive to thoughts about the past and the future. No broad motorways, shooting at speed from one unknown destination to another, weaving in and out of others whilst flashing past slip roads and overpriced-petrol signs. Just well-known, gentle flowing single carriageways, where I could pick my own speed and didn't have to be alert for sudden lorries or idiots in BMWs whose indicators, apparently, hadn't worked since the car came out of the factory. Just the tall, waving summer stems of Queen Anne's lace laying out a white background to the unfurling fingers of meadowsweet and the dots of rattle and buttercup.

Andrew was right, damn him. And we *had* had that conversation before. After the break-up of my short-lived marriage, when I had become a virtual recluse, swearing never to have anything to do with men ever again – excepting Andrew and Gregor, of course – and exhibiting a degree of insularity that, Andrew had told me, bordered on agoraphobia. Apparently, I'd started to let life happen to me, even during my marriage. I'd allowed my ex-husband, Hugh, to direct me and to dictate our marriage: where we went on holiday was up to Hugh. Where we shopped and what we bought were up to Hugh.

I hadn't explained to Andrew that Hugh was so exceptionally self-assured and convinced that his was the right way that trying to deviate from his path was like trying to avert an avalanche. A few muttered objections and complaints weren't going to do it, you had to have a spreadsheet and be prepared to give a presentation, with slides, as to why you should be allowed to do things your way. So, it was easier not to. To go along with the juggernaut of Hugh's personality and pretend that he'd swept me off my feet and just carried on sweeping.

I got back home, trundled up the stairs to my flat and shut the door thankfully. The summer sun, reluctant to allow dark a piece of the action at this time of year, was skulking down behind the spire of the ancient church; from my kitchen window as I filled the kettle I could see the sky staining red. The spire stood like a huge middle finger to the night, backed by the scarlet clouds, and I nodded approval of its sentiment as I made myself a sandwich. Greg and Andrew were hospitable, but shocking cooks. Tonight's sustenance had been a bowl of crisps and some cocktail sausages, and those had been shared with the burly heavy-metal boys. I was *starving* and Andrew's jibe about my gaining weight could be shoved up his carefully curated collection of artwork.

Just as I was about to bite into my impromptu meal, I heard a sound from downstairs. A muffled bump, as though someone had walked into a chair. A hasty look out of the window showed nothing amiss. The minibus was parked in its usual spot with no gang of youths attempting to hot-wire it. Nobody was hanging around suspiciously. But then the bump came again and I, mindful of the reason I was given the accommodation 'over the shop' (before I'd come here to work, the staff had managed to lock one of our clients in overnight when she'd fallen asleep in the toilet, which had been insufficiently checked at closing), I armed myself with the nearest thing to hand and tiptoed down the internal stairs to the door that led to the kitchens.

There were definite noises in there. Clonks and scuffs. Someone was inside. There was nothing much worth stealing, but then again, there was nothing much for the local kids to do, and long warm summer evenings tended to bring out menace and boredom like it brought out heat rash. I flung the door open, wielding my weapon, and announcing my presence in slightly muffled tones, as my heart was thumping so hard that it wouldn't let me speak clearly.

'What's going on?'

Ned, who'd been in the process of upending a packet of pork scratchings to tip the last into his mouth, jumped, choked and fell backwards off his stool. He landed, like a load of damp washing, out of sight on the floor behind the table.

I stood and stared. Seeing it was Ned had settled my heart a bit, and I now realised that the rolled-up copy of *The Yorkshire Post* I was carrying probably wasn't the burglar deterrent that I imagined. Eventually, his head appeared over the top of the table as he got to his feet. His dark hair was sticking out at angles, damp with sweat, and his face, when it moved within view, looked shocked.

'What are you *doing*?' He pulled himself to his feet and flopped, as though exhausted, over the tabletop.

'Investigating strange noises.' I tapped the newspaper cudgel on my hand, for all the world like a cartoon wife about to say, 'And what time of night do you call *this* to be rolling in drunk?'

Except Ned wasn't drunk and he wasn't rolling in. By the look of the equipment he'd got spread out on the floor, he was here replacing the dodgy element on the cooker.

'I thought you were out,' he said. 'I came over to fix this. You've been complaining about it all week.'

None of these statements were anything I could deny. He was perfectly right. Part of his job would involve a degree of 'handyman' work: mending small items, keeping the place in good repair. Just as part of mine involved cleaning, tidying, and replenishing the teabags. And I *had* been muttering grimly to myself about the cooker element, which only heated up properly when I wiggled the knob. I had to mutter it to myself, because the phrase 'wiggling the knob' had caused John and Will a fit of the most childish giggles and a retrospective examination of their marriages.

'Um.' I tapped the newspaper again. 'Well, I'm here.'

'I can see that,' Ned said dryly. 'Now you know it's only me, you can go upstairs again. I won't be much longer.' Then he turned his back, screwed up the pork-scratchings bag with what looked to be a degree of ferocity, and flung it down with the obviously defunct cooker element, laid on a towel on the floor.

Ned and I hadn't really had much to do with one another since our introduction. He seemed friendly enough when we interacted, but then we'd usually got a crowd of onlookers – even if some of them did have to look on through fairly thick spectacles. He'd been busy and I'd been busy; the summer meant that we were getting more drop-ins than usual, as people came into town to shop or just for company in the warm weather.

'I'm sorry,' I felt bound to say. 'I really didn't know you were coming over. I thought it might be burglars.'

Ned looked, ostentatiously, around the large kitchen space, quite clearly devoid of any items of resalable value.

'We were broken into once.' For some reason I carried on. 'OK, that was by a drugged-up idiot who mistook this place for a pharmacy and who was apprehended by the police staggering down the street carrying a decorative warming pan, but even so.' Once. Years ago, before I'd even worked here, when the building had been used only as a lunch club for the elderly.

'You don't need to keep talking,' Ned said, his voice echoing around the cooker's insides as he bent back to his task. 'I know you're upstairs as a security measure.' He looked at me over his shoulder. He was doubled up, half inside the big, recalcitrant stove, looking as though an absent-minded wicked witch had been called away mid preparation. 'As I said, I won't be much longer.'

I'd been about to offer him a cup of tea, but his tone was as cold as the inside of the oven. Or was it embarrassment? Which was ridiculous as it was I who should have been embarrassed; bursting in like an avenging angel armed with unbiblical newsprint.

Without another word, I turned around and went back up my staircase, closing the door to the little flat behind me with something that felt like reluctance. Was I so desperate for company that I'd wanted to stick around and watch someone fix a cooker? Maybe, I thought, as I reclaimed my sandwich, that should be my new hobby, forcing myself into situations where I was unwanted. I'd be good at that. The Hairy Boys, as I had taken to thinking about them, had been polite and accepting, but clearly slightly mystified at my presence in their game, despite Greg's assurances that it would be fine. My lack of any evident talent for, or real interest in, Dungeons & Dragons had scattered over the tabletop with the crisp crumbs.

No. Gaming would not be my new interest in life. Despite Gregor and Andrew's best hopes, it would not be the medium through which I gained myself a partner, a hobby and a life. I had tried and it was not for me. I needed another plan.

4

'So, how was the dungeon?' Joe asked, wilfully loudly, the next morning as I brought out a plate of homemade shortbread to add to the replenished teapot.

He'd casually enquired about my plans for the evening yesterday, and I had, equally casually, told him that I was off to play Dungeons & Dragons. Then I'd had to explain what Dungeons & Dragons was, as Joe and half the others had never heard of it. I couldn't believe that none of Lena and Margaret's innumerable grandchildren had ever played, mentioned, or otherwise had an interest in gaming, and had to conclude that neither of them actually paid much attention to what their offspring talked about, contenting themselves with nodding, smiling and counting heads.

Total number of grandchildren was what mattered, apparently. Their score was about equal, although Lena was slightly ahead on points as one had just qualified as a doctor. Margaret was coming up hard on the inside though, with the imminent birth of a great-grandchild.

'It was fun,' I told Joe, and then sidled off before he could quiz me any further. I had the awful feeling that he thought there had been either Devil worship involved – he watched far too much reactionary television – or something sexual. He'd read *Fifty Shades of Grey* and was quietly convinced that everyone else was 'at it, like rabbits'.

'Ah, Seren.' Holly came in, elbows indicating that she was speed-walking, whilst the rest of her body remained still. 'Could you pop out and help Ned? Mimi's having a bit of trouble getting out of the minibus, and you know some of these ladies aren't keen on men – well, *handling* them.'

Grateful not to have to go into detail about last night's gaming session, I went out into the car park where the day hit me in a burst of clammy light. Mimi was hesitant on the steps, and I offered her my arm to supplement her stick.

'They're a bit steep,' I said. 'A lot of people have problems. We should get a ramp,' I addressed Ned, who was standing a few metres away.

He, and Mimi, said nothing, and all three of us shuffled to the main doors like a minor branch of a Trappist order. Mimi's hands were knotted and gnarled around the joints with the arthritis that clearly caused her pain on walking. But, from her absolutely upright posture, she was not going to admit to it, or give in. I wondered how she got so immaculately dressed – she must have help at home, I reasoned. A family, out all day so Mimi was left by the roadside to be collected, like a dustbin on rubbish day. It was extraordinary how some of our clients were treated by their families as untidy extras; like an unruly dog that wasn't completely housetrained and needed to be socialised and exercised by someone else whilst they went out to work.

But then, I chastised myself silently as I lent my arm to Mimi to walk up the step into the centre, if you had to leave a dog alone all day, you'd get a dog walker in, wouldn't you? It wasn't kind to let them sit, solitary and unattended to, for hours on end. So surely it was just as kind to send your elderly relation to our centre?

I settled Mimi in the chair that had become her usual spot, near the window that opened out onto the tiny stretch of concrete between us and the antique centre. Holly had dotted a few pots about, and, at this time of year, the sun sliced between the buildings to make the flowers glow a Mediterranean red. Mimi sat silently and gazed out on this patch of terrace until it was time to go home, refusing all approaches from anyone. She'd accept a cup of tea and occasionally eat a biscuit or a small sandwich, but that was all.

'Can I talk to you for a moment?' It was Ned, appearing at my shoulder as I backed away from Mimi like a guard in the presence of royalty. Some of our customers had been brought up in a time when you didn't turn your back on your elders – it was a sign of dismissal, apparently, so I always bore it in mind with new people, even if it did make me bump into furniture.

'I'm a bit busy. I've got some buns to get out of the oven.' I reviewed my statement. 'Which is working much better now, thank you.'

'In the kitchen, then.' Ned followed me through. The kitchen was quiet and calm compared to competitive Scrabble, aches and pains and grandchildren. The big urn popped and steamed, a bee bumped mindlessly against the already open window and I'd arranged my nicest set of tea towels on the big hanging rack. *This is my domain,* they announced, in their multicoloured, National Trust glory. *I may not be allowed to hang pictures, but these will do.* Dunster Castle had flopped over and I rearranged it whilst Ned leaned against the island surface.

'I'm sorry about last night,' he said, in tones that made me profoundly glad we were in here and not amid the prurience of next door. 'I was rude and abrupt and you were only doing your job.'

I was a bit taken aback. People didn't often apologise to me. 'I, er, no, it's fine.' To give myself something to do with my face other than look shocked, I bent to the oven. The buns were a mild tan colour. Another five minutes.

'No. I was dismissive, and that really wasn't very nice of me.'

I had to turn round and face him now or I'd look as though I were trying to hide in with the buns. I stayed by the oven though. Those buns could overcook in a trice.

'I think we were both a bit surprised, weren't we?' After all, I'd not exactly been warm and welcoming. I might have *thought* about offering him tea, but I hadn't actually done it. 'I'm not used to anyone being here after hours. Oh, sometimes Holly comes by to pick something up, if we've had an open day, but that's not very often.'

I'd noticed that Ned wasn't hugely tall already, but now was the first time I noticed that his hazel eyes were made up from shades of yellow and brown with a hint of wariness about them. His hair was dark and neatly cut and his shirt and jeans were clean, but there was an un-ironedness about his clothes and a slight off-centre parting that made it look as though he wasn't bothered about how he looked. Now, as he lifted a hand and wiped an arm over his forehead, I noticed that the cuff button on his shirt was hanging by a thread.

'I overreacted when you came in, you see. You startled me and I... I'm not good at sudden shocks.' He gave me a grin that sparked from his eyes. 'Plus, you caught me with pork scratchings.'

I went with it. 'Yes, if you're trying to make an impression, eating pork scratchings is probably not the way to go.'

'Who says I was trying to make an impression?' But he spoke lightly, with a trace of humour in his tone, and he'd lost the defensive look. 'I thought I was being sufficiently manly by holding a screwdriver and looking as though I knew which end to shove in the thingy.'

'You just lost the advantage by calling the oven element a "thingy",' I pointed out. The buns were beginning to scent the kitchen with warm sugar and overheating raisins.

'But I fixed it, so you have to allow me that. Anyway, I'd better get on out there. Charlie has promised to show me his photograph album and I want to talk to him about his angina.' Then, in a movement of limbs that would have left Holly in the shade, he was gone, carefully closing the door between me and the customers, as though he thought I needed peace and quiet to get over his presence. Or maybe it was just to stop the smell of newly cooked buns causing a riot.

I got the buns out of the oven, left it on to heat the lunch through, and found a cooling rack. Shepherd's pie for lunch, already prepped and just needing a bit of cheese to top the potato, some peas to boil up and maybe a few carrots. My hands were already busy, readying pans and grater, while I thought about Ned.

It was nice of him to apologise. He hadn't needed to, his abruptness hadn't been enough to cause me to rewrite my opinion of his character this far, not that I really *had* an opinion. He was a fellow worker, presumably sticking around, unlike some of the volunteers who could be a bit fly-by-night when they realised that helping out older people wasn't a constant round of whist and crochet patterns. Being elderly wasn't a shortcut to losing all ambition or desire to experience the world, it just slowed down your ability to do it, that was all. Our clients were just as keen to attend music concerts, learn to speak Spanish and watch *Love Island* then gossip about it as anyone younger. Whist and crochet, to them, was for 'old people', a nomenclature that none of them, even Joe, were ready to assume yet.

* * *

Lunch was successfully negotiated, with a minimum of complaint, and I went to stack the dishwasher. I had a few bits upstairs to put in too, so I dashed up to my flat to fetch them. My kitchen was too small for a dishwasher and, whilst I normally hand-washed my few plates and cups, sometimes I'd shove some in the industrial washer downstairs to keep it full.

Whilst I was up there, my phone rang. This was an unusual occurrence. It normally meant that Andrew and Greg were having some kind of crisis and they needed me to adjudicate.

'Hello?' I answered the phone one-handed, the other being full of a tray of crockery.

'Seren, love, I've had an idea.'

'Andrew, I'm not sure I—'

'Y'see, we've got a friend, Mattie, you may have met her at the party, not sure, she was there but she does tend to be a bit on the loud side, for you, anyway. She's just asked me if we know anyone over your side.'

I breathed in. 'Over your side' could mean anything from geographical location to sexual orientation and I didn't want to commit to anything until I had a firmer grasp of my brother's intention. Well, I didn't want to commit to anything full stop, really.

'She runs dog training classes out at Appleton and her assistant has called in sick for tonight.' The juggernaut that was Andrew's conversational technique continued. 'She just needs a pair of hands and a body on the floor, and I thought, well, you want to get a new interest and some hobbies or somesuch, don't you? Dog training might be just the thing.'

I looked around me at the tiny flat, the resolutely pet-free nature of my entire life so far, and considered my previous experience with dogs. The absence of any interest in canines should have been glowing down the phone at Andrew. 'So I told her you'd be over there at seven,' Andrew finished, with a flourish that sounded as though he wanted congratulation.

'But I...' I began, with no idea what I was going to use as an excuse.

'I *know* you don't like going to new places and all that, but you know Appleton, and you know the hall, we used to go to dance classes there when we were small.'

He was right in one way, I did know the place. 'But I gave up dance when I was *seven,* Andrew!' I almost wailed. 'It's twenty-five *years* since I knew it!'

'You used to come with Sophie when she picked me up,' Andrew said reasonably. He'd kept up dance until he was seventeen, when his height meant he'd kept banging his head on the tin roof of the hall during the jeté. 'So, you do know it. Anyway. Seven o'clock. There will be lots of cute puppies there, apparently.'

Then he hung up.

The crockery rattled. It was only when my favourite bowl began jingling against last night's tea plate that I realised I was shaking. I didn't go to new places. I went into Pickering, occasionally, to get some bits of shopping that the online shop had missed. I drove to Andrew and Gregor's flat, because I could park right outside and go up with a minimum amount of exposure to outdoors.

New places unsettled me. I might get lost on the way there, or not be able to park the car, or not find the actual location and end up walking for hours.

But, on the other hand, Andrew was right, I *did* know Appleton. It had about ten houses, a wide road, plenty of parking and a village hall on the outskirts, which meant I didn't even need to go into the village itself. And I had decided I needed some kind of life, hadn't I? A hobby? An interest? Whilst I hardly thought that dog training was going to be my metier in life, my previous lack of any contact with dogs being a bit of a giveaway there, actually *going out* to somewhere would be a good start.

Knowing Andrew as I did, my lack of cogent argument would have been taken as acquiescence and he would already have told Mattie, whoever she was, that I'd be there, trembling with eager excitement like a – well, I couldn't think of any breed of dog off the top of my head, but I was sure there would be one that trembled with excitement – at seven on the dot.

I was going to kill him when I next saw him.

I descended the stairs and began to stack the dishwasher. Holly rotated her way in and stood beside me as I slotted plates into the rack. She still seemed to be in motion, even though she was standing still.

'Did you see that we're having the Kirkbymoorside Brass Band next month?' she asked.

'I did.' My voice echoed off the crockery in a sepulchral manner.

'I thought we might make a bit more of a "do" of it.' Holly's elbows indicated extreme excitement at this prospect by churning the air. 'Have an open day kind of thing, alongside the usual stalls. Sell a bit of baking, invite the rellies of our clients, hang a bit of bunting. You know the drill.'

I sighed. 'All right.'

'We could do with raising a bit of cash, with electricity prices going up and all, winter is going to hit hard.' Holly's tone had an edge to it, and I knew why. My flat had been converted out of storage space and, as such, was on the same meter as the downstairs rooms. My electricity bill was covered by costs and meant that I could have the heating on whenever I wanted and all the hot water I could use. It was, so far, the only perk of the job, apart from access to enormous numbers of knitting patterns and a library of second-hand paperbacks. 'We don't want to have to cut back our opening hours or anything, do we?'

With that slight hint of menace, like the 'dum dum dum' music halfway through a film, Holly oscillated her way back out of the kitchen and I carried on loading the dishwasher, shoving cutlery into slots with a good deal more vigour than was strictly necessary. It wasn't Holly's fault, of course. We *did* need to keep fundraising efforts high, to increase our visibility, give the local press an excuse to take photos of kindly townsfolk benefitting the elderly, and keep the wheels going round on this particular venture. I knew the local council, who owned the building, were just itching for us to fail; for our numbers to drop to an unsustainable level, and for the building to become available for sale for conversion into a set of luxury flats. They'd had a couple of goes five years ago, but local outrage – plus financial input from one or two families who would be at a complete loss as to what to do with Granny if we closed – had kept us open.

But open days meant – well, we'd be *open*. I'd have to spruce the whole place right through and bake more cake than Mr Kipling. Much of it would sell, but that didn't usually do more than offset the cost of ingredients and there had to be enough left over to stop the band members from fighting over the last sponge fingers, and to make a trifle for pudding the next day.

The horror of this potential event kept me from worrying about my evening engagement, until we'd closed our doors and I'd tidied up the main room. Ned was there, helping the last few people onto the bus. Many were collected by relatives on their way home, but those without transport would get the minibus back. Mimi was there, I noted, still silent, sitting by the window in the bus with her face averted from the rest of the chatty last leavers. Upright and stiff, like a guardsman on duty, she sat. As I shook a mat outside the door, I caught her eye. She was staring out across the car park and her composed face gave away absolutely no emotion, but I thought I saw, deep within that shuttered expression, a hint of trapped desperation. Then she snapped her eyes away from mine and began to stare at the doorway to the antiques centre, where there was nothing more fascinating to look at than a life-sized carved bear, chained to the railings.

That was it. They were all out, the place was tidy and I couldn't avoid thinking about my plans for the evening any more. Well, Andrew's plans for my evening, to be exact. I sat down at the big kitchen island and put my head in my hands. I was going to *kill* him.

There was a sound at the door and I looked up to see Ned coming back in with every appearance of a man who was going to put the kettle on.

'I thought you were driving the minibus?'

'Roger's taking it. He's got some things to drop off and he thought he may as well use our diesel.' Roger was the owner of the antiques place. He sometimes doubled as bus driver, especially when it meant not having to get his own vehicle out. It did mean that the gangway of the bus was jammed with pictures, a random assortment of purchases for some of the hotels further out on the moors and the large frame of Roger himself, but he was a useful, if sporadic, addition to our team.

'Oh.' I continued to sit, slightly annoyed now. The presence of Ned meant I couldn't have a good wallow in how unfortunate I was in my choice of sibling and how much I was going to hate the unplanned fifteen-minute drive I was being forced to do.

'Any plans for this evening?' Ned, cheerfully failing to read the atmosphere of 'piss off and let me suffer', filled the kettle. 'It's looking lovely out there. I thought I might head up onto the moors and take some photographs.'

I looked at him through my fingers. There was an almost fey air about Ned. Not only because he wasn't six feet nine and built like a filing cabinet, but his cheery and upbeat air came with a feeling that it could change in an instant into something weightier. Not in a threatening way, but as though he could switch from being randomly engaged at a superficial level to a sudden, much deeper, level of engagement. As though focus and sharp intent lay just below his surface.

'Whereabouts do you live?' I asked idly. I didn't really care, but it stopped me having to talk about my potential evening, which stopped me having to *think* about my potential evening. Honestly. Dog training. I was *so* going to kill Andrew.

'Oh.' Ned moved around the island, fetching the biscuit tin. 'Er. In a little place. Up in the moors.'

'But you're not local?' Mercurial, that was the word for Ned. Lithe and changeable, but moving along without leaving a trace of himself. I had no idea why I'd thought that. We were having the most superficial conversation it was possible to have, without discussing the weather, and yet I was getting the impression of – avoidance? As though he were flowing away from my words whilst trying to pretend to be deeply engaged.

'I came from London.' The tin was located. 'Has Holly told you about the open day? Do you have many of those? Sounds as though we're going to have quite a lot to do – apparently there's some bunting she wants me to turn out and hang. Nobody seems to know where it is or where to hang it and I've got the feeling that I'm being expected to go out and spontaneously bunt the entire building.'

I couldn't not smile. 'It's not a verb,' I said mildly. 'It's a noun.'

He smiled back. But still that hint of – *something*. 'Yes, I know. But it should be a verb. Why say, "I have to hang the bunting," when one could just say, "I have to bunt," and everyone would know what you meant? Economy of words, y'see.'

'Oh, yes, of course, you've been talking to Timothy, haven't you?'

Timothy was one of our 'occasional' drop-ins. He came over from Malton on the bus when the weather was fine and his sciatica wasn't too bad, and was, in his own description, 'overwhelmingly afflicted with prolix verbosity'.

Now it was Ned's turn to drop his head. 'Yes, yes, I have. And I had to borrow Joe's dictionary twice.'

'Have a shortbread. Honestly. The only thing that helps is lots of sugar.' I pushed the tin towards him. 'And if you ever need a rest, Timothy knows an amazing amount about the history of the *Eagle* comic. Get him on that subject and you don't even need to join in, he can monologue until—'

'Until the bovine lactators return to the domestic dwelling?' Ned looked up again and gave me a smile that held no trace of hidden sharpness. 'As Timothy would, no doubt, say.'

I snorted a laugh. 'Exactly.'

'So.' With a flip of his head, which made his hair flap, Ned was back to sharp. 'What *do* you have planned for tonight?'

I was weakened by the proximity of the biscuit tin and my forlorn state at my immediate future, so I told him. In fact, I think I might have gone into a lot more detail about Andrew and Gregor's plans for my future than I should have, because we got through half of the shortbreads and I would have to do some emergency baking before coffee time tomorrow.

Ned looked aghast. 'Why do they think you need to get a life? I mean, this—' he held out his hands to indicate the kitchen, but presumably meant the whole of my employment at the Pickering Day Stop '—is a full-time job and a half. Don't you only get Sundays off, same as me?'

'Yes. But that dating site they persuaded me to sign up for seemed to think that I'm only ever going to meet someone if I take up abseiling and shark fishing. And I don't... well, I don't like going out much,' I finished, with my voice descending into my trainers. 'So that's a bit of a drawback.'

'Do you *want* to meet someone?' Ned had hunched forward over the tabletop, almost as though he were crawling towards me on his elbows. 'Because, if you don't, why would you let your brother push you into dating?'

'Andrew can be very...' I groped for the word '... insistent. And he does think the way he lives is the only right way. It wasn't so bad when he was single, because he was too busy to worry about inflicting his lifestyle on me, but ever since he and Greg settled down, he's been on at me to do the same.' I sighed. 'At least he isn't trying to set me up with a big bearded Polish furniture designer.' I saw Ned's baffled expression. 'That would be too matchy-matchy, even for Andrew.'

Now it was Ned's turn to snort. Then he looked at the big clock on the wall behind me. 'Look, it's nearly half past six. You'd better get cracking if you're going to be dog training by seven. And I—' He stopped and became a blur of movement, quick as Puck. 'Goodnight.'

Then he was gone. I heard the outer door slam and then the sound of a car firing up in Roger's car park next door almost before his leaving registered. He'd even had time to put the lid back on the biscuit tin. But he was right. I did have to get moving. Running hand in hand with my hatred of going to places was a hatred of arriving in those places where I didn't want to be late. Wearily, I gathered up my things and headed out.

5

Mattie wasn't what I had imagined. From Andrew's description, I'd pictured a large, jolly lady in a tweed twinset, all bosom and booming voice, but she was, in fact, slender and dressed in jeans and a T-shirt. She was also pathetically pleased to see me.

'Oh, thank God,' she said, when I introduced myself. 'Bloody Melissa – that's my usual assistant – has gone and got herself a boyfriend and it's made her totally unreliable. At least if she'd broken her leg we'd have an end date for all this unpredictability. Well, unless she had to have it reset, of course. Sometimes these things don't mend as well as they should, you know.'

I nodded and agreed that, yes, putative legs might take a supposed amount of time to mend. But Mattie didn't really need me to converse with her, I just had to stand in front of her and nod, it turned out, and occasionally field a runaway sentence just as I had to field a runaway dog.

'Just stand at the back of the hall and be prepared in case anyone gets into a fight,' Mattie said, preparing to open the door. There were already the sounds of vigorous canine excitement outside. 'I think we've got nine coming tonight. They've all been before, except one new bloke who rang yesterday and asked if it was too late to sign up. Nobody's any trouble. Oh, except Alfie, of course.'

She did not go into detail, so I remained in ignorance as to whether Alfie was a dog or owner. My heart had only just settled after the journey, but my system was still full of the adrenaline of the drive. Andrew had been right, I had remembered the route and not been distracted or got lost, so it had gone better than I'd imagined, but when Mattie flung open the hall doors and four enormous dogs bounded in, owners ineffectually tugging on leads whilst a selection of feet and paws skidded on the polished surface I remembered from the dance lessons, I felt my breath catch in my throat again.

Everything was a confused mass of fur and voices and barking for a few minutes until Mattie regained control and the owners and dogs got over the excitement of socialising. She'd been right, I didn't need to have much input; my job was to field any dogs that got away from their owners during the Down Stay, and be an extra pair of hands to help Mattie. The owners, and, indeed, their dogs, all had a firm idea of what was happening once the initial barkfest was over and it was actually quite fun. 'Alfie' turned out to be a mischief-filled spaniel, for whom commands seemed to be more like suggestions, but once I'd retrieved him from the kitchen a couple of times, even he settled down.

Halfway through the evening, just as the owners were all enjoying a cup of tea and the dogs were wandering around the walls sniffing at chair legs in a way that meant we were watching with *very* close attention, there was a casual knock at the door and another dog walked in. In contrast to the Labs, spaniels and one pug, this was a Border collie, and his owner was just behind.

'I rang,' the owner said, identifying Mattie as the leader of the group, probably because she had a dog whistle around her neck and was the only one of us not holding either a cup of tea or a lead or, in some misguided cases, both. He was a thin, edgy-looking guy, wearing pressed chinos and a very white shirt. My brief exposure to dogs, which basically consisted entirely of the last half-hour, told me these were probably a mistake.

'Ah, yes.' Mattie bounded over. 'And this is Kez, am I right?'

The dog looked up hopefully at his name. He was black and white with yellow eyes that held an expression that looked vaguely familiar, but I didn't really get much chance to look at him because I was too busy trying to stop Alfie from eating all the biscuits. I'd not allowed for the fact that some dogs could be quite tall when standing on their hind legs, and Alfie's owner, a lady in torn jeans with a harassed expression, didn't seem to be able to stop him grabbing everything edible.

'Yeah. We got him for the kids, really. From a farm – he was no good with sheep so we got him cheap. He needs teaching.' The man went to put Kez's lead into Mattie's hand, but she pulled back.

'Oh, we do training with the owners. I don't take individual dogs, you see. You need to learn to manage him as much as he needs to learn to behave.'

Bramley, the pug, shoved his nose up my trousers at this point, so I missed the rest of the conversation, but I got it from Mattie after the class was over, as we tidied – and also mopped, because Alfie had got overexcited – and put the hall straight.

'He's my least favourite type of owner,' Mattie confessed. 'That guy who brought Kez. Bought a dog "for the children", which is now becoming a nuisance and he's decided it needs training. Poor love.' She shoved a chair back into place, and I was pretty sure she wasn't talking about the man who'd come with Kez. 'Thank you for coming. You were a great help. Just having someone else here makes it easier.'

'I didn't really do much.'

'You distracted Alfie from the biscuits and that's a major achievement. That dog is going to weigh ten stone if his owner can't get a handle on teaching him not to steal food. Or learn to put stuff out of his reach, which she seems to struggle with too.' Mattie sighed. 'But they're all getting on.'

'Kez seemed to do well. For his first time.' I'd watched the collie closely. With him and his owner being new, I'd been afraid that I might be called on to help in a more hands-on way, but the dog had picked up the commands almost without fault.

'Border collies are basically just looking for something to do with their brains.' Mattie finished packing away and stood expectantly at the hall door with the key in her hand. 'You have to keep their minds busy or they go bonkers. That poor lad is under-exercised and under-employed.' She sighed again. 'I really hope his family know what they've let themselves in for.' Then she looked a bit embarrassed for a second. 'Er, Seren...'

I braced myself. This sounded as though awkward questions were going to follow. I hoped Andrew hadn't prodded Mattie into trying to enquire into how likely I was to take up dog training. I couldn't see that doing much for my dating life, other than attracting men who wanted to be told 'No!' in a firm voice and to be kept away from biscuits.

'Mmm?' I tried to sound vague and as though I had to hurry away to my next, incredibly important, task. I shuffled my car keys from hand to hand, to add weight to the hint.

'Tony – that's Kez's person – has asked if he could come tomorrow evening for a "catch up" session. As he's joined the class so late. I wondered if you...?' Mattie trailed off and looked at me with a hopeful expression. 'It's just for this week,' she added quickly when I didn't leap at the chance with light-speed delight. 'Kez is giving them trouble at home. Tony's got three children and an out-of-control dog with children is a recipe for disaster.'

As Kez had shown no real signs of being 'out-of-control' during the class, other than a pronounced desire to round up the other dogs, I wondered if Tony and his wife had a rather overblown idea of 'out-of-control', and what they'd make of Alfie. I briefly imagined the three children sitting on the sofa in neat height order and silence, watching David Attenborough documentaries and eating prunes.

'Tomorrow...' I said thoughtfully, as though mentally rearranging my incredibly busy life to see if I could find a space. All that was written on the calendar in my kitchen was Midsummer Day, and then, in pencil, 'haircut?'. I was hardly working through a frantic series of dating opportunities and recklessly agreed-to outings. And much to my surprise, tonight had been fun, in a 'lots of ears to stroke' way. Mattie was nice and I found myself replying, 'I suppose I could. If you really need me.'

'Brilliant, it will just be to help out at the end of the hall.' Mattie was already locking the door as though my acquiescence had never been in question. 'I can normally do one-to-ones on my own, but with Kez being so new to training of any kind...' She pursed her lips. 'I really do worry about people who get a collie "because they're intelligent" and think they won't have to bother with training,' she said. 'They're intelligent. Not psychic.'

I got into my car and watched Mattie walk away up the road towards the village. She walked confidently, on her way back to, she'd told me, three school-aged children, a husband and four Labrador bitches, one of whom was expecting puppies any day now. It did cross my mind to wonder whether Andrew had somehow managed to bribe, not only Mattie, but also Tony and, by extension, Kez, into needing me for a follow-up day, but I dismissed that thought after a few miles. Andrew's desire for me to find a partner wouldn't go so far as to bring other people into his machinations. Would it?

Next day there were posters. Many, many posters, all over my kitchen, accompanied by Holly and her overactive elbows, and three volunteers.

'So, if you put them up around Pickering and then go out as far as Scarborough your way, Liz, and maybe down to Thirsk?' Holly was stacking the posters into piles. 'Anywhere you can think of. We're going to make this a Big August Bash: stalls, tea and cake, and, of course, the band will be playing.'

She was making the Kirkbymoorside Brass Band sound like a cross between a K-pop act and the reuniting of The Beatles. But then, this was Holly's job – fundraising, organising, keeping everything running – and she was amazingly good at it.

'I'm putting some bits in the local papers,' she went on, taking no notice of my arrival laden with used pudding plates. 'And *The Yorkshire Post* has promised to come out and do photos. So we want to make this a Day to Remember for everybody!'

Holly could pronounce capitals like no woman I'd ever met, I thought as the volunteers moved past me in a rustle of posters.

'Any thoughts about the baking? For the open day?' Holly

turned on me now. 'It might be a good chance for you to try out some new recipes.'

I looked up at her from the depths of the dishwasher. 'New recipes? Holly, you know our customers prefer the same old same old. New recipes just make them worried. They like knowing that we've got set dishes on set days and I don't want them to think I'm going to surprise them with Terrine Tuesday or anything.'

'Oh, well.' Holly shrugged. 'You do like your routine, I suppose, Seren. You've never been very adventurous, have you?'

'I'm off dog training again tonight,' I replied, stung by the tone of faint damnation in her voice.

'But you haven't got a dog. Have you? I'm not sure about a dog, not in your flat, it's very small and we may have service users who are allergic. A cat, maybe? Or a hamster, had you thought about a hamster, if you're lonely?'

'No. I'm helping someone train other people's dogs.' My voice bounced off the filter and it made the words sound dead.

'Well, as I said, it's not really adventurous, is it?' Holly picked up the remaining posters. 'Now I'm off to get these to Kirkby to put up in the shops.'

And off she went. After I'd left enough time for her to be gone, I muttered, 'You don't need to be adventurous to turn out forty thousand tray bakes and a "Guess the Weight" fruitcake.'

'I can imagine you don't.'

Ned's voice came from the other side of the kitchen, and made me jump so that I banged my head on the dishwasher arm.

'How long have you been there?'

He didn't answer, or advance, so remained just a voice somewhere behind the baking sheets. 'Why don't you pull out the shelves rather than climbing into the machine to fill it?'

'They're stuck.' I crawled backwards out of the dishwasher and stood up. 'This machine is probably older than I am.'

'Hmmmm.' When I'd reversed out, slamming the door and carefully not looking in his direction, he went on. 'Shall I have a look at them? Tonight? All my gear is still here from when I fixed the cooker.'

Now I turned. Ned was standing, leaning against the stack of cookware I'd had to take out of the lower cupboard to search for the special tin I made the brownies in.

'That would be nice, thank you,' I said.

'You could help? It might need another pair of hands.' He tipped his head and looked at me from under a loose flop of hair. He was smiling, but there was still that focused look in his eyes and I suddenly knew who Kez had reminded me of. It had been Ned. Both of them had eyes of a pale brown, Kez's so pale as to be almost yellow and Ned's a more human shade, but both sets held an intensity of stare that looked only one step away from going postal with the nearest blunt object. Or, in Kez's case, with really sharp teeth.

'Sorry, I can't. I'm dog training again tonight.' I did manage to sound a little bit sorry. *Was* I sorry? It had been rather nice last night, here in the kitchen with Ned and the shortbread and just the quiet of the hall beyond.

'Never mind, then. Just leave me the biscuits, and I'll be fine.' Ned grinned again.

There was a little pause. In the background, I could hear Joe trying to persuade Jim into a game of Scrabble and Tom and Will having a disagreement about something to do with Concorde.

'How did your photography go last night?' I asked finally. Ned was still leaning and I wanted to get to the cupboard again and put away the trays. Asking him to move didn't sound very polite so I decided to wait. He couldn't stay there all day.

'It was great, thank you. I got some wonderful shots of the sunset over the moors.' Ned shifted and I moved closer in hope, but no, he was just adjusting so that he could lean more comfortably. 'Why don't you take up photography? If you need an interest in life? It's very creative and you could always print the pictures off and make a display.'

'But I'd have to—' I began, then stopped suddenly. I'd been about to say that I'd have to go out, travel around. Be outside in places I didn't know, actually *get* to places I didn't know. I could hardly make much of a photographic display of the inside of my flat and the car park. 'It's not really my thing, sorry.'

Ned shrugged. 'I would never have put you down as a dog trainer either,' he said, but didn't press the point, for which I was thankful. 'By the way, lunch was delicious, thank you.'

I tried to hide my surprise at his praise. Apart from covert remarks about lumpy custard, or questions about whether I'd changed my recipe, as suspicious forks prodded around in gravy, I didn't get much feedback on my cooking. It wasn't out of rudeness, more habitude; our menu tended not to vary much, apart from seasonally, so that our customers knew what to expect. They weren't big on change.

'Seren!' Joe had opened the door a fraction and put his head round. 'Can you pop out here and tell Jim that, despite what John here may allege, I do *not* cheat at Scrabble? I just have an extensive vocabulary.'

Ned raised his eyebrows at me and grinned again. This time I grinned back. The grin made him lose that tight, concentrated look in favour of a bright-eyed anticipation, which also reminded me of Kez. But it made a trickle of warm complicity run through me.

'You do cheat, Joe,' I reminded him. 'But you *also* have an extensive vocabulary.' I went to the door and Ned gave me a wink as I left the kitchen. 'The two things aren't exclusive.'

* * *

There was an atmosphere of burgeoning excitement in the hall today. Even though we were a good few weeks away from our prospective open day, activities were already being undertaken towards it. Margaret was knitting again, adding small items to a basket by her side, ready to be put on a stall for sale. Lena had been taken away for the weekend by her family, and Margaret was obviously trying to get ahead before she came back. John sat beside her, in Lena's usual spot, doing something with sandpaper to wood. John made shepherd's crooks, which were much in demand at our sales. His woodworking prowess never failed to surprise me as he'd had a lifelong career in electronics and had, as far as I was aware, never been closer to a sheep than sitting next to Margaret's wool.

Mimi still sat alone and unmoving. She hadn't come up to the table for lunch either, although I'd offered to help her, or to bring the food to her chair by the window. She had declined, without speaking, just turning her head away from me, staring out over the concrete and tubs as though waiting to be rescued.

I thought I'd give her another try. 'Mimi?'

She turned, but only out of politeness. I could already see the shuttered look on her face.

'Everyone is going to be making things for the stall at the open day. Do you have any handicrafts that you like to do? It doesn't matter what it is,' I went on hastily as she began to avert her eyes, 'or how small. Grace makes little paper origami models and they go down very well.' Then my eyes fell on her twisted, arthritic hands, and I backtracked. 'Or if you can sing, we sometimes have someone do a solo along with the band?'

There was a moment of suspended movement, as though Mimi wanted to say or do something. One of her gnarled hands twitched in her lap, and her very blue eyes met mine as I held my breath for some word, some acknowledgement of a talent. Then the eyes lowered again, went back to the geranium tubs and the weed-scattered cement, and she shook her head very slightly.

'Never mind, then,' I said, and then worried that I'd sounded a bit patronising, but couldn't really think of anything else to say. I'd had a few, very one-sided, conversations with Mimi in an attempt to get her to speak; she seemed, not depressed exactly, but so self-contained that nobody else could get through. I'd received no more than small nods of acknowledgement of my presence and one or two smiles.

None of us had met the family she lived with either. Ned reported that Mimi lived on a farm out towards Farndale and was always standing alone at the end of the track when the bus pulled up, so he'd not had chance to ask anyone about how she was at home. Maybe her family would come to the open day? Although plenty of people seemed quite happy to leave their elderly relatives with us without ever coming by to check that we were the sort of people they *ought* to be leaving their relatives with. But all our clients seemed happy, and presumably took home stories of treatment no worse than the occasionally substandard custard or our throwing away of the *Fifty Shades of Grey* trilogy when there had been too much arguing about whose turn it was to read it.

I sighed and went back to the kitchen, from which Ned had, thankfully, gone. I straightened today's tea-towel display, Wild Flowers of the UK and Castles of Wales, and started putting the baking tins back in their cupboard now that the brownie tin had been discovered lurking right at the back.

In my pocket my mobile rang. I thought about ignoring it, but it was almost certainly Andrew, who would only ring back every ten minutes, so I answered.

'Mattie says you were a great help, well done, love.'

'Thank you,' I answered primly. 'I'm going back tonight too.'

'Yes, she said. Good, good. Look, will you come over here again on Monday? Greg's keen for you to give D&D another chance, and I want to hear how the dog training went.'

'But you've already heard. Mattie told you, and now I've told you too.' I jostled the baking sheets and used my elbow to clatter a couple of plates on the side. 'I can't really chat, Andrew, I'm busy here.'

'Ah, right, yes, sorry, forgot that you work strange hours. So, we'll see you on Monday, then, shall we?' and he hung up, leaving me thinking that only someone who ran a gallery so exclusive that you had to ring a bell to get in, and therefore only had about three customers a day, could call lunchtime on a Friday 'strange hours'.

Ah, well, I could use Monday to invite Andrew and Greg to the open day. They were usually good for a posh raffle prize.

'Do you need a hand with the teas and coffees?' John put his head around the door this time. They all regarded the kitchen as my domain and behaved as though I guarded it with a shotgun and tripwires, even though they were perfectly free to come and go as they wanted. 'Do you need a hand?' was code for 'Hurry up, we're dying of thirst in here.'

'I'll just be a minute,' I answered, and then looked at him. John walked with a frame that took both hands. 'How were you going to help anyway, carry them on your head?'

He snorted. 'I wasn't going to help at all. They just sent me to find out what was taking you so long and I thought it was politer to say it that way.'

I laughed. 'Tell them I'm coming.' And then, feeling like a put-upon below-stairs maid, I laid out the tea trays and began spooning coffee into cups.

PROPER SHORTBREAD

Now, the thing you really need to know about shortbread is – butter. Real, proper butter, none of that 'I Can't Believe It's Never Seen the Inside of a Dairy' stuff, or even the stuff that pretends to be butter 'with oils added to make it spreadable'. You don't need it to be spreadable. It has to taste of real, honest to goodness butter. Churned cream and maybe a bit of salt. Trust me on this.

You need 225g of flour (it should be plain, but, to be honest, I've made it with self-raising because I haven't always got plain flour in, and it's not a deal breaker), 225g of butter (I know it sounds a lot. It IS a lot. But you want a lovely, buttery biscuit, not mouthfuls of something that's just... there). Put these into a bowl. Add 100g of sugar – recipes always seem to say caster sugar but I use demerara or muscovado, because it gives the shortbread a caramel colour – 50g of ground rice and 50g of ground almonds. Mix it up with your fingers (I promise I don't have some kind of finger/pastry fetish, it's just that so much of my cooking is done with the hands!). It will start off bread-crumby but then start to clump up into a doughy, pastry-type mix. Lightly knead it together (but only very lightly), then put it into a greased and lined tin, about 30 cm x 25 cm or the nearest you can get, and press it down gently. I always prick the surface all over with a fork. I was told this keeps the top level, but I've no idea if it really does, I just do it anyway because it makes a nice pattern. Now stick it in the fridge to chill. I have cooked it straight away because I've been in a hurry, but this seems to make it less 'short' and more chewy, so I'd chill if I were you.

Pop into a warm oven (around 160 degrees C, you want it almost to dry out and bake, rather than cook too fast) for about half an hour. If you used caster sugar, it goes a lovely golden brown when it's cooked. If you use demerara or muscovado, it's this colour all the time and so there's a bit more guesswork involved. Take it out and let it cool, but not too much.

Once it's solid enough to handle, cut it into pieces. Don't let it get too cool or you won't be able to cut it without it shattering, and you end up with a plate of broken bits and crumbs. It should still be soft enough to draw a knife through without it breaking. So, cut the pieces and then lift them out VERY CARE-FULLY onto a rack to finish cooling and to go completely hard. If you've greased and lined your tin properly, you should be able to slide a palette knife underneath, or even a fish slice. You may have to sacrifice the first slice, but you get to eat that, so it's fine. Once on the rack, give the biscuits a dusting of caster sugar to make them extra crunchy, and prepare for the lot to vanish in far less time than it took you to cook them.

7

Tony was late. Mattie and I sat in the hall on a table, swinging our legs.

'So, how do you know Andrew and Greg?' I asked.

Mattie gave a couple of experimental blows to the dog whistle around her neck. 'I've known Andrew since university. Met Greg when Andrew introduced us and I got him to make a couple of pieces for our new place. He does a very nice line in functional utility furniture, doesn't he?'

I murmured agreement. I always thought Greg's furniture looked rather as if it had been a 1960s shopping centre in a previous life, but each to their own. 'Look, is this Tony now?'

A small, sporty car drove into the hall parking space. There did not seem to be any boot space, so I wasn't very surprised when Tony got out and revealed Kez sitting on the passenger seat beside him. The seat had been wrapped in plastic rubbish bags taped together.

'He seems to have forgotten everything he learned last night,' were Tony's first words. 'I don't think any of this talk about Border collies being intelligent is true, y'know. He's thick as a brick, this one.' He wiped himself down. 'And he sheds hair everywhere.'

Mattie just looked at me. Clearly nothing about Tony's attitude today had changed her mind about yesterday's view of him. 'Right, well, let's get inside and see what he remembers when he's back with us.'

'I don't need him to be obedient when he's with you,' Tony snapped. 'I want him to behave with me. Oh, and the wife and kids, obviously.'

I looked at Kez as he walked past me into the hall. There again was that familiar glitter in the eye, that sense of something repressed, that had reminded me of Ned. The dog turned his head as Tony half led and half dragged him over the threshold, and there must have been something about the light, because it almost looked as though the dog winked at me.

I needed to stop this. I was anthropomorphising a dog now. Perhaps I was going mad? Between dog training, Andrew, and my clients at the centre, nothing seemed to be under my control any more. I'd had my life as I liked it. My tiny flat, cooking for the clients, chatting to them, then tidying up and back up to the flat to read and then bed. Nice. *Contained.*

Now I was watching a collie with its front paws on a table staring at me as though I were being interviewed, and, when I'd once only had to look forward to a set of well-baked scones and a good fruit cake, now I also had to anticipate the Down Stay and being a wood elf in the company of hairy men.

This isn't me. I watched Mattie putting Kez through his paces. He seemed perfectly obedient to me, and even well trained for a dog that had only been to one and a half classes, but Tony was impatient and short tempered with him.

'Just sit *down!*' He snapped again as Kez capered in front of him. 'What am I supposed to *do?*'

Mattie had been distracted at the other end of the hall, so he'd addressed his question to me. I didn't want to confess that I had absolutely no idea. 'Maybe you're using too many words?' I suggested. 'Kez, sit.'

To my astonishment, the dog sat on my feet and gazed up into my face with an expression somewhere between eagerness and insanity.

'Kez, down,' I said, slightly weakly and experimentally. The collie went into the kind of lying down that looked as though it were waiting to be rocket-launched.

'He doesn't do that for me,' Tony said, slightly sulkily. 'Kez, come here.'

Apart from an ear twitch at his name, Kez didn't move from my foot.

'Oh, I'm sick of this.' Tony threw me a look that suggested he suspected I had the dog stapled to my shoe and a pocket full of treats, just to show him up. 'I'm going out for a smoke.'

His leaving the hall didn't make the dog change focus. Kez kept his eyes fixed on mine. 'Oh, up,' I said, because my foot was beginning to go to sleep. Kez 'upped'. He walked around behind me and came to sit at my side, pushing his sleek head into my hand.

'Thought he'd been trained already.' Mattie came over. 'He's just been playing Tony and the family up. Probably doesn't like them much. I've seen the type before. They want all the kudos for having a gorgeous, well-behaved dog, but do nothing more about it than sending the kids out to play in the garden with him, and winding him up.' She fussed Kez's ears. 'I'll have a word when Tony gets back in.'

But Tony didn't come back in. First we heard the car drive off. About five minutes later, Mattie's phone pinged a text.

'Tony says, "You can keep the bloody dog. The kids want a quad bike now anyway, and we're sick of the mess."'

We looked at one another, horrified, and then down at Kez. He looked up, and flopped his tongue out of the side of his mouth, as though he were grinning. 'That's horrible,' I said in a small voice. 'You can't just abandon your dog like that!'

'Oh, they can, and do.' Mattie picked up her phone again. 'You'd be surprised how often it happens. I'll call the Dogs Trust people to pick him up. I'm sure they can find him a new home quite quickly. Not as fast as if he'd been a pup, but he's only about eighteen months, someone will take him.'

A cold nose nudged the palm of my hand and I looked down to see Kez's unblinking stare. 'Poor chap,' I said and fussed his ears.

Mattie was looking thoughtful. 'He seems to like you,' she said slowly. 'I don't suppose…'

'What? No! I live in a flat!'

'As long as he gets plenty of exercise he'll be fine. And you're around all day, aren't you? He wouldn't be left?'

Hang on, wait, I thought. If I look after the dog, only for a few days obviously, just until Mattie can find somewhere to take him permanently, then I've got the perfect excuse not to have to go over to Andrew's and be subjected to trial by twenty-sided dice… 'I could look after him for a short while,' I said. 'But that's all.'

So that was how I found myself driving home with a dog in the back of my little car. He'd jumped in perfectly happily, sat hunched like a miser in the small boot, with his head over the back seat, and twelve tins of dog food from Mattie rattling around on the floor in there with him. Whilst *he* was happy, I was quietly cursing myself for being a pushover. I *should* have said no. I *should* have explained properly that the flat was tiny and didn't belong to me, that I didn't like being outside, let alone walking the miles that Kez would need. I should, firmly and calmly, have stood up for myself and refused to take a dog I didn't want to a home I didn't own.

But I hadn't. Of course I hadn't.

'I don't know what Holly is going to say,' I said as we took the roundabout faster than usual. 'She's only just told me I couldn't *have* a dog. I don't suppose you can impersonate a cat, can you? Or a hamster?'

At the word 'cat', Kez's ears twitched, but he didn't move otherwise. I met his eye in the mirror and I saw his tail wag.

'But it's temporary, you understand? I can't have a dog. I can't have *you*.'

The ears shrugged.

'And if I ever meet Tony or his dreadful family, I am going to give them what for on your behalf. How can they just leave their dog? I hope the quad bike...' I tailed off, running out of vituperative comments. Besides, I wasn't sure what could befall a quad bike. I wasn't even entirely sure I knew what a quad bike was. I thought it was one of those things the gamekeepers used to carry feed out to the pheasant pens, but that didn't seem suitable for children.

Kez didn't comment. He raised his chin from the back seat, moved further into the boot, and then I heard the unmistakable sound of a dog being sick over the carpet.

'Oh, that's just great,' I muttered. Yep, if Tony ever came anywhere near me, I was going to poke him vigorously with one of John's shepherd's crooks. Possibly. Or I might just be very, very polite to him, in an icily detached way. Yes, that would teach him.

8

On Saturday morning I got up very, very early, on the grounds that, if I wasn't likely to see anyone I knew, then nobody I knew was likely to see me. Or, more importantly, Kez, who, having been told he could sleep in the kitchen, got up from the end of my bed and followed me around the flat as I dressed in the half-light of the summer dawn. He looked anxious, but once I clipped on his lead and took him down the stairs, he lifted his leg against one of Roger's anti-ram-raid bollards and started to look more cheerful.

I'd not seen Pickering this early before. There was nobody about, and only one or two cars passed me as I cautiously walked Kez down to the big field behind the station where the steam trains would be huffing for tourists in a couple of hours. There was nobody in the field either, so I let Kez loose, whereupon he didn't immediately dash off in search of his old home as I'd been slightly hoping. He zigzagged about a bit, nose to the ground, and then raised his head and stared behind me as though I were being followed by the ghosts of every reluctant dog walker ever.

'Hello, you're out early.' The voice from behind me made me

squeak. Kez's ears went up and down but he didn't spring to my defence, the traitor. Instead, he watched for a moment and then went back to combing the grass with his nose, his black and white coat flickering through the undergrowth like light and shade in motion.

I knew who it was from the voice, but his appearance had astonished the words out of me. I turned around slowly.

It was Ned. Looking exactly as he did in the hall, slightly careworn, slightly scruffy but clean. Still a bit fey, like a nature spirit who lived in the woods that curved behind us and around the field, forming an arboreal arm into which the field snuggled.

'Sorry, did I startle you?' Ned asked, unnecessarily, because my mouth was hanging open and I'd got Kez's lead between my hands like a makeshift garotte. 'I was taking photos up in the wood and I saw you arrive.' He swung the camera he was holding up into my field of vision. 'I'm not a weird stalker or anything. Lovely dog, who does he belong to?'

Kez was now digging an urgent hole in the sandy soil, tail waving an eager hello to whatever was down there.

'Me, I think. For now, anyway.'

Ned cocked his head and raised his eyebrows, and again I was struck by his resemblance to the collie currently excavating the centre of the field. I couldn't just stand there, so I told him the story of the dog training and the negligent Tony, and ended with, 'So, I said I'd take him for a few days. Until Mattie can find him a proper home. But for God's sake, don't tell Holly.'

Ned and I looked together at the dog. He'd stopped digging and was lying a few metres away from us, with an expectant air.

'What is he waiting for?' Ned asked.

'I have no idea. I've only known him for a handful of hours, and most of those were spent with me telling him to get off the end of my bed.'

Ned looked down at his feet and I could tell he was trying not to laugh. 'Any success?'

'Not notably, no.'

Tired of waiting for me to intuit what he wanted, Kez ran over with his excavated treasure. It was a large rubber ball, sandy from its time buried by a previous owner. Experimentally, I threw it, and Kez, powered only by the sunlight that was splitting the trees and lighting the field, tore after it.

'Ah.' Ned raised his camera and clicked off a few shots.

'Is this what you do when you're not at our place, then?' I asked, for something to say, taking the slobbery ball from Kez, and hurling it out again.

'It's my defining characteristic.' Ned spoke from behind the bulk of the camera. 'I drive the minibus, help at the hall, take pictures and worry.' His hair flopped again and he gave me another sideways bright stare. I was almost tempted to throw the ball for him after Kez returned it again.

'Worry? What about?'

There was a moment of quiet. The black and white streak of collie tore out across the field again.

'Oh, this and that. Nothing much.' Ned sounded light, dismissive. But then those light brown eyes found mine and I noticed a webbing of lines around them. A tightening around the mouth, as though he wanted to smile but couldn't get it past something else, something that pulled the joy back inside him. He'd shaved, but not well; there were little patches of dark stubble dotting his cheeks and chin.

I dropped my eyes. There were things I wanted to say and questions I wanted to ask, but didn't know how to frame them. Into the slightly awkward silence, a bird sang bright and sharp.

Then Kez plopped the spit-streaked ball onto my foot, walked around behind me and sat firmly, neatly lined up with my left hand, nose up, waiting for further instructions. His tongue lolled, pink and warm, and he was panting. Clearly this ball chasing had been the most exercise he'd done in a while – Mattie had been right about Tony's family thinking a play in the garden would be enough exercise, and I wondered how much damage this energetic dog had done to their house in pursuit of a good gallop.

'Well, I ought to get back. I need to work out how to hide the dog from Holly until Mattie finds someone to take him.'

'Good luck.' Ned looked down at Kez, who was doing an impression of the World's Best-Trained Dog. 'She'll go spare if she sees him. Come on, I'll walk back with you.'

'Don't you want to stay and take more photographs?'

Ned looked down at the camera, almost as though it came as a surprise to find it still around his neck. 'I don't think these woods are going anywhere. Or this field. Or Pickering, in general. Has it changed at *all* in, say, the last century?'

I clipped Kez's lead on and we started to walk. 'Not much. No need for it to. We're based on farming so there's no real industry to lose and it's just an insignificant little market town so it never got bombed in the war. What were you expecting? I suppose it's very different from London.' Having someone walking beside me made me feel less – whatever it was I felt when I was out alone. Less like the world had pinned a target to my back, less afraid I might get unexpectedly lost walking in a place I'd lived for years.

'Yes.' Ned spoke slowly. He was watching the horizon, built of moorland hills behind the gentle slope of the town, topped by its castle like a derelict cherry on an over-whipped meringue. 'It's very different. But that's rather the point.'

'If you're going to have a change you might as well make it a big one?' Kez's claws were clicking on the warm concrete of the pavement. A few more people had decided to start the day now, wandering down the road in search of exciting diversions, or on their way to work, but Ned's presence made them feel distant, no longer out to jostle me.

'Something like that.' He gave me another cocked-head look. His hair was unevenly parted and looked as though he'd cut it himself. Added to the bad shave, he looked a little like a clean and well-spoken tramp. I wondered briefly if he was an ex-offender, housed somewhere on the north edge of the moors and given a job with us to ease him into society. 'Did you grow up here? In Pickering, I mean, not this bit of pavement.'

I laughed. 'Not quite. Andrew and I were born in a village near York. Our parents died when I was quite young and Andrew brought me up. He moved us here because the schools were close by and it's cheaper.' I had few memories of the house I'd lived in for the first four years of my life, and those memories were mostly of small, dark rooms that held an air of sadness. I'd realised far too late that I was remembering the aftermath of my parents' deaths rather than growing up; drawn curtains and crying. Andrew had only been twelve when they died and we'd been given to an aunt to bring up, but as soon as Andrew was eighteen, with a Life Plan and a university place, he'd taken over guardianship of me and we'd moved away. He'd bought our aunt a house in Spain and we visited twice a year, grateful, but not really loving.

'You were brought up by your brother? That must have been quite an experience.'

'Well, it made for some interesting embarrassments at parents' evenings.' We'd almost arrived back at the hall. The sun was glinting off Roger's warming-pan-filled window, and I noticed that ours needed a good clean. 'What am I going to say to Holly about this?' I pointed down at the dog, who was still trotting alongside me on a slack lead, like a Crufts Obedience Champion. I wondered what he'd done to Tony. 'I can't keep him hidden for long and she's bound to find out.'

'Maybe... maybe if he stays up in the flat, you can break it to her gradually? I mean, you're only looking after him for a few days, aren't you? He might even be gone before she needs to know. How did the dog-training-as-a-hobby go, by the way?'

'It was fun, but I don't think it's a life choice. I mostly just stood around and sometimes cuddled puppies.'

'Perfect job, then,' Ned said robustly. We were standing outside the hall, as though reluctant to go in, even though I'd unlocked the door and it was swinging open in the slight breeze that was also ruffling Kez's fur along his back, making him look like a canine tidal wave.

'Very unlike this one, certainly.' On the outrush of air from indoors I could smell stale dust and old cooking. I needed to air the place out more. And maybe get some fresh flowers in vases around the place, although Tom and Jim would probably complain that I was making the place look 'fussy'.

'Ah, this isn't so bad.'

We still stood, listening to Pickering bursting into morning life around us. A postman whistled in the traditionally approved fashion as he walked down the road, cars passed in spurts of music and exhaust and two ladies, obviously walking to work together, with their name badges glinting in the sun, squeezed past us and carried on, without pausing their conversation.

At last Kez, seemingly tired of our admiration of a building and the lack of any evident breakfast, tugged me over the threshold and clattered his way up the main stairs, which were lino-covered and utilitarian. 'I'd better feed him,' I said, apologetically although I didn't know why. Ned hardly thought I was going to stand on the doorstep with him all day.

'And I'd better get the bus out. Our clients aren't going to get themselves here. Well, apart from the ones who do.'

'It looks like a lovely morning for a drive up over the moors.' I had to call this over my shoulder, as Kez was towing me along the upstairs corridor, where there were two small offices and a store-room, towards my flat at the far end. He'd already got a clear mental map of where the food was kept.

I didn't hear Ned's reply. It was covered by our arrival at the flat, and Kez scratching at the door and whining, as though the door led to a smoke-filled room and someone begging to be rescued.

I fed Kez and then left him lying, once more, on my bed, with assurances that I'd pop up and see him during the morning. He seemed tired and content to stretch out on the mattress, but I went downstairs with my ears alert for any outbreaks of whining or howling. I could probably explain them away as problems with the plumbing, if Holly came around and asked. Some of our clients were losing a little hearing in the upper register and wouldn't be a problem, but there were still a fair few whose abilities were pin sharp. I needed to work out a cover story for them.

I started whipping up a batch of small biscuits to go with the morning coffee. Home-baking was one of our chief attractions, so I liked the place to smell of something on the go when everyone arrived. Ned had taken the minibus off on the collection run, but I could hear the door opening as those who came under their own steam went into the hall and resumed whichever activities they'd arrived early to get first go at.

Thinking of Ned made me wonder. I had told him a lot about myself, without getting much in return, and it was dawning on me that I was trusting the quiet and unbrushed man rather a lot for someone I'd just met and knew nothing about. What had made him want to come and work here, when he was clearly intelligent and obviously capable of more than driving a minibus and discussing 'How Things Used to Be' forty times a day whilst helping with crossword clues or assisting with the million and one small tasks associated with our customers? Our volunteers were nearly all retired themselves, a few years younger than our clients and not yet in need of our services, but still past the age of heavy lifting. One or two came to us, usually to gain a little experience back in the workplace before moving on to better – and better paid – things. My continuing in the role of cook/housekeeper without dashing off to York to work in a big hotel for more money was, as Holly always said, a credit to the charity that lay behind most of the funding.

I didn't like to tell her that there weren't that many jobs I was qualified for that didn't involve me driving every day or being in places I didn't know. Outside, where everything was too big and unknown, or in strange locations that I might get lost getting to. No. Helping and baking and living in the same place suited me down to the ground, even though the pay was woeful. My accommodation, electricity and food were largely covered, so I couldn't *expect* much in the way of salary, could I?

Idly, I wondered how much they were paying Ned.

Lunch was roast chicken and veg. We didn't open on a Sunday, so served a Sunday roast on Saturdays to make up for it, because there were fewer of our clients in at the weekend. Their families tended to be more present at weekends, so we only got those who lived alone and wanted the company, or those whose families worked unsocial days and hours. I had the feeling that Holly would also have liked to have been open on Sundays, if it hadn't been illegal to make me work seven days a week. I knew there were some clients whose home lives were less than optimal, who would have come if they could, and the odd confused one or two who forgot which day of the week it was and would turn up anyway, so the doors were usually open during daylight hours, whatever day it was. It wasn't as if I were going anywhere, was it?

'Lovely bit of chicken, that.' Tom patted his stomach, in a satisfied way. 'Nice crunchy roasties too.'

'Speak for yourself,' Jim mumbled. 'Can't be dealing with crunchy, not with my top set. But I did like the sticky toffee pudding, Seren, m'dear. Best I've ever had.'

'Gosh, thanks, chaps,' I said. It wasn't like them to offer compliments, or, indeed, any remarks about the edibility of my cooking, so it *must* have been good. 'I didn't do anything unusual today, just cooked the same as normal.'

'Your cooking is *always* superb,' Tom said firmly. He and Jim exchanged a glance. 'We just don't always tell you.'

I noted the look. 'So, why are you telling me now?'

Another look, and Jim muttered something into his shirt front. I raised my eyebrows. 'Ned said we should appreciate you more,' Tom said, eventually, going a bit pink around the ears.

'Did he?' I didn't know how to feel about that. I thought I felt a touch patronised, but wasn't sure. Was them telling me they liked my cooking because Ned had told them to any better or worse than them saying it without encouragement? I mean, they *liked* my cooking. Obviously. The clean plates and second helpings were the giveaway there, and did I need them to say it out loud, especially just because Ned had told them I needed appreciation?

But underneath these feelings there ran a tiny warm undercurrent of satisfaction.

'Are you sure you wouldn't like a small dinner, Mimi?' I asked the ramrod-straight figure gazing out of the window again as though the lifeboat were inching closer to the sinking ship. 'I could plate you up something for you to take home?'

She didn't even look in my direction, just shook her head slightly.

'Ah, leave the old misery be,' John said. 'If she don't want to be a part of all this, that's up to her.'

'Shhh.' Grace put a hand on his arm. 'I'm sure Mimi has her

reasons. You don't have to involve yourself in them if you don't want to.'

Tom bridled at the physical contact. I saw him look pointedly at Grace's hand, still on John's sleeve, with his lips practically inside his mouth, and I sighed inwardly. He hadn't quite got the message that his romantic interest in Grace didn't make her his property, and I wondered again about his late wife and the life she must have had.

Before pistols at dawn were called for, I broke up the potential love triangle with the tea tray before handing round the post-prandial teas and coffees, then dashing back up the stairs out of the kitchen to my flat. Kez was paddling around in the entranceway with a slightly impatient look.

'I *can't* take you out at the moment,' I said, pleadingly, into those light brown eyes. 'I don't want anyone to see that you're up here.'

Kez sat on my foot and gazed up at me, as though trying to will me to understand his problem. *Understanding* it wasn't the issue, alleviating it was, and I didn't know how to ask him to hold on a bit longer.

I gave him a treat and closed the door, tiptoeing back down just in case someone was hovering about outside the kitchen door listening for me. I had no idea why this would be a problem, because I was quite entitled to go up to my own flat during the day, but a raging case of guilt about the secret dog was clearly making me sensitive.

Ned was in the kitchen, making himself a coffee. 'Everything all right?' he asked, looking up at the ceiling in a questioning way, although what else he could have meant I had no idea.

'He's a bit... cross-legged,' I said. 'But everyone will notice if I take him out.'

'I could provide a distraction if you like.' Ned's coffee was clearly very, very strong. I could smell it all the way across the kitchen. 'Keep their attention for long enough for you to go out and back for five minutes and let Kez have a wee. I can tell them you've popped out for milk or something, if they ask.'

I shook my head. 'They know I don't go out.'

'What, *never*?' The coffee cup hung, suspended by doubt, midway to Ned's mouth. 'You were out this morning, though, when I met you.'

'Oh, not *never*, obviously not. I mean, I shop and I go over to Andrew and Greg's, and I went up to Appleton...' I trailed off. The Appleton outing was the entire reason for my current predicament, and Andrew was going to hear *all* about the position he'd put me in. 'But not casually,' I finished with, I thought, commendable brevity.

'Any particular reason?'

'No. And thank you for telling the clients that they should appreciate what I do, but I'm not sure I like them being guilted into saying so.' I thought changing the subject was probably for the best here.

Ned's eyebrows rose over the coffee mug. 'Oh? I'm not sure I "guilted" them, whatever you mean by that.' He swallowed a couple of times. 'But I did notice that some of them can have a tendency to assume we're here to serve them – a touch of "I pay your wages" syndrome, I call it. And I thought a little bit of valuing what we do here wouldn't do them any harm. Would you like me to take him?'

'What?' I was genuinely nonplussed. 'Take who?'

'Kez. The dog.' Ned jerked his chin at the ceiling. 'I'm not doing much at the moment other than letting Timothy throw his vocabulary at me and listening to Harry and Will argue about the undercarriage of the B-17 or something. They can spare me for a few minutes.'

I instantly felt sorry for accusing him of forcing the clientele to like my cooking. 'Oh. Oh, yes, please, would you?'

'Seren!' It was Joe from the other room. 'You said you'd give me a rematch.'

'Just coming!' I called back, and then, speaking quickly, 'The door's not locked. Right at the end of the passage. His lead is on the table. Just go down the main stairs at the far end, out of the front door, shove him back in when you're done and shut the door.'

'You don't lock your door?' Ned looked astonished through the coffee-scented steam.

'This isn't London. The outer doors are locked after hours, and anyone coming in during opening times would be quizzed to death about their intentions by the Neighbourhood Watch.' I nodded towards the hall. 'Besides, there's a dog up there.'

'True. You go and sort out Joe's Scrabble addiction, I'll take Kez for a quick romp.' Ned put the cup down. 'I've missed having a dog. I've not had one since I was a child.'

'Couldn't you have had one? People have dogs in London.' I was really trying to find out whether it had been circumstance, or prison, that had prevented him from pet owning. Ned's background was very much an enigma wrapped in a photography distraction.

'I was too busy,' he said. 'Not home enough.'

Well, that didn't really stop my wonderings. He could have been away from home for any number of reasons, and prison was still up there as my number one theory. Ned had a 'careful' kind of way with him, alongside the clean-but-scruffy appearance. As though he watched what he said all the time – maybe afraid of saying the wrong thing to the wrong person? I didn't really know much about life *inside*, apart from the occasional sensational news report or TV drama. But there had to be a reason for his watchfulness, his seeming to be processing everything really, really quickly, in case a reaction was needed. Like Kez.

'Where did Ned go?' Will and Harry were waiting for me as soon as I went back through. 'He said he was just going for a coffee.'

'He's... um... got one or two things to do around the place,' I replied, factually correctly. 'I'm sure he'll catch up with you again later.'

'Oh. All right, then.' Will went off to check the bookshelves, presumably in case we'd suddenly acquired a set of *Jane's All the World's Aircraft*, and Harry, looking annoyed at the ending of their squabble, sat next to Grace and tried to engage her in conversation, oblivious to Tom's eye-daggers thrown from across the room.

Joe was sitting by the table. 'Shall I get the board out, then?' I asked.

'Gone off the idea now.' Joe sounded a bit short, which wasn't like him. 'Maybe I should take up knitting, like the lasses.'

Margaret's knitting had nearly filled her container with little fairies, dragonflies and one or two unicorns. Margaret knew her market.

'Can you knit?'

Joe laughed, rather wheezily. 'Course I can knit! Your generation didn't invent girls doing men's jobs and vice versa, you know. I can darn a sock too, not that that's any use these days. Learned in the army.'

Out of the window I saw Ned and Kez strolling across the car park in the sunshine. Only Mimi was looking in that direction, and she didn't react to the sight of the pair. Kez was trotting beside Ned happily enough, pausing to sniff at lampposts and gutters, and it looked as though Ned was talking to the dog as they went.

When I heard the gentle door-close of their return, I made my excuses and went back into the kitchen. The aged and reluctant dishwasher had finished and puffed out steam when I opened it, but Ned had done a good job on the shelves. They slid out for unloading without difficulty. When he came down the stairs from my flat, having put Kez back, I thanked him.

'Well, it *is* my job.' He looked a bit embarrassed, running his hands through his hair so that the disturbed parting now looked downright hysterical. 'Thanks for letting me take Kez out. I'll do it again in the week if you like. Tomorrow you'll be able to take him yourself, won't you, with us being closed?'

'Yes, of course.' Where did I know, apart from the field, that I could take Kez? Would he get bored if I always took him to the same place? I'd have to get up extra early so nobody else was there to confuse me – could I take him there twice?

My expression must have looked grim, because Ned gave me a sympathetic smile. 'Look. I'll be in tomorrow, why don't we take him out together? I know a few nice spots, places I go to take pictures, where he can have a good gallop, and you won't be on your own – does that make things better? Not being on your own somewhere new?'

He was smiling, head cocked and his hair still standing at improbable angles. Friendly, open. But still, underneath, a stranger. Would a trip out be a nice gallivant into the countryside or the prelude to me being chopped up and distributed in bin-liner bags around the county?

'OK, your hesitation leads me to believe that you aren't over-whelmed with enthusiasm.' Ned headed for the door. 'It's fine. Just a thought.'

What was more terrifying, really? The thought of having to take Kez somewhere on my own, or a day trip with a possible murderer? 'I don't know you,' I said, and my voice sounded small, as though I were a five-year-old being asked to go and see some puppies.

He gave a small cough, a sound of surprised realisation. 'I'm sorry. Of course you don't. Just because I know I'm perfectly – no, not reliable, that's the wrong word – perfectly unlikely to cause you any harm if I can possibly prevent it, it's not a supposition any woman could or should make. I'm really sorry to be so thoughtless, Seren.'

He went out into the conversation-filled room beyond, without another word, and I felt the steam from the dishwasher drying my skin into hot tightness. It would have been nice to have had company to walk Kez, Ned was right. I wasn't so afraid when someone was with me, even if I was driving somewhere different, almost as though the presence of another person meant that getting lost or having to deal with crowds of unknown people wouldn't happen. And, if it did, there was someone else to deal with it. I could hide in the car or behind a tree, and someone else would sort out getting home. Was I desperate enough not to feel scared of the outdoors that I would possibly put myself in danger?

* * *

'Please would you come with me tomorrow?' I cornered Ned in the corridor. I'd waited until he left the room to escort John and his shuffle-walker to the toilet, because I didn't want to give any of our clients any gossip fuel. If they'd saw me having 'a private word' with Ned, the vacuum caused by the indrawn breath would have slammed every door in the building.

He leaned against the wall. He had to wait for John to come back out because the walker didn't negotiate the slippery lino floor very well, and the combination of shuffle and slide could precipitate the less mobile at a faster-than-wise speed. 'You've changed your mind?'

'Apparently,' I said tartly. 'It happens.'

'Wow.'

'Why is it so surprising?' We were conducting the conversation in hushed whispers. I was very well aware that John was probably trying to listen, and hoped that negotiating the facilities was preventing him from hearing.

'You always give the impression of being...' Ned made circular motions with one hand, as though searching for a word.

'Rotary?' I still sounded sarcastic and I didn't mean to, so I smiled to take the sting from my tone.

Ned smiled back. This was the first time I'd seen him smile so broadly; it stopped him looking quite so intense and made his face open out into a pleasant friendliness. 'Definite. Immutable.'

'You make me sound like a geological era.'

'I'll be over at nine. If it makes you feel better, we can take two cars, you can follow me. Is that all right?'

'Will you two stop flirting out there and let me come out of this damn toilet?' John's testy tones echoed from behind the door. 'I don't want to interrupt, but I've done everything I can legitimately do in here. I'm going to need to go again if you don't get a shift on.'

I gave Ned a silent nod and fled back to the kitchen, where I hid until the gossip died down.

* * *

'I mean, you'd defend me, wouldn't you?' I asked Kez when I went to check on him later. 'You wouldn't let some man murder me? Oh, this is ridiculous, it's *Ned*, and now the entire group knows that we're planning a day out together tomorrow, if anything *did* happen they would be over at his house like the Avengers. Probably. Although more slowly and with less Lycra.'

Kez's tail waved a plumed acknowledgement. His ears went up

and down, then folded flat to his head and gave him the sleek look
of a seal.

'And you do need a good run out. I wonder why I haven't heard
from Mattie yet. She must have found a place to take you by now.'

Ears up, ears down. And now, a cocked head to contend with.

'It's all right, you aren't meant to understand what I'm talking
about,' I reassured the collie, who had also gained a small wrinkle
between his eyes, making his white-flashed face look worried. 'Just
stay here and stay quiet. Only another hour until we close up, and
then I'll let you go out again.'

At the word 'out' the ears came up and stayed up, but my
leaving him caused a flop of disappointment, and I left Kez lying in
the hallway, disillusioned and with his head on his paws.

This was no way for him to live, I thought, going down the
main, lino-staired route to downstairs. A tiny flat, just big enough
for one person, if that person didn't want to collect anything other
than dust; there was no room for hobbies. A reluctant visitor to the
outside world, who preferred the safety and security of indoors.
And now, a Border collie, with a body like a coiled spring and the
intellect to dash downstairs and complete all the crosswords. It
was a situation that couldn't continue. I made a mental note to text
Mattie and tell her.

Holly was in the hall when I came in, gathering everyone
around her like moss accreting around a gigantic boulder.

'So, we'll begin setting up at nine,' she was saying. 'The band
will be here by twelve, we'll do a sort of opening ceremony thing,
and then have the stalls doing business whilst the band plays.'
She put the back of her hand to her forehead, like a Victorian
heroine, mid-vapour. 'Oh dear, I didn't account for rain. Is it likely
to rain?'

'If it does, it'll be torrential,' John said, happily the bearer of
bad news. 'Thunder showers and all.'

'Well then, maybe we'll keep the hall unlocked. Then if it rains we can just move everything indoors.'

Great, I thought. That means that, not only have I got to bake like a demon, I'll have to give this place a really good clean-out too. I might even have to dust the pictures.

'Where's Ned?' Holly went on, beginning a general gyration of worry. 'Ah, there you are. Ned, I think we might need to give this outside courtyard a bit of a clean-up so we can set the tables up out there.'

'I'm coming over tomorrow to make a start.' Ned was sorting some jigsaws in the corner, I saw now.

'Tomorrow?' Holly sounded shocked. 'But it's Sunday!'

'It's all right, moving the geraniums isn't against my religion.' Ned wasn't looking at her. 'I've got a few other bits that need doing and I can only do when the hall is empty.' Now he raised his head from the *Record Breaking Mallard* and *Thatched Cottages at Dusk*, which comprised our jigsaw collection, as though anything more exciting might be too much for our customers. He met my eye and winked.

I widened my eyes in warning.

'The leg is loose on one of these chairs,' he went on smoothly. 'I thought I'd get it sorted, rather than come back one evening and do it. As I'll be in town anyway.'

'Oh. Fine. As long as it doesn't go down as overtime. I must say, you do seem happy to put in these extra hours.'

Ned almost flinched. It was a strange movement, a twitch of the shoulders as though he'd been hit on the spine. 'I... like being here,' he said, eventually.

'Fair enough.' Now Holly was back to addressing her acolytes. 'Margaret, you said you'd run the handicrafts stall, yes?'

While they portioned up the open day, and, as usual, everyone volunteered to run the cake stall, I shuffled my way through to the back of the room towards Ned. 'Have you really got a house on the moors?' I asked. 'Because, if your living arrangements are... difficult you are quite welcome to borrow the shower up in the flat. Now and again. By appointment.'

He straightened away from setting the puzzles on their shelf. 'What on *earth* makes you think that there's something odd about my living arrangements?'

It was another *sotto voce* conversation. Anything Ned and I ever had to say to one another seemed always to be said in hasty whispers.

'It's all right, you don't need to tell me. I just wanted to say that the day's leftovers always go in the big tin on the top of the fridge – not the dinners and such, I have to budget for those so there aren't leftovers – but the baking and the sandwich bread. If you're hungry, take from there. I can turn a blind eye and massage the spending.'

Ned looked frozen in an astonished way, and I was acutely aware that Holly had finished talking, so I backed out of the corner and turned my attention to admiring Margaret's knitting.

I didn't know what had made me make the offer. The coming together of the clues, possibly. Ned's 'no fixed abode' look, with the crumpled clothes and messy hair. His being here at all hours, as though the alternative was the cramped loneliness of living in his car. The proximity, and general nosiness, of our clients meant that a more in-depth conversation would have to wait until we were alone.

What had made him flinch at Holly's mention of overtime? Didn't he want anyone to notice how hard he worked? Most people of my acquaintance, (all right, that was practically down to Andrew and Greg, but I still *knew* them), went on and on about the extra hours they put in in the gallery or workshop. Andrew seemed to regard it as contravening his human rights if he needed to be in after hours to supervise the delivery of some over-framed portrait of a young girl holding an improbable sunflower, and whilst Greg enjoyed getting his hands covered in furniture wax, he didn't much seem to like it happening on public holidays, weekends or evenings.

But then, I didn't want to provoke Ned with questions. Partly because the question of his murdering and dismembering me still hung in the air, but also... There was something about him that made me think 'fragile'. Oh, not in a 'might snap arms or legs or topple over' way, not like, say, John, whose ability to fall backwards was almost legendary, and had made us consider inventing him a 'wrap around' walking frame. More in a way that made me reluctant to give him a list of jobs that needed doing around the hall and its environs for fear of overloading him. So I'd been carefully feeding the information about broken elements and wobbly chair legs, one item at a time.

It now struck me as a slightly ridiculous way to carry on. Which made me feel awkward, which, in turn, made me feel embarrassed, so I avoided Ned for the rest of the day. I took Kez for a swift walk down the road when Ned was out with the minibus, so I didn't have to risk him wanting to come with me and provoking more awkwardness, and I was so keen to get the job done that it didn't really occur to me that the street was still busy. My attention was mostly focused on the dog anyway. He moved like a shoal of fish through a coral reef, winding his way through the legs of tourists who hung around the little town after everything had closed as though they were hopeful that, once the shops shut and the last steam train chuffed its cheerful way back from the moors, we'd suddenly unfold an open-air theatre, two cinemas and a host of cosmopolitan venues. In reality, we had several pubs and a handful of restaurants, and that was their lot.

The presence of Kez gave me something else to focus on, apart from my own vague worry, which helped. I didn't enjoy the drifting groups of people, but neither did they fill me with the worry that had clouded my existence since I could remember. I tightened my fingers on Kez's lead, as he towed me, unerringly, back to the field we'd visited in the early morning sun, and I wondered how he remembered. He probably regarded it as an oasis of off-lead running in a desert of being expected to piddle on bollards or fence posts, and he certainly behaved that way when we arrived, circling me with little yips of joy until I released the lead clip and let him dash away.

Why *did* I have this fear of the outside? Idly, I watched Kez and a black Labrador, which seemed to be unattended by humans, chasing one another through the grass, and let my thoughts run. I'd never been involved in any accidents, or any traumatic incidents that might have led to my reluctance to be outside. In fact, once our parents had died, Andrew had been very, very careful about making sure that I was always secure, never pushed into situations that scared me.

Maybe *that* was why? Maybe having Kez would make me keener to go out and about, and break out of my overprotective brother's shell?

Then I thought about how Andrew had wanted me to play Dungeons & Dragons, take up Internet dating and his unspoken but present desire to try to hook me up with one or more of the hairy, heavy-metal-band boys. None of that could be regarded as overprotective. Plus, his desire for me to 'get a life' had, so far, only resulted in me getting a temporary dog. No sign of a hobby, boyfriend, or any kind of life that didn't involve picking up poo and throwing slobbery tennis balls.

I sighed. The field was very pleasant, I had to admit. Fringed on three sides by woodland, and with the train track squaring off the bottom end, it had a shallow, reedy stream running through the middle and patches of exposed sandy soil that were providing trainee rabbits with digging opportunities. It looked like an illustration in a children's book, green and overhung with trees, and the sparkling water in the centre.

Kez clearly thought it was idyllic and I felt a bit mean when I clipped his lead on again and indicated that it was time to go home. There was an air of sagging disappointment manifesting around his ears, and a distinct slump to the black and white shoulders. 'It's all right,' I found myself whispering to him. 'We're going out tomorrow for a really good run.'

Great, I thought, as I wandered back to the flat, behind the homing dog. Now I've promised Kez that we're going out. I can't even pretend I have a headache and cancel on Ned, because it would disappoint the dog.

I needed to have a word with myself about anthropomorphisation.

9

The next morning I was up early, which surprised me. Usually, on my day off, I wallowed around, heavy with sleep, until mid-morning. My bedroom was so small that there was only room for my bed and me, no space for a bedside table on which to rest a cup of tea, so if I wanted breakfast or a hot drink I really had to get up, and this would eventually persuade me to the kitchen by lunchtime.

Today, sunlight-assisted, I was up by eight. It struck me that Ned had said he'd be over at nine, and I nearly talked myself into going back to bed, but the thought of him pounding on the door, and Kez's rotating desire for a wee, hauled me up. I gave Kez a quick sprint around the car park, which he clearly regarded as less than optimal because he positively planted his paws when it came to going back in, but was eventually persuaded with a mention of food, and I showered and dressed.

Then I sat and worried a bit. All right, following someone's car made it easier to go somewhere. But what if he lost me? What if other cars got between us and he turned off somewhere along the road and I missed it because I was behind a pantechnicon moving slowly along a rural road? What if he lured me to some out-of-the-way place for nefarious purposes? I thought about dialling 99 on my phone and leaving it in my pocket requiring only the final digit, then realised that I was allowing neurosis to get the better of me. For all Ned knew, I'd told the entire population of the county that I was going out with him. Not 'going out', obviously, this most definitely wasn't a date, just going 'out', which sounded better, in my head.

At my knee, Kez whined. He'd eaten his breakfast and was virtually pointing at a contract that had 'big, exciting outing' pencilled in for this morning.

'All right.' I opened the flat door, surprising Ned, who had his hand raised, ready to knock, and I realised that Kez had been telling me someone was out there. He hadn't barked, though. I wondered what Tony and family had done to train him out of barking at knocks on the door, then decided I really didn't want to know, and gave Kez a quick cuddle, which also had the advantage of meaning that I didn't need to look at Ned.

'Ready for the off?' Ned asked cheerfully.

Kez licked my cheek and waved his tail at Ned.

'I'll just find his lead...' I knew exactly where it was, I'd only taken it off a few minutes ago. But I felt odd, confused, at Ned's sudden presence, even though I'd been expecting it, and I wanted to get some air to my face before I showed it to him.

Kez was nudging at Ned's hand with his bullet-tapered muzzle. 'I'll wait here, it's all right.' Ned stroked the dog's head in an unthinking way, as though he was so used to having a dog by his side that he could pet it without paying attention. 'I'm keen to get going while the weather holds.'

'Is it meant to rain?' I dragged the lead off the table, where it lay coiled like a snake. Was I certain I wanted to do this? My heart seemed to have lodged itself somewhere just above my stomach, and the two organs were in league to make me feel faint and slightly sick, but, on the other hand, Kez was almost airborne with delight at the sight of his lead coming out again and the implied walk. I couldn't disappoint that eager-eyed intensity. Anyway, he needed a really good run or he'd start reassembling my furniture upside down or something. I couldn't help the guilt that I was keeping an illicit dog in a flat that was slightly too small, even if it *was* saving him from lonely boredom in rescue-centre kennels – or worse.

'I'm not sure.' Ned led the way down the main stairs, Kez's paws sliding with eagerness on the lino. 'But even my limited experience of Yorkshire leads me to expect that it's not going to be unmitigated sunshine for the next six months.'

'How far are we *going*?' I stopped, four steps from the bottom, and Kez nearly pulled me over onto my face.

Ned laughed. 'No, no, I just meant that we can't rely on the weather so we might as well make the most of it while it's nice.'

'Oh.' I felt stupid again. At a disadvantage. It all made me realise how unused I was to casual conversation that didn't involve questions about what I'd changed in the shepherd's pie and who had hidden the Scrabble board.

Ned didn't seem to notice. He held the main door for Kez and me, and we precipitated outwards into the gleaming day.

'You leave the door open?' Ned pointed to the side door, which opened directly from the car park into the hall and was ajar.

'On Sundays, yes.' I hitched my car keys out of my pocket.

'Aren't you worried about burglars?'

'Roger will keep an eye open. Besides, there's nothing really to steal, and nobody's going to break in in broad daylight. The connecting door is locked, so it's only the hall open.'

'Is that... better?' Ned looked cautious and also startled.

'Means nobody can get into my flat or the kitchen. Unless

there's a particularly brazen burglar with a taste for jigsaws and really old magazines, they wouldn't get much. One of the clients might turn up, getting the day wrong or just wanting to get away from home or something. I leave a plate of biscuits in a hidden location – they all know where they are, just in case.'

He gave me a long and considered look, but didn't say anything else. He'd parked his car next to mine and, as we both got in, I gave his car a quick glance. It was a small Audi, clean and presentable, and no sign of sleeping bags on the back seat or all his belongings crammed into cardboard boxes in the boot. So he probably wasn't living in there, then. Actually, today he looked rather less crumpled, in a nicely fitting T-shirt and jeans, with desert-type boots on. He hadn't shaved, but it gave his thin cheeks a more even appearance than when they were dotted with random stubble; today it was all-over dark growth, which made him look a little less fey and a bit more – no. It was just Ned.

'I thought we'd head over to the coast,' Ned called through his open window. 'Just follow me. I won't go fast.'

It's not the speed that worries me, I thought as I started the car and nudged out of the car park after Ned. It's the getting lost or the being a long way from home and something happening. But, from the boot of the car, Kez whined eagerly and smeared his nose along the rear window, and I realised that having a dog was not concomitant with staying at home all the time. Besides, that field was getting boring already and we'd only been there twice. In a week we would have mapped every single molehill and grass blade. Then I shook myself. No, in a week, Kez would be rehomed, of course he would, and I made a mental note to ring Mattie when we got back. I couldn't keep a collie, it was ridiculous.

Ned led the way up onto the moors. Despite my nervousness, I had to appreciate the scenery; whenever I could look away from the rear end of the Audi both sides of the road were draped in exuberant shades of purple and yellow as heather and gorse flow-ered frivolously into the sunlight. There wasn't much traffic so I needn't have panicked about the view-blocking juggernauts or the speeding sports cars getting between us. It was still too early for the tourist traffic and nobody else seemed to be about.

It had been a long time since I'd been out here, I realised as the hills suddenly opened to reveal a huge vista of moorland spread out below us as we crested a rise. A tapestry blanket of shades, covering an uneven bed of streams and hillsides, the heather boomed with the sound of bees and I could smell the honey-scent even from inside the car. It was glorious. But after that moment of appreciation, I felt the weight of the sky again, the sheer disorien-tating loneliness of the road stretching long and grey into the distance, and I speeded up again to stick more firmly to Ned's bumper. He had slowed down a little too, as a procession of motor-bikes passed us and whirred their irritated engines into the hori-zon, so we continued almost joined together, down a steep hill that made Kez slide up against the back seat, and then on over another rise, until I could see that the blue line hugging my right side wasn't mist, but the sea.

Down again, now through narrow lanes, and I was glad Ned was in front because there was no way of seeing if anything was coming round the tight bends and past the hedgerows. My hands were tight on the wheel and my palms were slippery with sweat by the time we crawled our way into a two-car parking space of beaten earth under some trees and Ned got out.

'Here we are,' he said brightly.

I looked around. 'Where the hell are we?' Soft green hills rose among loosely stoned walls, and the trees were small and mostly made of branch. 'It looks like the Shire.'

'No hobbits here.' He pulled a rucksack from the back seat of his car. 'There's a beach just down there.' A vaguely pointed finger indicated somewhere that could be the edge of a cliff. 'And you can let Kez run here. There's no road and no animals.'

Cautiously I unstuck my hands from the steering wheel, got out of my car and went round to open the boot. Kez leaped out, circled me twice, and then stuck his head into the undergrowth beneath the tree. I hoped that now wasn't going to be the moment that Ned produced the machete, because Kez had got too much mouse going on to defend me. 'There doesn't seem to be much of anything,' I said, still cautious.

'Well, you can't take dogs on the major beaches at this time of year.' Ned pulled the rucksack between his shoulders. 'I looked it up,' he finished, slightly smugly.

'So, what we've got is a *minor* beach? How does that work? Does the tide only come halfway in?'

Ned looked puzzled. 'Er. It's just not a tourist beach, that's all.'

I looked around, slightly ostentatiously. 'The lack of anybody else sort of gave that away.'

A beaming smile. 'Come on. Down this way. I came by the other day to take some pictures of the sun setting over the hills and I found this place – thought it would be perfect for the dog to have a run and...' He stopped talking so suddenly that I half looked for the whipping out of the giant knife.

'And?' I asked when he obviously wasn't going to dismember me.

'Nothing. Only, I brought a picnic. Just a small one,' he added hastily when he saw my mouth open. 'I just thought, you're always cooking for everyone else, you might like not to have to worry about food?' His head tipped to one side, questioning, and in exactly the same way as Kez was currently regarding me, although Ned wasn't peeing on a stick.

I swallowed. Murder wasn't usually accompanied by sandwiches and chocolate biscuits, was it? 'That's really very kind of you,' I said faintly. 'And you're right. It would be nice not to have to think about food for once.'

Another bright smile and Ned set off, leading the way down a muddied footpath where the trees closed behind us as though to prevent anyone seeing our exit. Kez trotted on ahead with his tail high, nosing at the grassy sides to the lane, and pretending that he knew exactly where we were going, but with one eye on our movements, should we suddenly decide to duck off the track.

The lane arched steeply over the brow of a hill and then curled down, opening out to reveal the edge of a small rocky inlet. A smooth curve of sand cushioned the waves that were rolling in to break softly against the sides of the bay and cliffs rose vertiginously to either hand. Beyond them, the open sea mumbled against boulders and wore its way under the edge of the land.

'It's beautiful,' I said, without thinking.

Ned slung the rucksack down onto a black rock, which edged a pool so clear that I could see tiny fish swimming away from his shadow. 'It's not bad, is it? And deserted too.'

'Stop saying creepy things.' I felt a bit more confident now that I really had stopped suspecting him of wanting to isolate me.

'Sorry.' Ned gave a grin that made him look boyish. 'I realise that this has been hard for you, but you've done brilliantly to get this far.'

I frowned. 'And there's no need to patronise me either.'

The grin died. 'No. Of course not. Sorry, again.'

We watched Kez, who was executing spin-turns in the sand, for a few moments. Then we both said 'sorry' again, at the same time, and it broke the tension into laughter. Ned started throwing seaweed-sticks for Kez, while I looked around the little bay, squinting into the brightness that was the sun on the sea, and up at the cliffs where gulls dipped and cried their squeaky-wheel calls into the wind. There wasn't a great deal of beach, maybe a couple of acres of shiny sand at the water's edge, then some powdery dry stuff dusting around the rocks at the bottom of the cliffs. The sun was high above our heads, arcing its way towards the land and burning any shadows to stubs, but the breeze from the sea was cool. I hoped that Ned wasn't going to suggest a swim. Even Kez, who'd run into the lacy breakers after a ratty bit of seaweed, had emerged to a good shake and showed no real desire to go back into the water again.

It was oddly peaceful. Oddly, because I was here with a man I didn't really know and a dog that wasn't really mine, spending my one day off doing something I would normally have told any amount of lies about previous engagements to avoid. But the coil of tension that usually held my shoulders straight had unwound amid the white noise of the sea and the ratchet calls of the gulls.

I felt *safe*.

Kez panted up to me and shook a rock pool's worth of water up my legs. Ned followed him, laughing and also looking more relaxed than I'd seen him look so far. He'd got sand up his arms and water marks on his jeans and he was laughing that proper laugh again, which took the lines from his face and gave him back that Puckish expression of imminent mischief.

'Well,' he said, flopping to sit on a rounded rock, 'the dog is enjoying himself anyway.'

'I am too,' I said, almost without thinking. 'It's lovely here.'

Ned sniffed. 'Probably just an influx of Vitamin D,' he said, looking at me sideways. 'You need more fresh air.'

'I get fresh air!'

'Moving the pots around in the car park doesn't count, you know.' He was still smiling. 'Sunshine. That's what you need. You're very pale.'

'No, I'm not.' I found I'd put a hand to my cheek. 'Am I?'

'Tom thinks you're anaemic.'

'Tom ran a business making cardboard boxes. He's hardly...' I realised that I didn't know the name of any doctors, apart from David Tennant and that wasn't really what I was going for here. 'Medically qualified,' I finished.

'They can google things, you know.' Ned was drawing in the sand by his feet with a tail of seaweed. Kez lay in the shade of the boulder, panting. 'Just because they're old, they're not moribund.'

I laughed, hollowly. 'Tell me about it,' I said. 'It's like having parents, en masse. "Are you eating properly? Have you met a nice man yet? You don't look like you're sleeping properly, you need..." whatever herbal remedy is currently being advertised on daytime TV.'

Ned wasn't looking at me. He was scribing complicated shapes in the moist sand, keeping his eyes firmly downward. 'Maybe they feel that they are sort of parents-by-proxy?' he said, his voice very level. 'You said your parents died when you were young? That must have been hard.' A pause. 'What happened?'

It didn't hurt to talk about. Strangely, it felt more like describing the plot to a soap opera than talking about my life. It had been so long ago. So long.

'I was four. Mum had been ill for a while. I don't remember much, just doctor's appointments and things, and then she was in bed for – well, I don't know how long, it felt like forever, and Andrew kept taking me out to do things because I wasn't meant to worry her. He was twelve, you see. He took me to the park. A lot.' I scratched my head, there was sand in my hair. 'I got really sick of those swings. Anyway. We came home from the park one day and Andrew went in to tell Mum we were back, Dad was in her room with her, I think. Then Andrew came out, really white. I remember that, I'd never seen a person go that colour before. I don't really remember much after that, just that Mum had died and Dad had had a heart attack when he found her, and they were both dead.'

There was a heavy silence, into which the gulls fell, screaming.

'That's hard.' Ned flicked me a look now. Bright and sharp. 'So, what happened then? You said your brother brought you up?'

'Oh, not immediately. He hardly knew how to turn on the cooker, it would have been a disaster. Come to think of it, I'm not entirely sure he knows how to work an oven now – whenever I eat there it's microwaved stuff. Waitrose and Marks & Spencer microwaved stuff, of course, because he has high standards, but still. Not fresh cooked.'

'I'm sure he tries.' Ned robustly defended my brother.

'Oh, yes, he has to. Greg can't cook at all, even the microwave defeats him. But yes. My dad's sister took us in, but as soon as Andrew turned eighteen he became my guardian, and I moved in with him while he finished university.' I twitched my head. 'And that's it. No scandal, nothing alarming. Just parents who died.' I kicked my toes into the sand, covering my trainers. 'It's only noteworthy because it doesn't happen very often. I'm sure in the old days, when there were orphans everywhere, nobody turned a hair at someone who'd lost both parents before puberty.'

'Probably not.' Ned glanced up at me. I saw his frown. 'Doesn't make it any easier when it happens to *you* though, does it? Oh, that's a hypothesis, by the way, I still have both parents extant and very much involved.' He looked back down at the scribbled-on sand. 'Too much so, sometimes.'

I tried to judge whether this was him wanting to talk about something, or a general comment about his family. 'Interfering-wise?' I asked.

Ned sighed. 'Little bit.'

'And that's why you came to Yorkshire? Asserting your independence?'

He sighed again. 'Sort of. It's – well, complicated. But, yes, I moved up here to get a new start, right away from the old life.'

'I thought you'd been released from prison.' I surprised myself with this confidence. I hadn't been going to tell him my first impressions of him, with his crumpled clothes and careful self-policing. But I *definitely* wasn't going to tell him that I'd suspected him of machete and murder.

'Oh, did you?' Ned half laughed at that. 'Actually, it does feel a bit like that, sometimes. Yorkshire is...' He flung an arm out wide, evidently lost for words.

'Sandy? Mostly dog?'

'Different. Not like London. You don't lock your doors, for a start.'

'We do. Just not quite in the same paranoid way that you do down south. I mean, I don't want my TV carried off to be sold in a pub by a man with a meth habit any more than the next person, but I don't lock all the doors and windows when I'm in the flat either. Besides—' I pointed to Kez, who'd flopped over onto his side and was stretched out like a hairy sunbather '—now there's him.'

Ned also looked at the dog. 'He's not exactly a Rottweiler though, is he?'

'No, but he'd whine a lot and then I'd know someone was there. I'm not usually far away. Mind you, he's going to go to a new home as soon as Mattie finds someone to take him.'

Now we were both looking at Kez. As though he felt our stares, he raised his head, looked at us, and flopped back onto the sand with a weary sigh.

'Are you agoraphobic? Or have you ever been?' Ned asked, seemingly casual, but I could tell from the sharpness of his look that he'd been trying to find a way to ask this for some time.

'Don't. You sound like Andrew. No, I'm not agoraphobic. I don't mind being outside, I just don't like being in strange places, or alone.' I looked up at the big sky, a blue sheet to the horizon. 'I'm all right when other people are there.'

'Any particular reason?' Ned stood up now, and Kez immediately leapt to his feet as though he'd been waiting for us to finally get the message that he was desperate for another run.

I shook my head. 'It's just the way I'm made, I think.'

Ned blinked at me, and I thought he was waiting for more confession, but there really wasn't anything else to come. I'd told the truth. No dreadful backstory, just a dawning realisation that I didn't have much confidence when I was away from home. 'Shall we have a look at this picnic, then?' he asked. 'Or would you like to explore the beach? I've got my camera. I thought I may take some shots of the cliffs.'

Kez ran a few indicative steps, then turned back to us, tail rotating.

'I think a walk along the beach sounds good,' I said, and, at the word 'walk' the black ears rose almost off the dog's head, even though he'd only just stopped dashing about in the surf. 'While the tide is out and there's some beach to walk on. When it comes in there's not going to be much space. Kez might have to sit on my lap.'

We walked up to the cliffs at the furthest extent, where the retreating tide had marked its place with hard, ridged sand like fingerprints. The cliffs here were darkly draped with wet seaweed at their base, and rose to pillared heights, shaded with streaks of seagull poo from evident nesting sites. Then, with Kez a black and white bird-hunting blur in front of us, we turned around and traced the edge of the tideline to the other side of the cove. Ned took pictures of the trees that crowded down to the rocks that formed the edge of the bay where we'd come down onto it, and of the wafer-biscuit formation of the boulders and their contained rock pools. At the far side of the bay the cliffs were slightly lower, less craggy and forbidding. They slumped their way down towards the sea edge, like teenagers being forced to go for a paddle, on ever-lowering racks of fallen earth topped with grass and shrubs, plants hanging on for dear life to patches of soil at gravity-defying angles.

The flowering gorse scented the air with a faint whiff of coconut, but the overwhelming smell was of seaweed exposed to the baking sky, and wet dog. Kez shook himself up my legs again.

'It's so quiet,' I said, eventually, when we'd run out of remarks to make about the warmth of the sun, the coolness of the breeze and the sandiness of the sand. For all that I'd begun to feel more comfortable with Ned, in the absence of evident murdery intentions and following my confessions about my parents' deaths, I hadn't been able to make any interesting conversation. And I still didn't know much about Ned.

'I suppose it is,' replied Ned, who was also evidently lacking in the 'witty repartee' stakes. 'But that's what I'm really liking about Yorkshire. You can be up on the moor where I live, and only hear birdsong and sheep. No sirens or shouting or music or loud parties.'

'Yorkshire is quite big though,' I said reasonably. 'I expect Sheffield and Leeds are full of sirens and shouting.'

'And that's why I chose to come here,' Ned said enigmatically.

We deepened the silence a bit more, by stopping talking. Kez skittered his claws across the rocks, nosing at the layers of weed but finding nothing worth investigating further.

'Right, picnic,' Ned announced, when we'd combed as much out of the little bay as we could. Our footprints gleamed wetly in the shiny sand, showing our progress up and down, and Ned took a couple of photographs of them, Crusoe-esque, the only marks not made by nature on this deserted beach.

He'd made a selection of sandwiches, there was some shop-bought cake at which I tutted lightly, and a packet of biscuits, which had melted together in the sun to form a massive slab of goo.

'Wonderful,' I said robustly. I did mean it. It was nice not to have to think about food for once, and Ned's thoughtfulness made me look at him slightly differently, even though I did have to repeatedly wash my fingers in the nearest rock pool to prevent my entire body becoming smeared in 'chocolate-flavour coating'.

Kez didn't beg for food. He didn't even really seem to notice that we were eating. Instead he went on a sortie that involved chasing some seagulls and then finding small caves that had been washed into the rock at the cliff base, into which he would stick his head. I wondered if he liked the echoes.

'He doesn't seem to be pining for his original family, does he?' Ned neatly folded the remains of our picnic back into his rucksack.

'Well, Tony had already adopted him from a farmer who found he was no good with sheep, so he's already had two homes. Maybe he doesn't think it's worth getting attached to anyone.'

We watched the black and white shape, now pottering along in the lace of the surf. The tide had turned and the beach was getting smaller by the minute. I whistled, so Kez obediently trotted over and put his wet sandy head on my knee.

'He's attached to you,' Ned said.

'I hope not. I can't keep him.' I brushed the sand off his furry head. 'He needs a life where he's not shut upstairs all day. He's far too sociable to live that way. And, besides, Holly might let me have one small cat but I don't think she's going to allow a hulking great collie in the flat.'

Ned shrugged, but smiled. I did have to admit that Kez seemed fond of me. He walked alongside me as we picked our way up the steep slope back to where we'd left the cars at the top of the lane, and occasionally nudged at my hand with his nose. But it could have been the fact that I was still lightly streaked with biscuit covering, of course.

'I'll lead the way back.' Ned leaned on the roof of his car. 'I've still got to fix that chair.'

'Oh.' It dawned on me that, for me, this had been an unexpected rare outing. For Ned it had been time taken out of other things he should be doing. Presumably. Although he'd not mentioned any previous engagements. 'That could wait, you know. Doesn't have to be done today.'

Ned gave me one of those smiles that said his mouth was amused but his brain was busily working on something else. 'I don't want to leave it, just in case someone sits down heavily and we have to extricate them from the wreckage. There's a fair few hypertension cases going on, and I don't want to be responsible for a stroke or heart attack because I didn't put a new screw in a leg.'

'That's very – responsible of you.' I got into my car and wondered. Ned was a bus driver and handyman, what did he know about the medical history of our customers?

We looked at one another through our open windows. In the back of my car, Kez gave off a powerful odour of damp fur, and lay down licking his paws.

'I like to cover all bases,' Ned replied cheerily. I only realised that this didn't really mean anything as I followed him out of the damp earth and undergrowth of the hidden parking space, and up along the pinched lane towards the main road home.

Who was Ned, really? There was a level of intelligence and consideration behind those light brown eyes that surely wouldn't be happy simply keeping the hall maintained and remembering which villages to pick up and drop off at. He'd hinted at a faster-paced life in London – had he really just moved here to avoid parental interference in his life? What was stopping his parents from following him here, if they really wanted to oversee his life to that extent? And why did he sometimes look so... so... *uncared* for? As though he didn't seem to feel himself worth the time to invest in an iron or a proper haircut.

As I followed Ned back to the relative safety of Pickering and the security of home, I found I was wondering more and more about the enigmatic handyman.

10

I put cheese in the mashed potato on Monday, and it nearly caused an Incident.

'If you're going to surprise us,' John said, indignantly poking at his plate, 'then surprise us with something we can leave out if we don't like it.'

'But you *do* like cheese!' I wailed. 'You *all* like cheese! I put it on top of the mash on the shepherd's pie and you like it!'

'That's different,' Margaret said, definitively. 'We expect it there.'

'*I* liked it,' Tom said robustly. 'Made a change. Nothing wrong with cheesy mash.'

'Nothing wrong with cheesy mash when you're *expecting* cheesy mash.' John held to his opinion and rallied support. 'Unexpected cheese is a step too far.'

I shook my head and collected the plates. Despite the unexpected nature of the cheese and the resultant complaining, most of them had eaten every scrap. Joe had left most of his dinner and Mimi, as usual, hadn't taken one, but the rest seemed to be moaning just for the sake of having something to moan at.

Ned helped bring the plates through. 'They all seem a bit irritable today,' he remarked as we loaded the dishwasher, now, thanks to him, by pulling out the racks.

'It's warm. They always get a bit tetchy when it's hot. I never know whether it's because they don't sleep so well or whether it's because they'd all secretly like to be out somewhere enjoying it.'

At the mention of 'going out' I remembered that I'd promised to go over and take part in another Dungeons & Dragons session tonight at Andrew's flat. Well, I was going to get my own back by taking Kez with me. He was currently upstairs, spread out on my bed, catching the breeze from the open window in his fur. Thankfully he still seemed tired after yesterday's running about and had been happy with a quick saunter up over the marketplace this morning.

'Maybe we should take them out?' Ned gave me a sideways look. 'Oh, not far. Just somewhere where they can sit outside if they want to. Get some fresh air.'

'But we haven't got a trip organised.'

'Wouldn't need to. Pop all that want to come into the minibus, drive five minutes – I mean, come on, this is Pickering! In five minutes we can be in open countryside. I'm going to ask them.'

He stacked his final plate and went into the hall. I held my breath and listened, but Ned's proposition was more warmly received than my cheesy mash had been, and ten minutes later we were loading almost everyone onto the bus for a drive out to Sinnington, where the river ran through the village and there were plenty of benches to sit on.

'How nice,' Lena commented to Margaret as they carried their knitting on board. 'An impromptu drive out.'

'Are you sure you don't want to go?' I asked Joe, who was flipping idly through the dictionary, searching for more dubious words to round up his Scrabble score. 'The ice-cream van might be there.'

'You're not going, are you?' Joe replied. 'Someone has to stay here to keep an eye on you. Make sure you don't start putting cheese in the teabags or something.'

I ignored him. 'Mimi? Would you like to go for a run out?'

I kept trying with her, although I wasn't sure why. She hadn't spoken a single word since she'd started coming, and she only drank the occasional cup of tea and ate morsels. Instead she still sat, hands folded in her lap and her eyes on the car park, until we helped her back into the bus for the journey home. Holly had muttered something about having a word with her family, apparently Mimi lived with a granddaughter and her husband on a farm out in the wilds, but I guessed that Holly would know that they'd probably stop paying for Mimi to come if they heard how little she got from the group.

Mimi shook her head, very slightly, and shifted her hands. I wondered if the arthritis was causing her acute pain, but there was no point in asking, she'd only shake her head and turn her eyes back to the tubs of geraniums and Roger's comings and goings next door.

So Ned took the bus full of those who wanted to go, all behaving as though they were usually kept in close confinement with no activity other than continual repeats of *Cash in the Attic* on the TV. I was left with Joe, Mimi and a handful of others who'd decided that they would rather stay behind. The hall was beginning to smell of the scones I was baking for afternoon tea, and I think they feared they might miss out if they went 'gallivanting', as they called it.

The quietness gave me chance to clean down the kitchen properly and pop up to see Kez, who, apart from occasionally raising his head to snap at a persistent bluebottle, seemed happy to continue occupying my mattress. I sorted out a few recipes that I wanted to try before the open day, and then took the tea tray through to the hall.

'Are you feeling all right, Joe?' I asked, when the old man didn't bustle up at the first clink of the sugar bowl. 'You're a bit off your food.'

'Just tired.' He raised his head from the dictionary and I noticed that he looked a bit pale and his blue eyes had lost their usual sparkle. 'I'm ninety, you know. Entitled to get a bit shabby round the edges at my age.' He picked up a fruit scone. 'I hope you haven't put cheese in this,' he added, with a touch of his normal acerbity.

'No, I haven't.'

'Well, good. I dunno, next thing there'll be cheese in the biscuits and cheese in the rhubarb crumble.'

'It was cheesy mash, Joe. Hardly an unknown culinary experiment.'

Joe grumbled on, picking the sultanas out of the scone and leaving them on the side of his plate, which was a shame because they were Earl-Grey-soaked sultanas, but maybe that was the point.

Almost as though they'd been summoned by the rattle of the teacups, the minibus pulled into the car park and its passengers bustled out. Ned looked a bit frazzled, helping those who needed help down the few shallow steps or up into the hall, and when the last person was safely installed around the tea table, buttering scones and discussing their adventure, he and I perched on stools in the kitchen and he put his head in his hands.

'Never let me do that again,' he said, with feeling. 'If I have any more good ideas, lock me in the understairs cupboard until they go away, please.'

'Tough crowd?' I asked sympathetically, and pushed a mug of

tea across to him. A burst of laughter came from the hall and he jumped.

'It seemed like such a good thing to do for them,' Ned went on sadly, talking to the tabletop. 'Little drive on a hot day, a sit by the river, maybe an ice cream if the van was there. And they were all right on the drive, but when we got there...' He shook his head.

'It's best to think of it like a school outing only with people who are old enough to smoke and drink,' I said, still sympathetic. 'Did they try to get into the water?'

'Some did. There was "competitive paddling".'

'Well, I'm sure they enjoyed...'

'Followed—' Ned raised his head and looked me in the eye '— by competitive ice-cream eating, competitive "walking up the hill" and two lots of "looking through windows and criticising people's curtains". I mean, I know they're a lively bunch, but it was like all human life, with the filters off.'

'Ah.' I pushed the mug closer to his hand and went and fetched the emergency scones. 'Is this your first exposure to wilful disobedience and reckless disregard in older people?'

'In the wild, yes.' He bit a scone. 'I've dealt with the elderly before, of course. But never...' He shook his head again. 'What's in these scones?'

'Earl Grey.' I sighed. 'Just pick the sultanas out if you want.'

'No, no, it's lovely.' Then he gave me one of those mischievous sideways smiles. 'And at least it's not cheese.'

'Don't you start.' I grinned at him. 'They're just people who happen to be older. And sometimes they play on that – "Oh, nobody's going to mind an old lady having a look at their garden," or "They've doubled their sales today, why should they worry about me having a 99 in each fist?" Was it that sort of thing?'

'*Exactly* that sort of thing.' Ned gave another shudder.

'They get bored.' I tried to explain. 'It's hard for them. They get parked here by their families or the people who are looking after them, and most of them don't even think they need looking after. But they know that they're not quite as agile as they used to be, and that they're more liable to injury, and I think the restrictions that their health puts on them can get a bit...' I waved my hand. 'And then they get patronised and...'

'And people put cheese in the mash.'

'That's part of it. They don't have total control any more. Imagine if you'd been completely self-sufficient for sixty, seventy years, and then someone comes along and says, "From now on you won't be able to drive or go anywhere alone or do without these five hundred tablets a day." And all that autonomy flies out of the window. So, when you get the chance to go off the rails a bit, you do.'

'I do know this.' Ned was looking at me as though I were lecturing him in Drinking Without Spilling, 101.

'So why are you surprised that taking them out somewhere different resulted in them coming over like a toddlers' outing?' I was a little bit hurt by the sharpness of his words. I didn't mean to patronise him, but *he* was the one acting as though our client base had ganged up on him. 'They had fun. I'm sure it was stressful for you, but they enjoyed themselves. Isn't that what matters?'

There was another burst of laughter from the hall. Clearly, the adventures of the afternoon were being recounted in glorious detail.

'They're just people, Ned,' I said, more quietly. 'They got old, that's all.'

Then I left him sitting over his tea and scone and went off to listen to the embellished tales of exploits and mischief, which were making a couple of hours in a very small village sound like a stag weekend to Ibiza.

EARL GREY TEA SCONES

Best for when you want to impress someone or you want a choice of scone – for example, they're perfect for an open day.

First you must prepare.

Make a pot (or mug) of very strong Earl Grey tea. The nice, expensive lemony sort is good for this, but if someone has given you some Earl Grey tea – surprisingly popular as a birthday present, because people think it's classy – and you hate the stuff, this is a good way to use it up. You can use loose or teabags, doesn't matter, just make it strong.

Pour the tea into a bowl (using a strainer if you've used loose tea) and add sultanas. About 80g is the proper amount but I just chuck in a couple of handfuls because I like my scones good and fruity and it doesn't seem to upset the recipe too much, however much you use. Leave these to steep for as long as you can. Overnight is best, but if you've completely forgotten that you needed to do this bit and you've only got an hour, it will still work, your scones just won't be quite as flavour-ful. Shove the bowl in the fridge out of the way otherwise you will catch it with your elbow and tip it over every time you go into the kitchen (that's a pro tip for you).

When you want to cook your scones, first put the oven on to pre-heat. I know nobody usually bothers with this, but for scones, which can be surprisingly sensitive, you really should. 200 degrees C for a fan oven, but a bit hotter if you don't have a fan. While the oven is heating, get yourself a baking tray and put a bit of flour on it, so that your scones won't stick, then get mixing. You want about 350g of self-raising flour and around 85g of butter. You don't have to be too precise, you are making scones not building a space shuttle. Rub the butter into the flour, by pinching off little bits of butter and sort of moulding them between your fingers into the flour until all the butter is gone (you can look up a YouTube video on how to do this, if you've never done it before). Don't work it too much, once the butter and flour look like breadcrumbs, that's enough, but you don't really want big chunks of butter left.

Into this crumbly mix, add a teaspoon of caster sugar. I say caster sugar, but nobody ever has any of this in their kitchen, ordinary granulated is fine, as is brown sugar or even Muscovado. Whatever you've got. Then drain your soggy sultanas as well as you can, and stir those in too. You can mix with a spoon at this stage, if it's getting a bit wet for you. Once that's all mixed, add some of the Earl Grey tea that you soaked your fruit in. Add a little bit at a time, because you don't want your mixture to go runny. It should look like Play-Doh, with a few crumbly bits that won't quite stick – so like Play-Doh that's been left out of the container for a few days.

If you've forgotten to save any of the soaking liquid, or if it's already all over the kitchen floor, you can mix using milk. Or you can use some Earl Grey and some milk, it's up to you. All Earl

Grey will make your scones quite dark, so maybe use half tea and half milk if you want the conventional pale scone appearance.

At this point, put your floured baking sheet into the oven to heat up. Being pre-heated means that the bottom of your scones will cook to perfection and not stay soggy.

When you've got your ball of dough, tip it onto a floured surface and pat it down (don't roll it out) until it's around 4-5 cm thick. Too thick and the middle won't cook properly, too thin and you won't be able to split them in half (but you can just shove two together and pretend). Then, using a cutter (or if you don't have any, the edge of a suitably sized drinking glass) press out little rounds of dough and put them onto a plate.

When you've used up all the dough, brush your scone rounds with some beaten egg. Just get an egg, break it into a cup and swiggle it around with a fork (or your fingers). Then, using a pastry brush, a corner of kitchen roll (or your fingers), moisten the top of your scones with a little bit of the egg, just enough to give a sheen to them. This will make the tops go brown and shiny. You can skip this bit if you really want to, but for showy scones, as for an open day or if you've got relatives round, you have to do this.

Now get your hot baking sheet out of the oven and quickly slip all your scones onto it before it cools too much, then pop them in the oven for about ten minutes. You should be able to smell when they are done, but err on the side of caution. Over-done is better than underdone with scones. They should look puffy and brown.

Take them out and let them cool, but not too cool if you're serving A Tea, people like warm scones because they know they are fresh. Being Earl Grey scones, these are best served with a 'sharp' jam, like blueberry or even lemon curd, and clotted cream (none of this 'whipped cream' nonsense, clotted or nothing, please).

11

'Oh. You brought the dog.' Andrew opened the door to me and immediately took two steps back.

'I can't leave him on his own all day and all evening,' I said reasonably. 'And besides, he's your fault.'

In the living room, the game was clearly already under way, and I was relieved. I'd deliberately delayed my arrival so that I wouldn't get caught up in the creation of the party who were, from the sound of it, currently raiding a citadel somewhere in a forest. There were trolls.

'Well. Everyone's here. You've missed the start.' Andrew swept me along the hallway and into the kitchen. 'You'll have to sit this one out, but you can pick up some tips. For next time.'

There was a whoop of laughter from the next room. It struck me that much of my life seemed to be like this now. Listening to other people laughing in another room. It was practically a metaphor if I dared think about it. By my side, Kez padded along, being A Good Dog. Occasionally he would look up and catch my eye, as though to check we were in the right place, because

Andrew and Greg's home had very few points of contact with mine.

'Keep the dog off the furniture,' Andrew said, unnecessarily, because I was hardly going to let Kez run riot over the antiques, even if he'd wanted to.

As we walked into the room where all the gaming was taking place, gaming stopped. Everyone was instantly drawn to the dog, as though he had magnets in his fur, and it was incongruous, watching seven large, hairy and tattooed men making 'ooza gu'boy?' noises. They were quite sweet really, I thought, as Kez smugly rolled over and stuck his legs in the air for a chest scratch and the lads practically fought over his attention.

'Isn't he lovely?' murmured Nate, who had dragons breathing fire over both forearms and indications at the neckline that his chest was covered in something skeletal.

'I'd love a dog.' Tommo, who played bass in the band and had hair down to his navel, said. 'But the missus won't go for it. Says it would end up being her who walked it.'

'She's got a point though, mate.' Jed petted Kez with hands covered in silver rings that probably weighed more than I did. 'With us having to spend so long on the road and rehearsing and all.'

'True.' Tommo stroked Kez's muzzle. 'Still like one though. Maybe one day.'

I sat down on something that was eighteenth century and thought about these lads' 'one day'. They'd be old, still tattooed, would they still wear their hair like an eighties glam rock act? And what on earth would they be like if they attended a centre, like our clients? Would they toddle on their Zimmer frames headbanging to death metal when they were ninety?

I hoped so, and the thought made me smile.

'We are playing,' Greg said eventually, quite sharply. 'We must go on. The quest is not over.' Reluctantly everyone peeled themselves off the floor and went back to the table and Kez sat and had a good scratch, sending a drift of fur into the air and making Andrew wince.

'I hope he hasn't got fleas,' Andrew said dubiously, holding a bowl of crisps.

'I don't think so. Anyway. He's not my dog. Mattie will be finding somewhere to take him,' I said firmly, although Mattie's resounding silence and current unreachability was making me nervous. I'd tried her phone a few times during the last couple of days and she wasn't picking up. But then, she was busy with children and dogs and puppies, I reasoned. She definitely wouldn't leave me with a dog I didn't have the space or time for on purpose.

'Hmmm,' Andrew said, as though I were lying, which, since the wh-ole 'Mattie' thing had been his idea, was a bit rich. 'Right then, Seren, love. You'd better tell me what you've been up to lately, as the D-&-D-ing and the dog training don't seem to be catching on as hobbies. Have you been out and about?'

I took one of the bowls of crisps from him, and found myself talking about yesterday's seaside trip with Ned and the forthcoming open day as though they were invitations from King Charles and a fortnight's white water rafting. Anything to stop Andrew from trying to find me another hobby. Behind us, the troll attack in the forest had resulted in multiple deaths and a lot of fighting. At least one person was sulking.

'Are you eating properly?' Andrew asked, looking down at the crisp bowl, now empty.

'Of course I am! Cooking is my job! It's you two who don't eat properly.'

'We eat out,' Greg called from across the table. 'There are many good restaurants in York.'

'It's not the same.' I'd repeatedly tried to interest my brother or

Greg in the cosy comfort of cooking. Tried to show them how satisfying it can be to wander around a kitchen knowing exactly what ingredients you had, creating new dishes or feeling the fulfilment of putting meals and cakes on the table. But, although they both enjoyed the results, neither one wanted to put the effort in and so we'd arrived at a situation where I brought home-cooked meals over for them to put in the freezer, or they ate at places with French or Mexican names, which served dishes that I could have knocked up in twenty minutes for half the price.

But then, Andrew had supported me when I'd gone through catering college and got all my hygiene and safety certificates, so I owed him the odd banana bread or peanut chicken.

'And who is "Ned"?' Greg surrendered the game to the lads, who had split into factions – those who wanted to eat crisps and talk about the unsuccessful quest, those who wanted to lounge back in their chairs and discuss their latest gig and the remainder crouching on the floor to flop Kez's ears or try to feed him the remnants of earlier sausage rolls.

'New bloke at our place,' I said shortly. 'Drives the minibus and helps out.'

'Is he good-looking?'

I shrugged. 'He's just Ned.'

Now Andrew bustled in. 'Tall dark and handsome? Although I should want more than a Do-It-All guy for my sister, I *am* aware that time is passing and choices are becoming limited.'

'He's... not bad-looking, I suppose. But he's just Ned. Not a potential love interest, sorry. You might as well try to marry me off to Joe, or Will or any of our other male clients.'

Greg snorted. 'You would be too lively for them.' And then a sideways look at me. 'Probably.'

'Please don't tell me you've considered it!'

'I just want you to have someone, love.' Andrew looked at the boys from the band, scattered around the room in their various poses. 'And you aren't making any inroads on your own behalf, are you?'

'I like being alone,' I said, aware that this wasn't completely true. 'It's peaceful. There are people all day at work, it's nice to go up to the flat and sit in the quiet.'

'But it's not a life, is it?' Andrew snapped. 'You can do that every day until you are old, and then what? Move downstairs and become a client while someone else cooks for you? Where will you live? Who will you talk to then?'

'People don't *need* to be coupled up,' I said reasonably, eating more crisps. 'Just because you and Greg are happy. I've already done the miserable marriage thing, and I know that it's better to be sitting in silence alone than sitting in silence with someone who just doesn't want to talk to you.'

A memory sprang into my mind of my husband, of whom Andrew had deeply approved, sitting over his phone while I'd sat in lonely impatience, wanting to tell him things but being 'shhsh'd' into quiet so that he could scroll the latest apps.

Yes. It was better being alone than knowing you were, but shouldn't be.

'And don't be snobbish, either. There's nothing wrong with people who do practical things for a living. I mean,' I added hastily, 'not that Ned is a potential boyfriend or anything, but you really shouldn't dismiss anyone who drives a bus or helps old ladies to walk.' Or holds their wool and talks to them about the music of the fifties, or plays endless games of Scrabble with a nonagenarian cheat, or tries to persuade the silent Mimi to talk. I didn't add all this because Andrew only saw what I did when he came on open days and, I think, believed my job to be something like Mrs Patmore in *Downton Abbey* – lots of ordering about of underlings and rushing about a huge kitchen to produce a swan or suckling pig. Surprise cheese was not on his radar.

'I'm sure there isn't.' My brother smiled over at his husband. 'When I met Greg he was building moulds for pouring concrete, don't forget.'

Greg's experimental period with concrete furniture had, thankfully, been short-lived. The results had been wonderfully stylish, all polished surfaces and rounded corners, and so heavy that it could only go in downstairs rooms with sturdy flooring.

'But I want you to be with someone who improves your quality of life.' Andrew lifted my hand as though to demonstrate. My nails were very, very short, because of hand-rolling pastry, and my knuckles were dry because I washed my hands so often.

'I love my job,' I said quietly, taking back my hand. 'I love cooking and I love talking to the customers. I like the idea that we're providing a home-from-home for anyone who doesn't want to be alone.'

'But you don't go *out*!'

'I don't *like* going out,' I pointed out, simply.

'I wish you'd learn that the world isn't as frightening as you think, Seren.' Andrew suddenly seemed to look inwards at a memory I couldn't share. 'I did pay for therapy, remember.'

It suddenly seemed that everyone in the room had been listening in, and I was subjected to six different views on therapy, how useful it was, and how much it had helped everyone present or their wives, girlfriends or other family members.

'I tried therapy and it didn't really work, did it? There wasn't much for me to say. I think it would work best if there was something to be overcome,' I said eventually, when I'd escaped with Andrew to their immaculate kitchen. 'There isn't. I've just never liked being in strange places by myself. If I was born with an aversion, why would therapy help?'

Andrew muttered something.

'Why don't you get a lovely range cooker put in here?' I changed the subject. 'A microwave and a toaster are not enough!' I ran a hand over the acres of gleaming brushed steel and marble that made up the beautiful kitchen. They'd had someone down from London to design it, and the worktops were from Italy, and I was overcome with envy every time I walked in there. But only at the style. The kitchen itself wasn't functional unless you just wanted Pot Noodle, toast and ready meals, although their coffee machine had cost as much as a small car.

'Different lifestyles, love.' Andrew was looking at me, slightly sadly, I thought.

'My kitchen might not look like the inside of an industrial warehouse, but at least I can knock up an Eve's pudding. Everything in here would stain, crack or mark if you cooked.'

'Which is precisely why we don't,' he said briskly. 'Would you like me to get a subscription to another dating site, now you've got things to add to your hobby-list? So you can make it sound as though you live a rounded life and actually, you know, *do* things?'

I reviewed my recent life. 'But I don't.'

'D&D with the lads, and dog training?' He tipped his head to one side and I was suddenly struck by how different it looked when Andrew did it, compared to Ned. There was something almost parental in Andrew's expression, a bossiness that spoke of him knowing what I needed from life. When Ned gave me that tilted-head look, it was sharp and seemed to always be asking a question that made me think. A laser-pointer of a look.

'Once. Well, twice for the dog training.'

'Look, there's people out there who claim "running" as a hobby when they haven't accelerated past a slow walk for twenty years. Unless you only want to meet D&Ders who are closely related to Graeme Hall.' He made a face at my frown. 'He's a dog trainer. On

TV. Tch, Seren, you can't even put watching TV as a hobby, and that's practically all anyone ever does!'

I took a deep breath. He was my brother. He was concerned for me, it was natural. Even more so since I hardly even remembered my parents, and he had brought me up through my formative years. It can't have been easy for him, trying to make a life for himself whilst caring for a 'difficult' teenager, but he'd done his best. And he'd always been there for me. 'I'll think about it, all right?' I said, trying to sound as though I would. Dating might not be so bad, if I could make sure I always chose where to meet and never had to go anywhere strange. After all, yesterday had been fun – walking on the beach and watching Kez chase the waves. 'I'll think about it,' I said again.

'You should.' Andrew gave me a little shake of the shoulders. 'You're too good to waste, love.'

'Being single isn't *a waste*.'

'Well, no, but I'm rather relying on you to breed so Greg and I can do the "doting gay uncle" thing. Take your offspring to ridiculous places and expose them to new experiences, and all that.'

'I believe that's the sound of my reproductive organs closing down,' I said. 'I'm not going to couple up and have babies just so you and Greg can act out a sitcom.'

Andrew beamed at me. 'Anyway. Probably time for Cinderella to make her escape. You might have to roll the dog down the stairs though, they've been feeding him on sausage rolls and crisps and he's practically circular.'

Andrew seemed to have come around to the idea of me visiting with Kez, I was horrified to note. I'd really hoped that he'd be so indignant about dog hair on the designer curtains and claw marks on the expensively stripped board flooring that I'd be excused from ever having to visit again.

I whistled, and Kez got noisily up from where he'd been being petted by what looked like the cast of *The Lord of the Rings*. How he knew that the whistle had been meant for him, I didn't know. It seemed to me that the dog was always waiting for me to indicate some kind of expected behaviour – as though he listened in to me all the time, as a collie-shaped spy satellite.

It worried me a little, as Kez jumped happily into the back of the car, how quickly both he and I had adapted. Because I most *definitely* was not keeping him.

12

A few weeks passed. Mattie continued not to phone me, although I did get to speak to her once, when she breathlessly told me that all the dog-rescue places and foster carers were full. 'It's... seven months... since Christmas...' she puffed. 'All the... Christmas puppies... have stopped being cute. They're all... into ten-month terrors.'

Kez, who was considerably older, and reaping the benefits of having passed his 'terrible teens' on a farm where, presumably, nobody had cared that he wasn't cute as long as he followed commands and attempted to work the sheep, rolled over on my bed and sighed. He'd filled out a bit more and wasn't the leggy ribcage he had been when I'd taken him on, which wouldn't have mattered except that he now took up the whole bed. I'd had to order him onto the floor last night and he still hadn't forgiven me.

'But I can't keep him!' I wailed at the wheezing Mattie. 'I live in a tiny flat and I already have to close the bathroom door if I want to go into the kitchen.'

'Sorry, Seren.' Mattie seemed to have reached the pinnacle of whatever she'd been doing and regained her breath. 'At least he's happy with you for now. Look, I've got to go, I've got twelve Labradors staring at me.' She hung up without giving me the chance to ask whether the dogs were eyeing her up as a trainer or lunch.

Oh, good grief. I sighed heavily and Kez raised his head. 'You can't stay here. I mean, even Holly is going to notice eventually,' I said to the white-blazed face. His ears rose and fell like speeded-up film of mountain ranges forming and eroding as Kez worked out whether or not I was talking *to* him or *about* him. Reassured that I didn't require any action on his part, he lowered his head to the duvet again, gave a blissful sigh and turned his belly to the ceiling.

'I suppose I could tell Holly I've got a poltergeist,' I mused. It would explain the mysterious thumps that Kez occasionally caused, that I passed off to our clients as being something falling off a shelf upstairs when they glanced ceiling-ward with agitated expressions. 'But I think Jim might already suspect.'

'You got pets?' Jim had asked. He was a recent addition to what Holly called 'our little family.' His own family had gone to the Algarve for six weeks, so he was coming daily for the duration.

'Er, no.' Kez didn't really count as a pet anyway, I thought guiltily. He was more like a flatmate who barked.

'Oh. Only a mate of mine swears he saw you walking a dog up at the big field the other day.' Jim looked at me shrewdly. He had blue eyes like little snips of cobalt in a white-bearded face and, if it hadn't been for his stick and bad hip, I'd have put him somewhere around fifty. He was eighty-three.

'That was Ned's dog,' I said, panicked. I couldn't afford to let any rumours get to Holly. Whilst I doubted she'd throw a cook/housekeeper out onto the street, she could lay down the law about Kez staying, and then finding him a new home would be down to me. If even Mattie, with her contacts, couldn't find anywhere for him to go, then I presumed Holly would be within her rights to order him to be put down.

'Oh. OK.' Jim wandered off. Joe, who'd had a resurgence of Scrabble lately, cornered him for a match and the two of them sat mumbling at opposite sides of the old table.

Mimi limped in. She'd been in the loo for so long that I'd started to wonder if I should tap on the door and ask if she was all right, but I suspected that she shut herself in there to be away from everybody.

'Hello,' I said brightly to her, as she sat herself, slowly and stiffly, in the chair that was definitively 'hers', by the window.

She gave me that familiar half-smile of recognition and laid her hands in her lap.

'Look.' I had an idea. 'Mimi, I really, really want an opinion on these new blondie things I've baked. Everyone else is too busy. Please would you try one and let me know if they're even passably edible? I don't want to unleash a repeat of "Cheesy Mash-gate" if they turn out to be too sour or too chewy.'

It was a little bit of a fib. If I'd brought out a new sample of baking it would have been like the sack of Rome, leaving nothing but a few crumbs and a despoiled baking sheet, but there wouldn't have been much critical thinking going on. The best I could have hoped for would have been 'very nice, love,' and then some complaints about raspberry pips stuck in dentures.

Mimi regarded me levelly for a moment. Like Harry, she had very blue eyes, although hers had the faded blue of much-washed denim. Then she gave me a small, sharp nod, which so overcame me that I almost forgot what my excuse had been, and had to dash to the kitchen to regroup.

'Mimi just communicated with me,' I said as I passed, happily breathless, by Ned, who was helping Margaret with a jigsaw on the big table.

He immediately left off trying to sort pieces of sky in the box and followed me. 'What did she say?'

'She didn't *speak*. I asked if she'd give me an opinion on the new blondies I've baked and she nodded.'

'Nodded.' Ned sounded less than impressed.

'Yes. But it's more than she's done this far. I mean, it's been nearly a month and she's done no more than small smiles and the odd head inclination. *Can* she talk, do you know?'

'Holly seems to think so. Although, apparently, her grand-daughter can be a little bit hard to reach to check these things out with.' Ned rested his elbows on the island unit as I hauled a steaming tray of baking out of the oven. I'd only made a small, trial batch, just in case. 'They look good.'

'It's a new recipe, and I tweaked it a bit. Now I'm worried that it's going to be horrible, so I'd rather not face the wrath of Joe and Will et al. if they aren't quite right.'

'You could have asked me to taste them for you.' Ned gave me that tilted-head look again.

'I don't *actually* need anyone to test them.' I lowered my voice. 'I mean, I'm pretty good at knowing what will work, and I will try them myself first, obviously. But I thought it might be an excuse to get Mimi interacting, even if it's just a little bit.'

'She always looks immaculate, doesn't she?' Ned sort of changed the topic. 'Hair done, beautifully dressed, all that. I wonder how she's managing, with the arthritis. Bearing in mind how hard it is to get in touch with her family, I can't see that they're getting her up and sorted for the day before she gets on the bus.'

'Farming people, I heard,' I said, still keeping my voice low. I didn't want anyone out in the hall to hear us discussing one of them. We had to talk about them, of course we did, there would be briefings and updates from Holly and her busy elbows, especially if there was a change in a health status or if someone needed specific medication to be taken at certain times. We weren't a medical facility, and we could only deal with clients who were self-reliant and independent enough not to need personal care, but we would remind them about pills or insulin timings, and keep a general eye on long-term conditions. But nobody needed to hear themselves or, even worse, someone else discussed as though they were objects rather than people.

'Yes. Isolated old place. Lots of barns and...' Ned was obviously straining to the end of his agricultural knowledge '... sheep and things like that.'

'In which case, right now they'll be out on the hills a lot. Prime time for getting the hay and silage done and not a lot to spare for Mimi. Maybe that's why she's here.'

The blondies steamed their fragrance into the boiled air of the kitchen. Any minute now the scent would waft under the door and a ravening horde would collect. There was a hefty thump from upstairs and Ned looked at the kitchen clock. 'Nearly three. I'd better get Kez out for his afternoon constitutional.'

We'd fallen into the pattern of Ned taking Kez out during the day. It had happened so easily and rapidly that I'd hardly even noticed that it had become a pattern. Every day at ten, twelve and three Ned would make his excuses or just slip away out of the hall, dash upstairs to my flat and take the collie for a half-hour sortie around the streets of Pickering or, occasionally, for a dash around the field. I did the early morning and late evening walks, and sometimes, if I couldn't sleep, a bonus night-time stroll. I was also working in some basic 'sit, down, stay' stuff, but since Kez already knew what those things were, and would obediently run through them for me without seeming to tax his intellect greatly, I was beginning to think we might have to move on to something more advanced. Brick-laying or calculus or something.

'Right. Thank you.' I was preoccupied with the baking, cutting the newly emerged blondies into neat squares; judging their cookedness from the resistance the puffy surface gave to the knife and looking critically at the amount of raspberries scattered through the mixture. But even so I saw Ned give me another of his looks as he passed me, heading for the stairs. He seemed to want to say something else but my activity and the switch of attention had put him off. Ned often gave me that impression though. We chatted quite a bit, but it was usually superficial stuff unless we were discussing a client's increasing needs or any other concerns about our jobs. We didn't talk about ourselves much, past the odd question about siblings or childhood holidays and things like that. Ned already seemed to have deduced a great deal about me, and I was still so creased with embarrassment about having thought he lived in his car that I didn't like to reveal my prejudices any further. And he helped me with Kez, which seemed to suit all three of us.

I heard his footsteps over my head, the creak and swing of my door opening, and then the click of Kez's claws on the boards as the two of them exited from the far side of the flat so they could go out, unseen, through the main entry door.

I continued to slice the blondies, and wondered how long I could keep a secret dog, and whether I ought to start trying to find him a new home myself. But the market seemed to have been flooded with post-Covid dogs, who had done their puppyhood in houses full of people working from home or furloughed, and were now struggling to come to terms with silent homes and people whose lives had regained the desperate dashing about that had, presumably, prevented them from getting a dog in the first place.

A leggy, weirdly-intelligent collie, who'd already been through two homes, was probably not going to be anyone's first pick. I didn't know how long rescue centres would keep him before having him put to sleep if he couldn't be rehomed, and the thought of lovely Kez, with his geographical ears, his sharp eyes and the reassuring nose in my hand, being put down made my eyes prickle with tears.

Just because *I* couldn't keep him, didn't mean *nobody* would want him, surely?

I put a blondie, cut into small segments, into a plastic box and took it through to Mimi. I didn't dare put it on a plate, it would have vanished in a veil of crumbs before I'd got through the doorway. The smell of fresh baking was already causing rumbles of discontent about 'teatime being late' (it wasn't), and hopes that I wasn't attempting some newfangled recipe that might contain suspect ingredients like quinoa or spelt or diced walnuts, for which virtually everyone seemed to have an unreasonable hatred.

Mimi was still in the position I'd left her. As angular as a draughtsman's T-square, with her chin averted so that her gaze fell across the open space of the car park that lay between us and Roger, and was mostly the scenic vista of the side of the minibus, two concrete tubs and a delivery of ancient furniture. Roger had heaped it up by his back door and paid it occasional visits with a spray can of insecticide and a dubious expression. As a view, it lacked a certain something, but I supposed it contained nature and movement and was probably about as interesting as watching her fellow clients knitting, doing jigsaws or debating the pros and cons of modern aircraft and *Love Island*.

As Ned had chosen to take Kez along by the river today, the view also contained Ned and Kez. Ned was clearly talking to the dog, as Kez had his head turned up so he could see Ned's face and his ears were doing the rise and fall that meant he was listening for trigger words. His elaborately plumed tail was held high and waved an occasional acknowledgement as the two of them followed the path, broken only by the odd taut-lead moment when ducks had the temerity to exist.

Mimi flickered her eyes from the window to me, then back to

the window again, as though she was trying to force Ned and I into the same field of vision. One eyebrow had tilted, I noticed. 'Er, yes. Ned's just going for... a walk.' I wondered if I ignored the presence of the dog, would Mimi assume that Kez was a given? I tried to distract her. 'Here's that blondie I mentioned. Could you tell me if it's all right?'

I held up the pink plastic box like a supplicant. Mimi hesitated, then dipped long, elegant fingers, bulging with the twists of arthritis, into the box and delicately extracted a morsel of cake. She wore a wedding ring, I noted. Gold, but with the thin, darkened look of a ring that had been in situ for so long that its presence was almost forgotten, as though it had become a part of its wearer. There were no other rings or adornments on her hands, but then maybe she didn't like to draw attention to them. Lena had studied nail art when she retired, and would do the nails of anyone who asked, so most of the women, and a couple of the men, sported flamboyantly coloured fingertips, some with gold-leaf designs. Mimi's nails were plain. Unvarnished.

Mimi laid the tiniest crumb onto her tongue and then sat, mouth closed and no apparent chewing for a second. Then her cheeks worked briefly and there was the tiniest moment of brightening in her eyes as the sweetness of the white chocolate and the tartness of the raspberry hit her tastebuds. She swallowed, then turned her gaze to me, as I still stooped in front of her like a beggar with a plastic bowl.

She nodded. Just a small, sharp nod again, but this time she was looking right into my eyes and there was an expression that I found hard to read. Perhaps an acceptance or an agreement – as one craftsman to another, appreciating artistry and creativity.

I let out a puff of breath. 'Thank you,' I whispered, and this time it was less of a 'get Mimi to communicate' and more gratitude at the acknowledgement that she had given me. It was something I didn't often get. Oh, they'd thank me for dinner, or offer comments (usually uncomplimentary) on the contents of today's fish pie, but it was rare that someone recognised the effort involved, unless Ned had had a word with them about appreciation. Whilst heavy-duty kitchen aids took a lot of the grind out of the actual work, adding flair or those little extras that gave a dish a bit more oomph than the average supermarket ready meal was all down to me. And nobody, generally, noticed.

So Mimi's low-key nod was practically equivalent to Prue Leith coming round and shaking my hand, or Mary Berry being caught with her head in the cake tin.

I went back to the kitchen and prepared the rest of the blondies for the tray, made a pot of tea and carried it all through to the hall, by which time Ned had returned Kez to the flat and reappeared among us as though he'd never been gone.

Nobody remarked on his absence. Ned's brief seemed so widely spread that he was liable for anything from tidying the minibus to overhauling the dishwasher, so, apart from his Kez-walking, he'd often be hidden away in various corners doing things with wrenches and screwdrivers. I kept out of the way. I had the horrible feeling that if Holly could consolidate our roles into one, she would, so I didn't want to know any more about the business end of a spanner than I had to, just in case. Ned seemed to have a similar lack of interest in cooking, so I reckoned that demarcation was still working for us.

I served tea, and the blondies were received about as graciously as what they called my 'experimental phases' usually were. A bit of cautious sniffing, some face-pulling and then, once the first brave souls had taken a bite and not dropped dead on the spot, disappearance. As the plate emptied, I looked over at Mimi and found that she was watching me with an expression that might have been a very slight smile on her face. I returned it, and she went back to looking out of the window but, I felt, with something of an air of satisfaction about her.

Maybe that was the secret, I thought as I carried the tray back to the kitchen. Maybe Mimi just wanted to feel that she was seen. Distinct. We tried, we really did, to treat every one of our clients as an individual, but there was a necessary amount of 'lumping together' that went on occasionally, where we had to regard them as a unit. Perhaps Mimi felt that homogenisation more than the others? I made a note to mention it to Ned and Holly.

I'd put the tea things into the dishwasher and set it running when Ned came in carrying a few loose cups and spoons that had been dotted around the hall during the day's session.

'They're all wondering who you're trying to impress with the new recipes,' he commented, sliding the crockery into the sink and starting to rinse it through.

'Just practising for the open day,' I said, hitching myself onto a stool.

'That's what I said.' He put the mugs upside down on the draining board, where the vibration from the dishwasher made them rattle against the stainless steel like false teeth attempting to chew through the surface.

'Anyway, who the hell do they think I'm trying to impress? Harry? Oh, please tell me they're not trying to match me up with Harry? He's got at least fifty-odd years on me.'

Ned averted his eyes and made free with today's tea-towel display – The Wildlife of the Orkneys – to dry his hands. 'I think it's me,' he muttered into a matching set of puffins.

'What, they think I'm trying to seduce you through the medium of baked goods?' I felt my cheeks get a bit warm at the thought.

Ned just gave a somewhat truncated shrug and kept his face turned away. 'Apparently.'

'I don't know whether to be amused, horrified or slightly insulted that they think my charms are purely limited to my cooking.' I tried to settle on 'amused', but feared that my body might be giving away 'embarrassed and misunderstood' vibes.

'To be fair to them, they are mostly of the opinion that "platonic" means "things served on a plate".' Ned turned around and now he was smiling. 'They don't really consider that a man and woman can be in the same vicinity for longer than a few weeks without falling deeply in love. I blame those paperbacks.'

We'd recently had a donation of books from the local charity shop. The covers had indicated that the books had been hanging around since the sixties, and tended towards floral covers featuring ladies in twinsets or ball gowns looking wistfully at men with interesting facial hair.

'We could burn them,' I suggested hopefully.

Ned tipped his head. 'Are you saying that in the old-fashioned sense of "let's have a conflagration of a literary nature" or in the modern sense of "we could set up our customers to be definitely answered with no chance of comeback"?'

I suppressed a smile. 'Yes. Both of the above.'

Ned held up a sudden hand. 'Have you noticed something?'

I started paying attention. Beyond the rattle of the cups and the vibration of the dishwasher, there was nothing but the sound of birds in the eaves beyond the kitchen window, the movement of passing traffic and our breathing. 'They've gone quiet.'

'We'd better find out what they're up to. Should we?' Ned seemed suddenly hesitant. 'Or is it a good thing?'

'When they *all* go quiet, it's never a good thing.' I slipped off the stool. 'Be prepared for blood.'

Ned flinched again, but I didn't have chance to wonder why. Cautiously, I opened the door between the kitchen and the hall, where the silence had a breath-holding quality, such as may be experienced if a bride were walking up an aisle or a new type of KitKat was being announced.

Everyone was turned towards the middle of the room. And there, sitting happily on two copies of *People's Friend* and a jigsaw box, was Kez.

'You didn't shut the door!' I hissed over my shoulder at Ned, who was trying to peer past me.

'I did! At least... no, I'm sure I did.'

'Well, you can't have done! Look at him! He must have come down the main stairs and come looking for us.'

Kez's tail was waving a wide circle, brushing magazines and the box lid – an improbably highly coloured picture of Bamburgh Castle, another recent donation – into a meniscus of happiness. His ears were cocked and he was happily blowing my 'Ned's dog' story out of the water.

'Where did this one come from?' I heard John mutter.

'Maybe he's a stray who's wandered in?'

'But the outside door's closed.'

Kez lay down and then rolled over, exposing his furry belly to the ceiling. There was a short chorus of 'awwwww's. I elbowed Ned.

'What are we going to do?'

'Seren told me it was Ned's dog.' A slightly accusatory tone in this.

'Then what's he doing here?'

'Maybe Ned brings him to work with him and he stays up in Seren's flat. Not kind to leave him at home all day, after all.'

'Let's stick to that story,' Ned whispered to me. 'It will cover us for now.'

We opened the door further and went into the room. Kez was having his head petted by Lena, while everyone else had gathered around as though observing a rather picturesque road accident.

'He's Ned's dog,' I said as we walked in. 'He's supposed to stay upstairs, quietly.'

Kez got up, shook himself, and then came to sit beside me, with his muzzle shoved into my hand. He ignored Ned. But then, I probably smelled of cooking.

'Er, yes,' Ned said, brave in the face of the evidence. 'He's mine. Er.'

Kez snuggled further into me. Another couple of people came closer. Jim bent down and stroked the long fur that lay, cape-like, across Kez's shoulders. 'He's a beautiful dog.'

Kez's tail waved an acknowledgement of his beauty, but his face turned up to meet my eye. The golden eyes looked a little bit happy to see me, and also a little bit guilty, until I smiled, when the tail waved more energetically and the nose dug its way into my palm.

'And he really seems to like Seren,' Margaret observed. 'More than Ned, in fact.'

To distract them from coming to any conclusions, which would only have been correct, I gave Ned a ferocious stare, flicked between him, the dog and the circle of people who were beginning to take on a kind of 'acolyte' stance.

Ned pulled a face at me and then said, 'His name's Kez. He's not really my dog...' I elbowed him, and he went on smoothly. 'I was given him to look after for a while but I'm away from home so much that I've been bringing him over here during the day. I hope nobody minds.'

I waited. Surely someone was going to pull a previously unheard-of allergy out of the woodwork, or a concern that the dog might suddenly go mad, attack us all and then dash out to conduct a barbaric riot through Pickering high street.

Nobody said anything. Eventually, one quavering voice said, 'Is it hygienic?'

'It is if he stays out of the kitchen,' I answered firmly.

'Oh, well then.'

But now Kez had moved. He'd left my side, again without a single glance at Ned, the traitor, and strolled unerringly across the room to where Mimi sat. She was watching us all, but without going so far as to turn around; she had her head half tilted in our direction, and Kez put his head in her lap. His tail rose as though winched, and wagged a slow greeting.

A thin, twisted hand touched the top of his head. Following on our earlier blondie moment, this was practically Mimi asking us all if we'd watched *Strictly* last night, and what did we think of the local news scandal?

I let out a breath.

'I think we got away with it,' Ned whispered as we retreated back towards the kitchen, leaving everyone making a big fuss of Kez, who seemed perfectly happy to sit with Mimi and be doted on. 'I'll take him back upstairs in a second.'

'And make sure you shut the door properly this time,' I muttered back. 'We can't have him appearing in our midst all the time, like a canine apparition. What if Holly had been here? We could both lose our jobs.'

'She wouldn't dare.' Ned kept the door ajar, one eye on the room beyond. 'Where else would she find two people to put up with this lot six days a week for pathetic pay?'

I'd actually thought the pay was rather generous, considering my rent, electricity and food were included, so didn't reply.

'And anyway,' Ned went on, 'if he really were a dog I'm just looking after, and I brought him over daily, and he sat upstairs in your flat, where's the problem?'

'I'm sure Holly would find one,' I said darkly. 'She can be surprisingly stringent. There may be, I don't know, by-laws or something. What if someone was allergic? Or had a phobia about dogs?'

'If he were upstairs, it wouldn't matter.'

'But he's *not* upstairs!' I almost wailed. 'He's out there now, flaunting himself and being petted! There are two women out there who are grandchild-deprived right now! He's going to be lucky to get out without a full knitted layette and a matching set of bootees.'

Ned raised his eyebrows. 'Are you, maybe, catastrophising just a little?' he asked. 'I mean, he's not your dog. You *want* him to get a new home, don't you?'

I had a sudden midnight memory, of lying in bed, awake in the dark, listening to the distant buzz of silence and the occasional hum of a car down the main street. Nothing but night and owls and the weight of a dog that seemed to increase fourfold in the night, across my feet. The way Kez would raise his head if I sat up, checking whether it was time to get up or not, and then flop himself back down to further pin my legs to the mattress.

'Yes. Yes, of course I do.'

'Well, this might just accelerate matters, then,' Ned said briskly. 'And you said you wanted to get a hobby. A dog is a hobby, isn't it? Walking and training and – all those other canine-related activities?'

It crossed my mind, briefly, that Ned might have not closed the door properly purely to precipitate this moment, but then couldn't think of one single benefit to him of doing so, and changed my mind. 'Yes, right up there with self-flagellation and ironing socks,' I said. 'Dogs aren't hobbies. Another living thing isn't a "hobby". You might as well say that having a baby was a "hobby".'

'I'll take him back up, then. The hobby.' Ned gave me a smile.

I heard the chorus of 'ahhhh's as Ned went through to remove

Kez from his worshippers, and then the buzz of conversation as the two of them left the hall by the main door, for the stairs.

'Miss our old Sammie. Golden retriever, best dog ever.'

'Ah, we had one of those. For the shooting.'

'My Bill had spaniels. Wouldn't have them in the house, mind.'

'My eldest grandchild, Em, they've got a dog. Fluffy little thing. She's expecting a baby, did I tell you? Dog's awfully good with kiddies, apparently, but I've told them to keep an eye on it. It had my knitting wool once.'

Not one of them seemed about to raise a complaint; at least, not a complaint that ranked higher than the usual background level of complaining, and I blew out a silent sigh. Ned was right, we did seem to have got away with it, but it also did mean that I needed to accelerate the removal of Kez. Someone was going to mention this to Holly, and the thought gave me a dry, powdery feeling in my mouth.

13

Later that evening, we piled those who weren't driving themselves home onto the minibus. I helped Mimi to her seat and then was accosted by Jim.

'Is Ned coming back for the dog, then?'

I was completely at a loss for a moment. 'Why?'

'Well, usually when he's driving us home, he takes the minibus on and then comes out again in the morning. But he's left the dog.'

'I need my car this evening,' Ned said smoothly over my shoulder. 'So I have to come back. No point in making Kez sit in the bus all the way round the moor to just come back here.' He picked John's walking frame up, folded it down, and tucked it alongside him.

'Oh, I see.' Jim sat down, edging himself into a seat. 'So the dog stays with Seren when you're out and about?'

'Mmmm.' I handed Margaret her knitting bag.

'We could take him for a walk tonight,' Ned whispered to me as we passed in the aisle of the bus. 'Now I've got to come back anyway?'

I thought of my solo walks with Kez around the tiny market

town in the evening. Shops shut, pubs open, a slow coming-and-going of cars as people popped into takeaways and restaurants, and twos and threes chatted on pavements. Our dusty, clicking progress over the pavements, with Kez bobbing his head to sniff bollards and kerbs and occasionally tugging me towards a supercilious cat on a wall. All under the low, milky sky into which the church tower reached at the top of the hill.

'That would be nice,' I said vaguely. 'It will make a change.'

'OK. I'll be about an hour, dropping off the crew.' Ned swung himself into the driver's seat and I climbed down the steps to watch them go. Everyone waved, well, everyone except Mimi, who focused on the far horizon with her hands folded over her bag, and I remembered her small signs of pleasure today, at the sweetness of the blondie and the dog's head in her lap.

She just might be thawing. Very, very gradually, but it was something.

When I got back inside, Kez was sitting in the middle of the hall again.

'How the hell did you get here?' I asked him pointlessly. He circled around me a couple of times, with little yips of joy, clearly indicating that it didn't matter *how* he was here, the point was that he expected me to be delighted at his presence. 'Come on, back upstairs.'

The ears drooped. The delight evaporated. Kez clearly thought that 'upstairs' now ranked with 'here, sit in the oubliette with not a trace of sunlight, a persistent smell of damp and the presence of many rodents' and I instantly felt guilty. After all, there was nobody else here now. 'All right. Stay in here. But quietly.'

Wag wag. Then he began a happy nosing among the sofa cushions for dropped crumbs. I started to tidy the room alongside him and it was actually surprisingly pleasant to have company, even if the company did keep emerging from corners chewing things I'd rather not know about. So I talked, chatting away to Kez with observations about the scruffiness of the trim on the sofa, the slightly worn rug that needed replacing, and then I found that I was telling him that Ned was coming back and we'd take him out for a more interesting walk than his normal evening ramble.

'Maybe we could go to the sea again?' I burbled, reply-less, as I changed the tablecloth for a clean one, and swept the last of the jigsaw pieces into the box. 'Have a change of scenery where you can run about a bit.'

Kez sat in front of the long window, near the feet of Mimi's chair, and gazed out at the sun, lowering itself now to throw witch's-hat shadows from the geranium planters against the back door.

'It seems a shame not to make the most of these nice, long evenings,' I monologued on to no reply but a gentle tail-sweep. 'I mean, the field is all very well but it's not wildly scenic, is it? And the marketplace is fine if you just want a quick wee and a sniff, but...' I trailed off, coming to a sudden realisation as I clutched the grubby linen to my chest, entangled with a final piece of the sky from the last puzzle.

There was a whole life out there. Not just beaches, but moorland and towns – cities even. Mile upon mile of life, rolled out around me. Things I hadn't seen, unless Andrew had taken me somewhere on a short-break holiday, or that my brief husband-experience had forced me into. So many places. And all of them would hold a kind of beauty.

The remaining jigsaw piece dropped to the floor and I had to abandon the tablecloth in a scrunched heap on the table in order to get down and pat the carpet in search of it. All the time, my head kept whispering at me about all the things, all the places I was missing. It was a very strange feeling. I'd known that there was a world beyond Pickering, of course I had, I'd even seen some of it, but always when someone else had provided that safety cushion.

But what was I afraid of, really? Getting lost? There were satnavs and maps and Google and road signs, and, after all, Britain was an island – a fairly big one, but I could only go *so* wrong before I hit coastline and had to turn round. How lost, in reality, could I actually *get*?

These thoughts weren't completely new. Every so often I'd have a resurgence of confidence like this. Sometimes I'd even go so far as to pull out a map from the tattered collection tucked in the back of the bookcase here, so that our customers could relive old road trips or give detailed instructions on how to avoid the A303 by travelling via Dorchester. I'd flatten the map on the table and look at the names of places, Alnwick, Ripon, Windermere, running them through like a chant in my head. Places I could go to. And I'd even half start planning a journey, running my finger along the promising lines of road from our tiny blob of town, out over the hills or down through the cities... and then I would look at the acres of paper filled with nothing and withdraw. Too far. Too much space. Too much to go wrong.

But this was stupid! I was a perfectly confident driver. I could manage the York ring road, which put the fear of God into many a more experienced navigator; the Hopgrove interchange held no fear for me. *Because I knew where I was going.* Always the same route, direct to Andrew and Greg's flat, take the small side road around the back of the minster and park in their little car park. No fear. I'd been doing it for years. And before that, always the known ways, often by bus as I hadn't passed my driving test until after the collapse of my marriage and my coming here to work.

'This is my life,' I said, still crouching on the floor. Kez came over and pushed his bony head underneath my chin, nudging me to sit, whereupon he perched himself awkwardly in my lap. 'This place. Pickering. The road into York. This is *it*, Kez.'

Intelligent yellow eyes peered into mine. It occurred to me that the dog could snap at any moment, rip half of my face off with one bite, and yet I wasn't afraid of that. I could be scared to drive twenty miles down the road to Scarborough, where the most pressing horror would be getting caught by a big wave and having soggy socks, yet the prospect of being rendered blind and lipless by a dog attack didn't even register. 'Human brain,' I said, resting a hand on the dog's ruff. 'Go figure.'

His mouth gaped and two rows of shiny, sharp teeth emerged. They were followed by a wet pink tongue, which licked my chin. The nearest thing I'd had to a kiss for – how long? I snorted a laugh. This was pathetic. *I* was pathetic. No love, no life, no hobbies; here I sat, forever tidying and cleaning and cooking, like a perpetual housewife with no house and no husband. Just. This.

'Why are you down there?' Ned's voice drifted across the room. He'd come in round the front again. Kez didn't move from my lap, he just wiggled his bottom as his tail reacted to Ned's presence, and rested his head on my shoulder.

'I was tidying up. Then I started thinking.'

'Oh?' Ned came in. He seemed to feel that it wasn't right to tower over me, if Ned's slightness could ever be said to tower over anyone, and he crouched down. Kez waggled a bit more but stayed where he was. 'Anything in particular striking you?'

I sighed, but couldn't contemplate dumping my thought processes onto Ned. It was all too complicated to explain anyway – my desire to do things that I was held back from doing by some nebulous and irrational dread. 'It's pretty grubby down here. I'm going to have to go round with the carpet cleaner this weekend.'

'But not tonight. Tonight we go exploring, yes?' Ned tangled his fingers in Kez's fur, scratching the dog under his chin, and his nose rose from my shoulder and stuck up in the air like a pointer, enjoying the rubbing.

'Exploring? I thought we were just taking the dog out for a

walk.'

Now Kez reacted. He clambered off my lap and began circling, over to the door then back to us, then down to the door again. He was saying, very clearly, that it was time we stopped chatting about this 'out' thing, and started actually doing it.

'Well, yes. That's what I meant.' Ned was still squatting beside me and I was still sitting, both of us trapped in dog-petting poses although the dog in question was now attempting to encourage us out by giving little high-pitched yips. 'Exploring. Out. Same thing.'

'Not really. I mean, I go out to Boots, or the bakers. It's hardly "exploring". Unless I really can't find the sliced loaves.' It was comfortable on the floor. Relatively speaking, obviously – my back was unsupported and the carpet wasn't nearly thick enough to cushion me from the tiling underneath, but it all seemed very safe and predictable compared to that sudden word 'exploring'.

'Look. I'll drive. We can put Kez in the boot and take him up on the high moor for a walk. I can take some photos, you can – do whatever, then I'll bring you back here. I told everyone that I needed the car tonight, so I really ought to make that happen.' Bright eyes twinkled at me. 'How does that sound?'

Someone else driving. That was slightly easier, I didn't need to navigate my own way out and back, and if we got lost it wasn't quite so frightening when someone else was there. Particularly when they gave off 'capable and practical' airs, like Ned did. 'Why are you so desperate for me to go out?'

The question took me by surprise. Clearly it caught Ned on the hop too, because he rocked back away from me a little and turned his attention to Kez's increasingly demonic dashing up and down. 'What do you mean?'

'Is Andrew paying you to get me out of the house or something?'

'I've never met your brother.'

But he remembered who Andrew was. Which meant he paid attention to what I said. 'Sorry. I know that. But first the beach, then, well, now. I'm beginning to feel like a winkle and you've got this pin and you just want to wiggle me out of my shell.'

Ned stood up. 'You said that you wanted hobbies. That you wanted to get a life.' He turned a small circle. 'Unless all your hobbies are going to take place in here, which really only leaves you with crochet, knitting or reading Dan Brown novels, then going out is rather the order of the day, don't you think?'

I'd just compared myself to a winkle, which was possibly the most unflattering thing I could have said. Plus he was perfectly right, I did want a life. I wanted *something*, anything, to make me not just Seren who did the cooking. Something that made me look like an individual who had thought processes and didn't just exist to do the same thing over and over, like a Sims character.

Ned was watching me. Even though I wasn't looking, I could see the angle of his chin, slightly dotted with dark stubble, and the flop of his hair. He was waiting for me to have an answer, and I didn't. Telling him that, yes, I wanted to get out more and do more things, but the outside away from home was frightening and I didn't need a life *that* badly, felt like cowardice. Especially when there was Kez to consider.

'All right. Where shall we go?'

I saw the edge of his smile. Kez yipped again, accelerating towards a full bark. 'Come on. I'll show you.' A hand came out to pull me to my feet, and I took it, feeling muscles that were surprisingly powerful for a man who drove a minibus and fixed chairs. For a second I felt the oddness of physical contact, and then it was over and gone and I was up and dropping that little bit of sky puzzle yet again. This time I left it.

* * *

We loaded Kez into Ned's Audi and then Ned opened the passenger door and removed his camera equipment from the seat. There were posters for the open day in there too. 'I suppose we should put some of these up as we go?' He unrolled one and studied the polychromatic lettering. Why the designers of these things seemed to treat an open day for an elderly day-care centre in the same way as a pre-school playgroup, I had no idea. 'It's coming up fast.'

'There tend not to be a lot of noticeboards on the moors,' I pointed out.

'There are villages. If we pass one, and they haven't already got a notice up, then I volunteer you to dash out and tack one to the board. That way we'll be keeping Holly happy, won't we?' Ned handed me the sheaf of papers, all tightly rolled and guaranteeing that I'd need to use a decorative amount of drawing pins to stop them pinging themselves off any boards and scrolling themselves off across the moors, to be eaten by sheep.

'I suppose so.'

Kez was airborne with excitement now. He bounced up and down as we climbed into the car and I settled the posters on my lap, his mouth gaping with delight and his tongue making occasional sweeps that splattered drool around the inside of the car boot. Ned didn't turn a hair.

Ned wound down the window, letting in the smells of the warm evening air: petrol and hot tarmac to start with, but rapidly increasing amounts of the spicy, sweet scent of heather and the almost burned smell of bracken that was passing its ferny green best under the drying sun. There was also a redolent amount of hot dog fur and I didn't think that I was quite as fragrant as I might have been if I'd been given the chance to shower and spritz myself with something nice, but Ned didn't remark on any of this. He just steered the car north and we climbed our way up across the hills to the moors.

I didn't say anything either. I just watched out of the window as moorland spooled its way out in front, led by the sticky ribbon of road into the purple-furred distance. The bright pinpricks that were the windows of other cars coming towards us diminished, until we were high on a stretch of rising ground, parked on a green square of sheep-nibbled grass beside a tumbling river. There was no other traffic and barely any sound at all, apart from a long-whistling curlew poking its way through the sky above us, and some cheeping dots in the far gorse bushes.

Ned turned the engine off and Kez sat to attention. 'What do you think?'

'It's lovely.'

'There's an old Roman road running along over there. Shall we see how it's holding up?' Ned opened his door and Kez tried to climb through from the back.

I said, 'Kez, sit down,' and the dog immediately flopped his bottom back onto the carpeted boot, looking slightly surprised, as though his body was obedient without his brain being involved. 'Good boy.' It felt impolite not to acknowledge his good behaviour, and he evidently knew he was being praised even though I wasn't looking at him, because I could hear the tail sweeping a layer of fur across the floor.

Ned stopped, halfway out of the car. 'Are you all right?'

How did I explain? I knew it would sound stupid, with the moor lying benign and smooth, tuffeted with spikes of bog cotton waving in the breeze, and bees dive-bombing the heather. 'You won't... leave me here?' I said cautiously, trying to judge his reaction.

'Why the hell would I do that?' He stopped trying to get out of the car and slid back into the driver's seat. One hand rested back on the steering wheel and I noted that his fingers were long, almost artistic. Curious hands to be nailing chairs and screwing racks. 'We're here to take the dog out, not to play an extended game of hide and seek.' A quick look flashed my way across his shoulder. 'You're not agoraphobic.' It was a statement.

'No. I just – worry about getting lost.'

'So you think I might dive off into the bracken and leave you on your own on the moor?' He sounded curious, rather than amused, which, given that it was, quite frankly, ridiculous that he would drive off without me unless he was far more sadistic than he'd given any sign of being, was reassuring.

'Mmmm,' was all I could say. Not definite, not really confirming his suspicion, but allowing for a little bit of doubt.

'You see this road?' Ned pointed at the gleam of black tarmac, patchy in places and giving off an air of second-hand chewing gum tackiness in the evening heat.

'Yes.'

'If you get lost, follow that. It's about five miles, straight road, back to Pickering. Bit of a hike, but better than being out here all night. Now, shall we get this dog out before he digs his way through my spare tyre?' He was out of the car again, this time closing his door as though he'd made up his mind that I would follow.

So I did. Keeping my eye on the road all the time, as though I feared it would perform some *Alice in Wonderland* stunt and coil up to ping out in a new configuration if I took my eyes off it, I got out and felt the cool air on my cheeks with a sense of amazement.

'It's so... open.' A small stand of trees alongside the river were the only things that broke the horizon. The rest of it was ironed smoothly into pillows of purplish grey, diminishing into the distance.

'Have you not been out this way for a while?' Ned opened the boot and then leaned into the back seat to fetch his camera equipment, while Kez bounced over to me then went and widdled on a gorse bush.

'Not for a long time.' When I'd been younger, Andrew had taken us out for drives over the moor, of course. Changes of scenery. But once he'd got settled into the city, into his career and his relationships, I had taken a rightful second place. My husband had disliked the outdoors, or at least an outdoors that didn't come with a full phone signal and good Wi-Fi coverage, and so there had been no need to venture out under this huge sky.

'Come on, then. Roman road.' Ned pointed with his thumb and we set off along a springy grass track bordered by bee-hummed heather, with Kez's nose to the ground in front of us, searching out sheep poo and snapping at the occasional insect. Behind us the river poured its way over grey rocks, in a toffee-coloured torrent, and an insistent cloud of small flies filled in the gaps.

Ned went slowly, as though to reassure me that he wasn't about to dash off and vanish, turning occasionally to click his camera. In front the hill rose too steeply to show much of a view, unless a small wooden stile and an information board about the Romans in Yorkshire was suddenly going to be picturesque.

'So you've never really liked the outdoors?' Ned asked conversationally as we watched Kez's white-tipped tail protrude from a tufty mound, which probably held rabbits.

'It's always made me nervous, yes.'

'But you don't know why?'

'We've had this conversation, Ned. No, I don't know why. No, I don't remember a traumatic incident and neither does Andrew. It's just who I am, that's all.' It prickled at me, Ned's insistence that there must have been some inciting incident for my dislike of being outside alone. 'Some people are just born with phobias, you know.'

'Hmmm,' he said. Not on a rising question of disbelief, but more as though he was thinking about it. Why the hell should Ned think about my vague neurotic fears? It was none of his business.

'So, why did you leave London and all its conveniences?' I asked, rather sharply, to illustrate to him how annoying it was to be questioned about something that you just did, with no real consideration. 'This is all a bit of a culture shock, I should imagine.'

'I needed a complete change.' Ned gave me a short, sideways look, as though summing me up.

'Tired of seeing yourself in the local paper with the caption "Have you seen this man?"?' I still sounded a bit waspish, but he laughed, which further reassured me that the whole 'living in the car, prison, machete' background that I'd dreamed up for him was far from the truth.

'Let's face it, this is a big improvement on city streets, isn't it?' He flung the hand not holding the camera wide to indicate two small brown birds bouncing one another out of a bush and the discoloured lace of elderly bracken. 'Space, and time.'

'You're not Doctor Who, are you?'

Now he laughed, a slightly bitter laugh. 'No. No. Definitely not. Look, you sit over there and I'll take a picture of you and Kez, if you can get him to sit next to you.'

'Of course I can.' I moved to perch on a handful of rubble and whistled to the dog. He hesitated for a moment, with his head up and the wind in his ears, then came shuffling over with his fur pulled every which way by the breeze. 'He's very obedient.'

'He is, isn't he?' Ned moved around, framing the shot. 'But he didn't behave for his previous owner?'

'No. I wonder if he just wasn't happy there. He doesn't look like the sort of dog that would be happy with children pulling his tail and garden walks only, does he? Maybe he played them up on purpose.'

Kez sat beside me and I put an arm around his shoulders. He gave my chin a quick lick and then leaned against me in 'devoted dog' pose. His eyes were on the horizon but his ears were acknowledging my presence, swept back and listening. I felt a sudden warm wash of affection for him, and squeezed his furry body closer to mine, which brought another chin lick and a momentary glance of amber-eyed adoration. His mouth had fallen open with his tongue rolled out like a carpet, and he looked as though he were grinning.

The thought of taking him to a dog shelter suddenly seemed like betrayal.

'There. Some nice shots for you to put on the dating sites. Now let's get on right up to the high point and look at the view from there.'

There was that hand again, pulling me up again. Wrist to wrist, and that feeling of fragile artistry in Ned's long fingers and strongly muscled arm. I had another sudden jolt of the incongruity of this slight, intelligent man being a handyman and driver when there seemed to be so much more to him underneath. But he didn't want to talk about his past. I'd noticed the adept way he'd sidestepped my question about his leaving London, when that would have been the time to tell me about family pressure or terrible crimes. He'd come here 'just because'. And I wasn't buying that for a second.

But, in case there *had* been dreadful crimes in his past, I didn't bring it up, not out here when I was armed with only a slightly wayward collie and a lot of fresh air. It could wait. Forever, perhaps, I realised. I was enjoying this, Ned's happiness at the wide spaces, his desire to take pictures of things and show me the moor. He was, I was coming to understand, astonishingly good company, but then I didn't have a great deal to compare him to, my most recent company being octogenarian, a heavy-metal band or related to me. Oh, and a dog.

We walked along trenched turf to a somewhat patchy surface, where fists of stone had been laid, come loose, rolled about a bit and then resettled into a mosaic of grey rock and grassy infill. The ground still showed the outline of a road, but only traversable on balloon wheels and only then if you really liked hearing the bones of your neck crack.

'This road has been here for two thousand years, give or take,' Ned said, obviously noting my 'well, it's hardly the M25, is it?' expression. 'None of us are going to look our best after that length of time. Plus, I suspect the local farmers have been prising bits off it to fill in mud holes for most of that time.'

'Just being around for a long time doesn't make something noteworthy though,' I said, watching Kez dig in a desultory way at a promising hole in the soil.

'Do *not* tell our clients that.' Ned gave me a big grin that made him suddenly look younger, and I realised that I'd got used to the somewhat 'pinched' expression he usually wore, as though worry was constantly pulling at his skin from behind. 'They all think that getting to over seventy should entitle you to special treatment.' Then he frowned for a second. 'Actually, thinking about it, that's what *I* think too.'

'Ah, they aren't so bad. Well, maybe one or two of them can be a bit tetchy, but when you listen to the lives they've had, it's not really surprising. Some of them remember the war, and life afterwards could be pretty tough too. My dad...' I stopped suddenly.

There was a long pause that stretched between the bees' wings and the birdsong. My mind had fallen into that gap, unwarranted.

'Your dad,' Ned said, gently. Not a question, not as though he was about to quiz me about my family, he was just repeating what I'd said, in case I could have forgotten.

'My dad. I vaguely remember – he was born not that long after the war, I think. Late nineteen fifties, maybe? I can just remember him telling me that his mum saved up rations? Something like that. I haven't thought about that for years,' I added, wonderingly.

'Your brother doesn't talk to you about your family?' Ned had stopped walking. Between his fingers, a heather stalk was being stripped of its bells, restlessly.

I stopped walking too. 'No,' I said softly. 'No, he doesn't.' And then, adding hastily, 'I mean, I quite understand why. He was twelve, he found them both dead. It's the sort of thing that sinks into your psyche, I should imagine. Talking about it would make him relive that, and I wouldn't want to put Andrew through that sort of pain.'

'And how about the aunt who brought you up until your brother took you over? Did she not talk about them either?'

Suddenly the world was too wide. The sea-blue stretch of sky, taut over our heads like a well-erected tent, was too big and the roll and fall of hills seemed to dip and dive, featurelessly, as though there were nothing else beyond, just this endless stretch of moorland until death.

I sat down, suddenly. Kez turned his head from the gorse-bush sniffing, and came over, pressing his warm body into me for a second and wafting me with his great fan of a tail.

'Are you all right?' Ned bent towards me. The little sprig of heather fluttered, denuded into a bare stick, between his fingers.

'Yes. Yes, sorry. I just… caught my breath there for a moment.' I gave a little laugh. 'No idea why. That's weird.'

'Was it something I said?' Ned perched down beside me on the slabbed rock of the Roman road. The surface was warm from the sun, even though the sun itself was casting itself down towards the far horizon like a bather diving into an unseen sea.

'No, I don't think… I mean, I'm not sure. You only said something about our aunt and I...' I shook my head, trying to dislodge the memories. 'I was just trying to think. I don't remember her talking about our parents at all either, which is strange now I come to think of it. I mean, we'd lost our mum and dad, she was our dad's sister – *why* didn't she tell us about them?'

I tried my hardest to remember those six years, between our aunt taking us in and Andrew being old enough to have guardianship over me, when I was ten, and not much came to me.

'Tell me,' Ned said, his tone still level. He didn't sound alarmed by my sudden collapse, or curious about my family remembrances. He seemed more... more as though he *needed* me to talk.

'It's just striking me as odd, that's all. Why can't I remember more? Our aunt was single, older than dad – she lives in Spain now. Andrew bought her an apartment in one of the Costas and she lives in splendid retirement with a whole host of other retirees who've turned it into England in the Sun.'

'But that's all *now*.' Ned threw the heather stem off into the undergrowth. Kez gave a happy bark and ran off after it. 'What about then?'

I frowned, as though bringing my brows together would summon memory. 'A big, cold house – there wasn't any central heating. Aunt Sophie never married and I think she'd inherited the house from Dad's parents...' I tailed off again, trying to slot pieces together. It was worse than doing one of Margaret's jigsaws: too much sky and not enough bits with identifiable pictures on.

'Were you loved? Secure?' Ned took the soggy stalk from Kez, who'd bounded back with it hanging out of his mouth, with an expression of extreme satisfaction.

'I don't know. Not *un*loved, certainly, just, maybe, a bit... *resented*? We were cared for, fed and clothed and given pocket money.' I scrunched my face up, harder. 'I used to buy comics, I think. And sweets.'

'And your brother?'

'Oh, I didn't buy things for him,' I said, and then realised what Ned meant, and laughed. 'It's really weird. I mean, I know Andrew was there, he slept in the little room in the attic. I remember, it had a big window that opened out onto this kind of balcony on the roof and I was really jealous because *I* wanted a window I could climb out of but I had to make do with an ordinary one that looked over the street.' Another little laugh escaped. 'I hadn't thought of that for years. But I don't really remember much about Andrew back then. He was out a lot, I expect, being a teenage boy. Plus he was working really hard to get into university. There must have been money, I guess, from Mum and Dad, because he bought a place for us to live in as soon as he finished uni.'

'You should ask him,' Ned said briskly, flinging the soggy heather stem away again and watching, with a slightly resigned expression, as Kez took off after it. 'I wonder how we stop him bringing it back?'

'Stop throwing it away.' I seized the change of subject with a near-religious fervour. 'He must think it's his job.'

'Maybe I could hide it when he's not looking?' Ned once more took the, now very soggy, stem, and shoved it in his pocket. After a few moments waiting with head cocked, Kez decided the fun was over and went off to nose along a rabbit trail again.

I stood up once more, feeling my legs slightly wobbly. *Why* were they wobbly? Cautiously I took a few steps as my muscles firmed up and felt better. I'd probably walked too far. After all, although I'd started doing far more outdoor exercise since I'd taken charge of Kez, most of my physical exertion before had been cleaning and tidying, running up and down the stairs and hanging posters. Scrambling over rock-strewn stretches of moorland hadn't featured enough for my legs to have strengthened. Yes. It was just the walking. That was all.

We reached the highest point of the road and turned to face the sunset. It wasn't true sunset yet, there was another hour or so before the light would go, following the boiling ball of sun down behind the distant hills. But the sky was already decorated with blood-red streaks of cloud dragged across the horizon, and the few shadows that were visible were long and sepulchral, spread morosely behind us like pouting infants on a long walk with no ice cream in sight.

Ned raised the camera and clicked away. I rotated on the spot, picking out distant landmarks in the serrated range of hills. There weren't many, we were too far and too high to see most of the local towns, but familiar scoops told of their locations, and a faint blue shimmer hinted at the sea.

What, after all, was I so afraid of? Like Ned said, I could just retrace my steps to find my way home. Most of the roads across the moors were straight, or, at least, weren't branched like a labyrinth, needing a ball of string and a sturdy approach to bull-headed beings to escape. I'd lived in the area most of my life, knew the names on the signposts, even some of the more obscure, Viking-related Waths and Tons. It was lovely out here, with the scenery and Kez trotting about and clearly enjoying himself hugely. *So, what was I so afraid of?*

Because I couldn't deny that I was. Despite the presence of Ned, despite the smooth roll of road visible into the far distance, I could still feel that tug of dread at the back of my mind. Consciously I was relaxed and enjoying all this, but my heart was on watch for the need to drive adrenaline around my body, my nerves all standing by for the signal that we had to go Full Hysteria. As though I were existing on the edge of some precipice – safe for the present, but only one misstep from the plunge into the abyss.

'Ready?' Ned made me jump, I'd been so lost in my self-examination. 'I've got some lovely shots. I might print a few up and bring them in.'

'We could sell some? If you think they're good enough? At the open day?' I tore my mind back from the tipping point. 'We could display them on the back wall, put prices on them. People often get a bit buy-happy at events, we get cleared out of anything that will sell. Someone once bought all the cushions,' I added, remembering that we'd also had to refuse to sell the rug and some of the crockery. 'You could do a 50-50 split? Half the proceeds to you and the other half to the fund.'

We'd turned now and were making steady progress downhill, stepping carefully over the missing blocks of paving whilst Kez roamed on ahead in search of rabbits.

'That's a good idea. I've got some other prints too, things I've been photographing since I came – I could shove some of those in some cheap frames and put them up for sale.'

'We need to drop off a few of those posters on our way back.' I waved a hand at the car, a burnished, gleaming dot at the bottom of the hill, next to the brown line of the river. 'Before they all uncurl and plaster themselves over the inside of your car.'

'And to justify our trip out?' Ned threw me a shrewd look. 'If anyone asks?'

'No,' I said in a tone that said that was exactly what I'd been thinking.

'They all think we make a great couple, you know,' he said conversationally. 'But then, neither of us has much competition, do we?'

'You're not married, then?' I realised that this was the first time it had so much as crossed my mind that Ned might have a Significant Other, and a sharp needle of guilt worked its way between my ribs. He'd asked me so much about myself, about my upbringing, and I didn't even know if he had a wife or husband tucked away in his 'house on the moors'. I knew he'd worked too much to have a dog, and that was pretty much it.

Ned gave me the tight smile again. The one that looked as though he was biting back a lot of words that wanted to come out but mustn't be allowed. 'No. I'm... I *was* a bit of a workaholic and it rather put the stop to much of a love life, I'm afraid. But you – you were married before?'

'Yes. Badly. Unhappily. I think I really only married Hugh because Andrew was settling down with Greg. We were never particularly well suited, but we tried.'

'What went wrong in the end?' We'd reached the end of the roadway now and stepped down over the moonscape of broken rock onto the smooth strip of grass. Some rabbits bounded away and Kez gave chase, in a half-hearted fashion.

'Nothing. We just realised that we were straining ourselves to find anything to talk about. No big betrayals, no *EastEnders*-style screaming matches or cheating. Just a sad fizzle into forgetting birthdays and him being out all the time.' I sighed. 'Just one of a million sad stories. So I found myself the job at the hall, moved out, and the last I heard of him he'd gone to live in London to work in PR.'

'A fitting end,' Ned said cheerily.

'Oh, nobody really deserves PR, do they?' I found I was laughing.

'Maybe not.' Ned fumbled in his pocket, drew out the chewed and leafless heather twig and dropped it on the ground. 'But selling some of my photographs would be good. If you think anyone would buy them.'

'Our clients bring their families and their families bring everyone they can think of.' I remembered back to our last open day sale, at Christmas. 'You have to remember that not a lot happens in these little market towns nowadays. It used to be

Market Monday and lots of dances and "dos" at weekends, but now, unless you travel through to York or Leeds, there's not a constant round of entertainment. An open day with a band for people to twirl along to and tea and cake will bring out the crowds.'

The handle of the car door was hot under my fingers and the sandy strip of grass looked dusty. Somewhere far off over the hills, a tractor grunted its way up an incline, engine roaring over a baked harvest.

'Let's go back via every village hall you can think of.' Ned popped the boot of the car and opened it right up to let the heat out. 'They're going to have noticeboards outside, aren't they? We can do a kind of mercenary attack, only with posters.'

I got into the car and sat on the hot fabric seat. Inside, I was smiling slightly. Ned seemed to want to prolong our evening out and it was giving me a warm feeling unrelated to the heat from the sun. He might be a touch reluctant to talk about himself, but he was still good company and I had enjoyed myself more than I had anticipated.

The wobbles were under control now I was sitting down. Safely contained in a car that would take me home – no abandonment, no terror. Kez jumped into the boot smoothly, Ned closed it up and came round to the driver's seat.

'There's a village hall about a mile that way.' I pointed back down the road. 'Then if we go along the little back roads, we'll go through a few of the more isolated settlements. They might not have a village hall but there will be a post or a gate we can pin posters to.'

'Excellent.' Ned started the car and we bumped slowly forward off the grass onto the reassuringly straight road.

In the boot, Kez spat out the heather stalk again, and looked smug.

14

'My nephew used to play the trumpet.'

'Bet that was popular with the neighbours.'

'I think they thought it was an improvement on the recorder. Those things should be banned, squeak squeak squeak. It was like a musical bloody rodent.'

Jim and Tom were bent low over the crossword in today's newspaper and discussing, from what I could gather, the forthcoming visit from the brass band. The Kirkbymoorside Brass Band had something of a local reputation and had been over at the Christmas do playing carols, which had brought out the press photographers. As I'd told Ned, there wasn't a lot else newsworthy going on in these hot, dead-end days of summer. We'd only be usurped for front-page news if someone blew up a steam train.

I laid out the tea things and brought through another batch of new recipe scones. Grace and Lena were doing a jigsaw on the table, so I put the tray on a small stool next to a chair, where Joe was sitting looking thoughtfully into space. Will and John were discussing aircraft, at least, Will was discussing and John was looking at the tea tray with undisguised longing. Margaret was pricing up knitted dolls, pinning scraps of paper to each with a sharp poke through the chest area that made me wince, and Mimi had moved from her usual seat by the window to sit out of the direct sunlight, on the sofa.

It was hot. We'd got the big windows open to the car park to let in whatever air found itself passing by, but all we were getting were dust and noise from the lorries rumbling past on the main road at the other side of the building. The geraniums had wilted, despite Roger dashing out every half an hour with buckets of water, and the paint was peeling off the stack of chairs he was upcycling by the back door.

In the hall, the air smelled of warm bodies and perfume, of talc and hairspray. Every now and then the kitchen allowed a puff of baking scent through, when someone opened the door, but mostly it smelled like a coach trip.

'I hope they play some swing tunes.' Lena leaned in to help the men with a clue. 'Nice to have a bit of a boogie. Reminds me of being young, at the dances.'

'You were never young, lass.' Jim snorted.

'I was too! Used to come to the dance, regular as, mid-fifties it will have been. That's where I met our Wally.' She looked sternly at Jim. 'Some of us had a bit of life in us, back then.'

'Aye, and some of us were working at fourteen,' he replied. 'No time for that dancing nonsense.'

'When the band comes, we'll show you how it's done.' Lena looked up. 'Won't we, Peg?'

Margaret looked up from the amateur voodoo. 'We will,' she said happily. 'Our youngest plays the cornet in the band, I've put in some requests.'

'Not much good if they only play it on the cornet.' Jim sniffed. 'We want the whole lot joining in.'

Margaret snorted and jabbed a knitted fairy in the head with such force that it made me pull a face. Somewhere, Titania now had a dreadful migraine. 'It will be fun,' she said, definitely.

'Scone, Joe?' I held out a plate.

'No, thanks, love.'

'Are you feeling all right?' I looked at him with concern. He'd been very quiet lately, and the incidents of aggravated Scrabble had dropped right off. 'Do you want someone to take you home?'

'Nay, lass. I'm just tired, that's all. It's the heat. Alabaster,' he added.

'Alabaster?' I wondered if he was having some kind of speech disruption.

'It's the answer to twelve down. Alabaster.' He nodded towards the crossword. 'Stupid buggers, they'll never get it.'

I gave him a stern look and went out into the kitchen to fetch the large teapot. Ned had come in and was washing his hands. 'It's even too hot for Kez,' he said. 'A quick once around the block and he was wanting to be in again. Maybe we could take him down to the river tonight, when it cools down?'

He was looking at me hopefully, and I had to admit that the idea of a paddle and a stroll along the riverbank sounded wonderful. I'd just been about to agree, when there was a heavy sound and breaking china from the other side of the hall door, and someone shouted, 'Help!'

I dumped the teapot on the table and dashed through. Joe had fallen forward, out of the chair, to the detriment of the plate of scones, and now lay sprawled on the carpet, looking small and very old.

'Joe!' I moved over, through the worried crowd milling around the fallen shape like cattle around a paper bag. 'Joe, can you hear me?'

I had my first-aid certificates – it was a condition of working here. Security checks, first-aid qualifications and the ability to cook, that was all this job required. I moved Joe gently into the recovery position, and then, suddenly, Ned was beside me.

'Call an ambulance.' He thrust his phone at me. 'Now.' He was feeling under the old man's jawline, bending over and talking in a low tone, explaining what he was doing as though Joe were awake and complaining. 'I'm just checking for your pulse – that's good, a little bit thready though.' Another glance at me. 'Ambulance. Quickly.'

It wasn't like Ned at all, this crisp ordering and taking charge. Ned was usually diffident and quiet, the kind of man who worked away in the background, unnoticed and unremarked and now – here he was taking over a situation as though this were his real job.

I dialled and summoned an ambulance while Ned called isolated words like 'hypotensive' and 'unresponsive' across the conversation. Harry gathered the watchers together and marshalled them into a corner of the hall away from where we worked on Joe, where they milled about collecting static from the carpet with their shuffled feet and anxiety.

Joe lay still under Ned's careful hands. His skin was very pale, he was usually quite pallid, but when I bent down to help cover him with a crocheted blanket from the sofa, I could see small patches of unshaven hair and little nicks in his cheeks. Joe, who was usually so careful about appearance – 'can't go about looking like one of these modern lads, all beards and earrings, that would never do' – had been letting standards slip.

Ned moved Joe's head gently onto a pillow and met my eye over the fallen shape. I was a little sweaty, taut with the stress, but Ned – Ned was grey. There were beads of sweat on his forehead that seemed over the top, although it was hot it wasn't sub-tropical, and the hands that carefully tucked the cushion under Joe's ear, were trembling. He looked like an alcoholic being ushered into a cocktail party after a year's abstinence.

'Ned? Are you all right?' I asked softly.

A sudden shake of his head. I didn't know if he was replying in the negative or just indicating that he couldn't talk, and then the ambulance was there. Two burly paramedics in full uniform with a stretcher and a calming patter, full of light jokes and capability. They'd crated Joe, still unconscious, into their vehicle and borne him off towards York hospital almost before we could tell them what happened.

Neither Ned nor I could go with him, as we weren't family. I think that the paramedics thought that Joe might need resuscitation in the ambulance and didn't want us to see, but anyway it wouldn't have been sensible to go and leave the other one having to calm down the remaining group, who were all keen to fear the worst.

Even in this heat the tea had started to cool, so I took the pot into the kitchen to refresh it, leaving Margaret, as the last person to have been talking to Joe, to lead the conversation into how he hadn't been looking right lately and it was probably a heart attack. Look at his diet and he never exercised, did he? Not like Tom there who was always up and down keeping his arteries open. Plus, at ninety, old lad had probably just had enough, after all, this heat was enough to see the fittest person off.

It was practically a hubbub out in the hall, and the kitchen was peaceful and relatively calm. I carried the big teapot through and was about to put the kettle on again when a small squeak from the far corner alerted me to Ned's presence.

He was sitting on a stool, back to the wall, squeezed in against the big fridge freezer. He had his feet up on the seat, knees under his chin and his arms over his head, like a child fearing punishment, and he was sobbing.

'Shit. Ned.' I put the kettle down and went over to his corner. 'Hey. What's up?'

Huge, terrified eyes were raised to mine. His hair was plaited with sweat all along his forehead and his mouth was pulled into an irregular shape that evidently wouldn't let words out, because, after a strangled noise that was more like a howl, he stopped trying and put his head down again.

'I'll get some tissues.'

There were none in here, not even any kitchen roll, so I tore up the stairs to my flat. The front door was just opening as I got there and Kez, with his paws on the handle, emerged, tiptoeing on his hind legs, into the hall.

'You can open the door?'

He dropped immediately to all fours in the gap, in a pretence of innocence that made me smile despite everything. I should have realised that a push handle wouldn't provide much of a barrier to an intelligent dog, I thought, as I fetched the tissues from the coffee table and then hastened back down the stairs with Kez now trailing me with a slight air of shame.

In the kitchen, I hastily ushered the dog through into the hall, where his presence caused an instant switch from the doom-laden inevitability that everyone seemed to be currently cycling through, then I went back to Ned, who hadn't moved.

'Here. Tissues.' I handed him a snowball of paper. 'I'm just going to ring Joe's family and let them know he's been taken to York, and then you and I...' I stopped. Ned's whole body was shaking. 'I think you should talk to me,' I finished.

My phone call would give him chance to compose himself. To think of what he wanted to say, because I had no idea what could have precipitated this level of emotion. We were *all* fond of Joe, but Ned's reaction seemed to be that of someone who had lost their whole family in front of them, not made an elderly man comfortable until the arrival of the professionals.

I looked up the contact number for Joe's family and rang his grandson, who promised to pass the message on to the rest of the family, and to head to York hospital as soon as he could. Then I called Holly, who would make any other calls necessary. It was really her job to alert the family too, but she was at headquarters in Acomb, doing paperwork and dealing with insurance, and I hadn't wanted to run the risk of family being the last to know.

Then I had to deal with the problem that was Ned. Ned, who'd seemed so practical, capable and not in the least highly strung, up until now.

I'd made my phone calls in the hallway where it was quiet and I had a reasonable amount of privacy. When I hung up from reassuring Holly that the family were on their way to the hospital and that there had been nothing further that we could have done for Joe, I found myself slightly reluctant to go back into the kitchen. A breakdown like Ned's could only have been caused by some extreme flooding of emotion – everything suddenly becoming too much, all at once. Which might, in turn, lead him to walk out on the job. Which would mean, I slowly realised, no more Ned hanging out in the kitchen stealing cake fresh from the oven, or arguing about pluralisation over the Scrabble board. No more little journeys out with Kez and a camera to show me a view, no more daft conversations as we laid out the tea things.

No more Ned. And suddenly that was a horrible prospect.

In the kitchen, he'd opened the window and was sitting at the worktop, rearranging the pots of growing herbs that sat in the sunlight that filled the room late in the day. He'd watered the parsley too.

'Ned?'

But the shutters were down. He'd assumed his normal expression of vague concern and was giving nothing away as he fiddled the chives back onto their saucer on the window ledge. Whatever emotion had overwhelmed him, it had been pushed back behind the barriers and a superficial jollity had taken its place. 'Your herbs are running to seed here, look.'

'Yes, I don't get to use them enough. They—' I jerked my head towards the door that separated us from the end-users '—complain if there are "green bits" in food. I can just about get away with chives, occasionally.' I joined him at the window. 'Except for Tom, who wants jalapeños in everything, but I think he only does that to impress Grace. They give him horrible indigestion. Ned—'

'Kez is out there. I can hear them all cooing over him again. It seems he's taken a lot of the tension out of the air.' Ned interrupted me.

'Yes. You know he's opening the door to the flat himself? I'm sorry I accused you of not shutting it properly – it looks as though he's learned to press the handle and let himself out. I really am going to have to get hold of Mattie and find him a new...' I tailed off. The sudden thought that I could find myself back in the flat alone again, and without Ned down here to talk to, or Kez to lie on my feet at night, made my heart ring with a hollow emptiness. 'He's too clever by half,' I finished. I didn't know where to go from here. Ned didn't want to talk, but I didn't want to ignore his breakdown – it felt as though there were things he needed to say but didn't know how to frame them to make me understand. I couldn't push him, but talking might make things easier. I'd been here before, with clients, holding secrets, keeping things close to their chests, sometimes things that had burdened them for most of their long lives.

I decided to use the approach that often worked with them. Cast it off, give them the freedom to talk or not talk, give them space. They'd often come around to mentioning things, once they'd learned that I wouldn't judge and would be led by them; that I wasn't going to force any issues or insist that they 'dealt with their trauma'. I was here to listen, if they wanted to talk.

'Shall we take Kez down to Sinnington tonight?' I flipped the kettle back on. 'Down by the river?'

'Is that where I took the crew on that outing?' Ned's voice sounded lighter. I couldn't see him, I was too busy remaking the tea, but his tone also seemed to hold an ounce of gratitude. I silently thanked all my past clients: Eileen, who'd been sexually abused as a child ('You just didn't talk about it then.'), Wilf, whose disabled sister had disappeared one night during the war ('She was never spoken about again and I got a backhander if I asked Mam what happened.'), Bert, who'd lived in such poverty that water had come from a collective well and whose brothers had died during a diphtheria outbreak ('My mother never got over it. She was never right again.'). I'd learned from them how to handle confessions that wanted – *needed* – to be made, but that couldn't easily be brought into conversation.

'Yes. If we walk a bit further upstream, through the woods, there are some nice places for Kez to swim.'

'Nobody fighting over ice creams?'

I half laughed. 'No. It's a lot quieter once you get out of the village.'

'And if you haven't got a dozen mortal enemies with you.'

The kettle boiled and I tried to think of what to say next. Ignoring Ned's emotional outburst would only work for so long before he might start to think that I was going to pretend it never happened. I'd just opened my mouth, with absolutely no idea what was about to come out, when Ned jerked his head up and looked out of the window.

'We've got visitors.'

I recognised the car pulling into the car park. 'It's Andrew and Greg. I wonder what's brought them out of town. They don't usually like to be this far away from shops selling handmade brogues and bubble tea.'

I refilled the teapot and took it through to the hall, where Kez was being the centre of attention as hard as he could, lying sprawled across the matting whilst several people rubbed his tummy. He cast an eye in my direction to see if I would object and, when I didn't, gave a sigh and waved his legs more energetically. Ned followed me and became subsumed beneath a conversation about TV schedules. It seemed that everyone had talked out the Joe panic whilst we'd been in the kitchen and I hoped, for Ned's sake, they weren't going to revisit it for a long while.

Andrew and Greg, apparently, had come to peer through Roger's window rather than visit me. I caught them both eyeing up the pile of peeling chairs and cupping their hands around their eyes to cut out the glare as they tried to see what was inside without the very obvious, but clearly 'not done' expedient of actually going in and asking Roger.

'Ah, Seren!' Andrew seemed surprised by my presence. 'Hello.'

'We have come to look for tables.' Greg was slightly more forthcoming. 'Andrew does not like gaming taking place on ours.'

'That is *not* what I said!' Andrew carried on peering. 'I'm just worried for the surface of our current table and I think a more practical solution would be to have a separate gaming room, that's all.'

'What I said,' Greg said smugly.

'And we wondered whether Roger might have something suitable. Old, but not too expensive, that we could restore to have in the flat.'

'And we are not at all here to see your new man.'

'Well, maybe a bit.' Andrew looked a little ashamed, but only a smidgeon. 'But Roger seems to be closed.'

'We've just had a medical emergency, so it might not be the best time,' I said, wondering whether Ned had regained sufficient composure to be subjected to my brother. 'Joe's just been taken to hospital.'

'Ah, well, I hope he recovers soon. Perhaps just a cup of tea, then?' Andrew looked hopefully towards the open doors into the hall, where the curtains flapped in what tiny bit of breeze had managed to gather itself. 'And cake?'

'All right. Come into the kitchen. I'm not sure everyone can take any more excitement today.'

I ushered them around the building and in through the front door, like official visitors. I wasn't quite sure what Holly's stance would be on having family pop round during working hours, so wanted to make everything look as formal as possible, just in case anyone asked.

Greg sniffed appreciatively. 'You have been baking.'

'Greg, I'm *always* baking. It's like having to appease really tetchy gods through the sacrifice of cake.'

'Mmmm.' He started eyeing up the racks of tins on my shelves. 'Where is your Ned, then?'

Andrew elbowed his husband and a furious look was exchanged. They had clearly been discussing me, my lack of life and the only possible man to be crossing my horizon who wasn't over eighty.

'Oh, he's... around.' I wanted Ned to have maximum time to recover before he ran into the twin obstacles of Andrew and Greg.

'I hope he's not imaginary,' Andrew said sternly, checking the oven for any immediate baked goods.

'Of course he isn't. The scones are in here.' I pushed the tin towards him. 'And there are some rock buns in that one over there, the one with ducks on.'

I made them both tea, but was absolutely not going to pander to them, so they got the usual Yorkshire tea made in mugs, rather than the Earl Grey hand-blended mix that I always got when I went round to their flat. Andrew looked sideways at the chunky clay with the slogan 'I Love Tea', but Greg seized his cheerfully and swigged like a builder.

'Roger will be in, you know. Pop round and ask him about tables.' I tried to hasten their visit to its conclusion.

'In a minute.' Andrew looked me up and down. 'You're looking a bit stressed, love. Everything all right? No sudden desire to take up paragliding or cave diving?'

'No. And I'm not stressed.' I suddenly realised that I was, actually, very stressed indeed and these two pitching up and demanding home cooking wasn't helping. 'I told you, we've had a medical emergency, plus we're trying to gear up for the open day.'

Greg raised eyebrows over the rim of the mug. 'Open day?'

I handed him one of the posters that were busily rolling themselves into cigar forms on the kitchen island. 'Here. Stick some of these up at your place, will you? I think Holly has the rest of York pretty well covered.'

Andrew tutted. 'I know it's your job, Seren, but – well, it's your *job*. Is there really nothing more exciting for you on the horizon? You've not booked a holiday cruising the fjords or taken up with a deep-sea diver called Ken or anything?' He looked around the kitchen, thick mug in hand, as though emphasising the grim inevitability of my situation. 'You behaving like the downstairs maid is not going to get you a partner.' Then, catching Greg's eye, 'Well, only in some fairly specialised circumstances.'

'Andrew, I'm *happy*. I love my job and my flat and having nothing more pressing to think about than whether we've got enough sultanas in. I don't *want* to have to start worrying about trying to fit a man into my life when I don't really get enough free time anyway!'

Then, of course, Ned walked in through the door, plunging straight into the middle of my assertion that the last thing in life that I wanted, or needed, was a man. 'Ah,' he said.

He was, I was pleased to note, not showing any sign of the previous emotion. He'd got a soggy and tea-stained cloth in one hand and some bits of broken china in the other. He looked far more downstairs maid than I did.

'Andrew, Greg, this is Ned,' I said weakly. Everyone 'hello'd' and Ned put the broken china in the bin.

'Thought I'd clear up in there.' He jerked his head at the door. 'Before we close.'

Andrew was eyeing Ned up and down as though Ned were a racehorse he was about to buy. Greg, on the other hand, had caught sight of Kez through the swinging door and burst his way through into the hall to make a fuss of the dog. 'Seren, your dog is in here!' he called back happily over his shoulder. 'I thought you were keeping him hidden in your flat?'

The pleasant buzz of conversation came to a crashing stop for the second time that afternoon. I met Ned's eye, feeling the panic rise again and sending the bun I'd had in my hand raining down onto the side in a hail of crumbs and cherries.

'Oh, bugger,' Ned said. 'I'll just go and...' He dropped the tea-soaked cloth and hastened back into the hall, where the silence was ringing like a great big bell.

'We told them all that Kez belongs to Ned,' I explained to Andrew, who'd managed to eat two rock buns in the time this had all taken. 'Because I'm not supposed to have a dog.'

'Ah. Whoops.' Andrew looked slightly guilty and I wasn't sure why, because it hadn't been him letting the cat out of the bag.

'Maybe I'd better go and remove Greg from the scene of the crime, then. We ought to go and check out the table thing, too. The boys will be over again on Monday and I just can't endure them spread all over the marquetry.' He swallowed hastily, drained his mug and went to the door to make earnest beckoning motions at Greg, who was down on the floor rubbing Kez's furry tummy, whilst everyone gathered around and looked down on them, like a canine-orientated Olympus.

As soon as Andrew and Greg had headed off to annoy Roger, Ned and I shut ourselves in the kitchen for a hissed conversation.

'Bloody Greg! What can we do?'

'They don't seem overly worried about actual *ownership*.' Ned glanced at the door, indicating our hall full of now gossiping clients. 'They've sort of shrugged it off.'

'But they *know*! What if someone says something to Holly?'

'Look, they all seem to love Kez.' Ned perched up on a stool. 'Let's worry about what Holly will say if it actually happens. I don't think anyone will be raising a complaint right now, and Holly's got too much to worry about with this open day looming. After all—' he gave me a sideways look '—you may have found him a new home before Holly finds out.' A grin flashed. 'I'm going to start the chucking-out procedures. You tidy up and then when I get back with the minibus we can take Kez out for his swim.'

The thought of being somewhere other than the hall suddenly seemed appealing rather than terrifying, and the idea of cool, shady trees and flowing water as a view, as opposed to the grim geraniums and Andrew and Greg squabbling in the car park, sounded blissful.

'All right.'

Ned looked out of the window. 'Why are they trying to get a table into a car?' he asked idly.

'It's a long story. A heavy-metal band and immaculate lacquer work feature.'

Ned just nodded. 'And that's your brother?'

'Yes.' We both stared now, at the two men arguing over a jutting table leg that wouldn't quite fit all the way into their car. Greg was shouting in Polish and Andrew was shoving and heaving and getting dust all over his chinos. As we watched, the last centimetre of table slid in, and there was much door slamming and dust whirling as they left.

'You're not much alike.'

'No.'

Ned seemed to shake himself. 'Right. Home time. There's only a few drop-offs tonight, Mimi and Will and Harry, the others have all got arrangements made, so I won't be long.'

'Take your time. I need to wash that bit of carpet where Joe spilled...' I tailed off. Neither of us wanted to remember Joe's collapse.

'Right.'

We both stayed where we were. The air felt heavy with something other than the smell of roasting or baking for a change, as though there was a lot of potential in here for us but we didn't know what to do with it. I felt the words in the back of my throat, wanting... *wanting* to explain the complicated, fractious, loving, dependent relationship that I shared with my brother, built up over years of his having to deal with a tween and then teenaged sister as a very young man trying to come to terms with being gay. There had been a *lot* of shouting; accusations and truly dreadful language that had circulated around our little house like dust and a set of irritatingly irregular side tables. But we understood one another now. At least, I understood him. Andrew seemed to have difficulty grasping that I could be happy in a life that consisted of a menial job and no partner.

'Going now,' Ned said at last, and pushed his way back into the hall, from where the sounds of bag-collection and farewells could be heard. I looked through to say goodbye, and saw Mimi, back by the window in her usual place once more, twisted fingers stroking Kez's ears, almost thoughtfully.

Kez saw me, but didn't move. He looked incredibly complacent.

15

After everyone had gone, I straightened the place and foam-cleaned the carpet where Joe had dropped his tea. It needed doing, I couldn't let the stain set, and yet it gave me a horrible feeling that I was trying to expunge his existence from the room. As though this can of carpet cleaner and stiff brushing were some kind of Derren Brown mind trick that would make us all forget that Joe had ever been here. We'd lost clients before, of course we had. Working with those who'd sometimes been pensionable longer than I'd been alive, it was an occupational hazard. But we rarely lost them in full view. Normally they would decline, going downhill slowly and inevitably, inching little by little towards an end by only coming twice, then once, a week. Staying for shorter periods and being collected by earnest friends or relatives, whose names they would forget. Then one day we would realise we hadn't seen them for a month or so, and then Holly would get up a collection for funeral flowers, and they would drift from our memories into the crowd of grey, half-remembered faces from the past.

It made hearing our customers laugh and have fun whilst they were here more important, somehow.

I patted the carpet dry, then tidied round the nearly completed jigsaw on the table, stacked away the books and magazines that had been left on chair arms and between cushions, and rounded up the stray cups and mugs that dotted ledges and shelves. Then I stood and watched the dust slanting along in front of the windows where the sun still sliced its way into the room, and mused on the fact that there was this much dust in *all* the air, but I could only see it where the sun shone. There was probably a metaphor in this thought somewhere, if I dared to look for it.

I flicked the damp cloth in my hand. No. There was no point in looking for similes and aphorisms in life when I didn't need them. My life was just fine. I had a job, I had a place to live. I had money – not just my salary but an allowance that Andrew paid me, being money from our parents' insurance policies that he had invested so wisely that we both had interest to help us along in life. In his case, this seemed mostly so that he could add to his ridiculous collection of retired furniture, and mine sat in the bank and occasioned letters from the manager about setting up long-term yields and things, which I ignored.

This was life. It would do. And, most importantly, it didn't require me to drive unknown roads, be in unknown places or have to navigate anywhere. As long as I didn't lose my winning way with shepherd's pie, and kept the sultana-to-cherry ratio constant in the scones, I could be here for life.

Holly rang, to report that Joe's family had visited him in York hospital, and that he was sitting up drinking tea and annoying everyone on the ward. He'd been dehydrated, which had caused his collapse, and the hospital were keeping him in until they were happy that he was drinking plenty, and were pumping him full of precautionary antibiotics to thwart what Holly delicately called 'a possible water infection'. The news made the inside of the hall brighter, and the stain on the carpet less ominous, although talking to Holly whilst watching Kez sprawl illegally on the sunny step must have given my responses a slight tinge of guilt, because she uncharacteristically started asking me questions.

'How's the planning for the open day going, Seren?'

'There isn't *that* much planning to do, you know, Holly. We'll borrow the trestles from Roger as usual, set up in the car park, open the hall in case it rains and we have to hurry the stalls inside. The band will turn up and play, everyone will drink tea, buy things and go home. What more is there to it?'

'Bunting ready to put up? Everywhere buffed and ready?'

I looked around the room. The edges of the sofa cushions were looking a little worn and shabby, and there was a bit of a track along the carpet where everyone came in through the front door. The curtains could do with a wash and some stitches put in at the top, where the fabric was weakening, and some of the magazines still featured the death of Prince Philip. 'We've got a couple of weeks to get the place spick and span. It will be fine.'

There was a small pause. Then Holly spoke again, her voice slow and more considered than usual. 'We really have to make this one count, Seren. There's more talk about closing us down and saving council funding.'

'How much do we really cost the council though? People pay to come, and the charity helps fund the rest.'

'Yes, but there's the electricity costs and the fuel for the minibus. And the fees don't really cover much, the charity has to increase its contribution every year, what with your wages, and Ned's, and we're really, when it comes down to it, a drop-in centre that goes over and above. They're talking about opening the residents' lounge in the old people's care home in town and just moving the drop-in centre there. They won't serve meals, it will only be tea and coffee, but it will have the same purpose. And be cheaper.'

My stomach dropped.

'The council do own the building, so they could decide to sell from underneath us. But if we have lots of local support – well, they can *still* sell from underneath us, but a lovely big turn-out might indicate that they'd have a fight on their hands, and they don't need a fight right now. So a really smashing open day ought to buy us at least another year.'

Only Holly used words like 'smashing'. Even our oldest clients knew dated terminology when they heard it.

I held the phone silent against my ear for a moment and stared out at the car park, the wilting geraniums and the twirling fairies of dust. The threat of closure was almost annual, but Holly had never sounded so worried before. I'd quietly speculated that she'd got some dirt on the local councillors that she was prepared to use if necessary, but maybe the statute of limitations had expired.

'The band is always such a draw though, and you can hear them from miles off. That and fresh baking usually gets us a good crowd.'

Holly blew down her nose and ended the call with a rather forlorn goodbye. I saw that Kez was getting up to greet Ned, who'd just returned the minibus to its station alongside Roger's ever-growing pile of furniture. I hoped he was going to move that before the open day, otherwise we were destined to greet guests in what looked like the aftermath of a particularly savage whirlwind.

Ned diligently hung the minibus keys where they belonged, and then rubbed his hands through his hair. 'Right. Let's get somewhere cool.'

While I locked up what needed locking, he put Kez into the back of his car and then waited for me, leaning against the metal-work and looking out across the bits of Pickering that were visible from here, mostly the church, and the rising gradient of old build-ings clinging to the hillside. The final steam train of the day whistled its way out of the restored station like a ghost of past times, and I could hear the sound of the little town emptying. No all-night bars, no clubs or twenty-four-hour supermarkets here, just late evening peace under the relentless press of summer heat. In winter, the town was deserted from 5 p.m., apart from people doing their last-minute supermarket shop, but that was how I liked it.

I thought about telling him that Holly had reported Joe was doing well, but decided to wait. Ned seemed calm, even happy, and I didn't want to remind him. Not just yet.

'Don't you ever feel claustrophobic?' Ned asked without looking at me as I went across the car park. 'Don't you sometimes want to decide to go and see a film at eight o' clock at night? Or buy all the ingredients for an exotic recipe at midnight?'

I looked at him sternly. 'Netflix exists for a reason. And cooking is my *job*, and besides, you've seen the way our lot react to the exoticness of cheese in the mash. Do you really think I'm going to be staring at cookbooks in the evenings and thinking what I really need is fifteen grams of galangal root and some star anise? They'd lynch me if I did that to them.'

'Maybe.' We drove out of the car park. Dusty cars full of sea-tanned families dotted the roads, returning to holiday cottages and hotels, so we had to wait at the junction. 'So, what was your plan B if you hadn't worked here? Were you always going to cook?'

'Pretty much. Andrew invested a lot in putting me through catering college and some cordon-bleu courses, and it's the only thing I've ever really wanted to do. But...' I stopped. I wasn't sure that this hot metal box, full of the smell of Kez, and Ned with his bare forearms resting on the steering wheel, was really the place for admissions.

'Go on.' Ned gave me a sideways grin, watching the oncoming stream of traffic. 'I won't tell.'

Why was I keeping quiet? What did pipe dreams matter? It was a bit like telling him what I would do if I won the lottery. 'I wanted to open a baking school. Teaching people to make really good bread and cakes, maybe some cake-decorating classes.' I relaxed into my area of interest. 'So people could come and learn how to make brioche and pastries and proper cakes. I know you can teach yourself from YouTube, but it's not the same as having someone there to answer your questions and look disappointed alongside you when your loaves turn out like breeze blocks.' Then, warming to my theme, 'People aren't taught to cook any more. Parents don't have time, schools don't have the money, so everyone is pretty much left to pick it up themselves from recipe books and the Internet, and it can be daunting. I'd like to teach people from scratch, how to make things they've only eaten in restaurants.'

Ned laughed and I wondered if he was keeping me talking about myself in order to prevent me asking about *him*. The Ned who'd cried, crumpled and broken, in my kitchen earlier this afternoon had been a million miles away from the ordinary, beginning-to-be-slightly-freckled Ned here beside me, with his white shirt untucked and sleeves rolled above the elbows; relaxed and mischievous and not minding the big collie in the boot, dribbling on the back seats. There was a little of the air of the schoolboy at the end of term about him today, but that might have been the shirt, with its open collar and hanging hems.

'But you haven't gone for that yet.'

'No premises. I'd need somewhere with lots of parking and maybe where I could hold weekend schools, that type of thing, with accommodation. I haven't got a house and the flat is too small, even if Holly and the council would let me use the kitchens here, which they wouldn't.'

We buzzed along the road out of town, covering the few miles faster now the traffic had cleared, and found the village quietly basking in the sunlight that filtered between the big trees along by the river. Two boys kicked a football to and fro along the green, and half a dozen small children were splashing in the shallow river by the bridge, watched over by a gossiped-out pair of mothers sitting quietly on a bench with their legs stretched out in front of them.

It was a scene that probably hadn't changed for fifty years. Maybe even more. The old houses that ringed the green centre were the same, the dust-flecked birds that were bathing on the sandy banks were descendants of birds who'd chirruped there for aeons. The river would have bent its slow, deep way between the trees down from the hills and out beyond the bridge for millennia. I felt a sudden tickle of impatience, and then suppressed it. I *liked* things old-fashioned and the way they used to be. Change wasn't always for the better and 'a good thing' and all that, however much we were told it ought to be.

Ned bumped the car into a spot near the river, and we got out, hearing the children's squeals and full-volume conversation as soon as the air hit us. Ned frowned.

'It's all right. We can walk along by the river. It's always really quiet once you're out of the village because the river gets deeper,' I said. Kez sat upright and alert, ears flicking now and then at the sound of the children playing. I wondered if he missed his erstwhile family, but remembered his quiet contentment spread out in the sunlight and his happy regularity of habit. He would have been fine with the chaotic noise of family life, but he did seem to prefer an established routine and no sudden moves.

Rather like me.

We left the car reflecting the sun in metallic pinpricks and set out along the well-worn bridle path that ran along the flattened side of the river, where floods caused local householders terrified moments every winter. Despite the recent lack of rain, there was still a hoof-pocked mud line down the middle of the track and we carefully avoided it, whilst Kez ran, uncaring, his feathery legs collecting the damp soil and his nose in conveniently placed piles of horse poo.

Ned seemed relaxed, so I thought now was as good a time as any. 'Holly's really worried about our future,' I said. 'She rang to say that Joe is fine and he'll be out of hospital by the weekend and then got into her annual "we need to bring in public support" speech.'

Ned had his hands in his pockets and was picking his desert-booted way along the drier ridge of path, whilst I wandered a horse's width away on the top of the bank where the trees kept the river at bay. 'Joe's all right? That's brilliant. What was wrong?'

'Dehydration. And possible urinary tract infection. Not that Holly said that, because I think she prefers to think of all our clients as smooth plastic below the waist, but, yes. Joe's all right. I mean, he's ninety, anything could turn serious at his age, but he's got rambunctiousness and bad spelling on his side.'

Ned smiled down at the toes of his boots. 'That's good.'

Overhead, the leaves shivered in a breeze that didn't reach us. Kez lifted his leg on a broken bit of branch whilst giving me side-eye as though I were about to forbid him, then trotted off down the path ahead of us, his long-edged coat agitating like a midnight duvet. An oncoming couple, strolling hand in hand behind an eager terrier, moved aside to let us pass. We were walking so far apart that they had to draw right to the grassy side of the path, either that or walk down the muddy middle, and the two dogs gave one another a nod of acknowledgement, then we were separate again, having done the polite Dance of Passage.

Ned looked at me. 'I'm sorry,' he said. 'About earlier.'

What did he expect me to say? Did he think I'd berate him for losing control, when it had obviously been an emotional moment for him? Or was I supposed to shrug and mutter, 'Doesn't matter,' when it quite clearly *did*? In the absence of knowing how to reply, I couldn't do any more than regard him steadily, which, given the unevenness of the path, was a recipe for disaster. I tripped over a tree root and plunged to my knees. 'Ow!'

'Are you all right?' Ned crossed the width of the path, hurrying to help me back up again, while Kez turned back from his nosing along the hedge line to loll his tongue at me and give me his keen amber stare.

'Yes, just caught my foot.'

'You're not hurt?' Ned levered me up by my forearm and then stayed standing close, still holding my wrist.

'Only my insufficient pride.' I was reluctant to step away. Above us, the trees susurrated another breeze through and the light twisted and danced, making the path seem to shift.

'Are you sure?' Ned's hand was on my elbow now, almost as though checking for fractures. 'You didn't turn your ankle?'

The moving light, filtered through a summer's growth, made his eyes look very dark. 'I'm not a Jane Austen heroine,' I said, with a careful amount of levity. 'I don't think I've ever "turned my ankle" in my life. If I have, I've just turned it back and kept going.'

'You've got leaves in your hair,' he observed, and now his other hand was brushing lightly against the side of my face. I could feel my heart shouting at me, pounding a message I didn't understand into my ears.

'Ned, I...' Was I nervous? I didn't really know. Happy at this physical contact? Well, I wasn't disgusted by it, wasn't pulling back. In fact, I might have taken the tiniest step forward, feeling his hand shift on my arm and the fingers move to push the hair back from my face.

'Seren.'

'Coming through!' Two very large horses burst onto the path from the stretch of woodland beyond, stepping their heavy way along the muddied track. Their riders, a pair of jodhpured women in sturdy hats and body-protection like an armed-response squad, smiled at us as they guided their beasts past us with a sudden smell of warm horse and a press of attendant flies. We stayed standing where we were whilst the plop of hooves and voices went by, but the moment was gone, and we started walking again once the swishing tails and conversation had moved further down the track behind us. Every so often the treeline beside us broke to show us a steep incline down to the water's edge, an incline along which Kez was alternately pelting and panting up and down in a graph that closely mimicked the rate my heart was going.

'Ned.' I started a sentence I wasn't sure about. His touch just now had felt more welcome than I wanted to admit, even to myself. Calm, capable, friendly Ned. Who had broken down catastrophically for reasons I didn't understand. Did I *want* to understand? Or would I rather brush off any complications and carry on with my life as it was? Or ask awkward questions and, perhaps, find myself pulled deeper into something that was currently making the back of my neck prickle with potential?

Did I want my life to change?

Then I saw Kez, trundling his way back up the slope yet again, zigzagging his way after a squirrel or a bird, happy tail held high. He had come into my life and changed things and, apart from making me fret about what Holly was going to say, things hadn't gone too badly there, had they? I'd never considered myself as a dog owner and yet – here we were.

'Ned,' I said again, more firmly. 'I think you should talk to me.'

We were through the woods now, bursting out into the sunshine and open glint of water, where a field newly planted with trees ran down to the river's edge. The trees poked like plastic-wrapped sticks bearing one or two leaves out of the top of their protective sleeves. It was like suddenly becoming a giant and looking down on a miniature forest.

'I want to,' Ned said slowly. 'I *should*.' Then he stopped.

'Look, let's sit down. Kez can toddle in and out of the water and the ground here doesn't look too wet.'

Without thinking I grabbed at his sleeve and he turned towards me, an almost balletic manoeuvre that made me realise again that he wasn't much taller than me and had the slender frame of one who was constantly on the move.

'Please, Ned,' I said and my voice was quiet beneath the sound of wind soughing through the junior woodland behind us. 'Just let's – talk.'

He collapsed down onto the sandy riverbank, as though giving in, and, as I was still holding his sleeve, I had to go down with him or risk ripping his shirt off, which was a move further than I was prepared to go, just at the moment.

Kez came over to stare in our faces, but when it became obvious that we weren't eating anything, or about to start flinging sticks, he went back to trundling happily along the bank in search of terminally careless rabbits.

'I want...' Ned started, staring off across the river as though in search of escape. Then he stopped, shook his head and said, 'I feel like I – like *we* – could begin something here. And I don't want to make a total prat of myself.' A flick of a look, as though he was trying to catch me with a disgusted expression or something. 'Would I be making a total prat of myself, Seren?'

I had let go of him now, but there wasn't a lot of space between us. What space there was contained sandy soil where the river-bank edged between field and water and, intermittently, a collie nose.

'I don't think so,' I replied, equally slowly. 'But I need to know things. I can't – I mean, you're *around*, but you never seem to be quite *here*, does that make sense?'

'Ah. The International Man of Mystery thing is working for me, then?' He gave me half of a grin, still keeping his gaze out across the water, where a large boulder caused the river to break and eddy in brown swirls, like a 1960s carpet.

I laughed. 'But not for much longer, before I'm back to assuming that you've got a machete and a hundred bodies in the basement.'

'Well, no. I'm not *that* interesting, I'm afraid. It's just an old, old story and I'm just another victim.' He stopped and shook his head. 'No. No, I'm not a victim. That's wrong. I'm just someone who got caught up in things I couldn't handle as well as I thought.' Now he looked at me directly. It was still just Ned, of the minibus and screwdriver, but there was a curiously focussed look about him now. As though the Ned I knew had been possessed by the spirit of someone edgier, someone with secrets.

'You're not a bank robber on the run, are you?' I sieved sand between my fingers. Its grittiness was pleasingly tactile. 'Who wants to renounce a life of crime and go straight?'

Ned looked taken aback. 'Do you really think a bank robber could pass the DBS checks?'

'Well, no. But you could be using the identity of your dead twin brother who was a policeman in order to present yourself as a pillar of the community, so that when your true identity comes out we all accept you as "just Ned" and there's a party and everyone forgets that you did armed bank robberies.'

'Wow.' He went back to staring across the river. 'You have thought about me *way* more than I ever thought you might.'

I realised that this was, in fact, the case, so couldn't reply.

'It's nothing like that. It's a lot less interesting, really. But have you ever thought about leaving off the cookery, and writing crime drama?'

Another grin in my direction and then he was pulling small pebbles from the riverbank, unthinking, throwing them to plop into the shallow, shifting waters at our feet. Kez, after a brief attempt to retrieve the first two, which involved much bubble-blowing and ridiculously wet ears, went off back in search of rabbits.

'I'm a doctor. *Was* a doctor.' Ned was scrutinising the river, his eyes tracing the path of those thrown pebbles with that brown stare of concentration that made him look so much like Kez. 'Specialising in geriatric medicine.'

My mind instantly conjured up scandal, Ned being accused of some awful crime, being thrown off the Doctors' Register or whatever they did when they sacked you from doctoring. Then I thought of the Ned I knew, careful, methodical Ned who would surely never be guilty of anything worse than pinching the buns fresh from the oven.

'You *were* a doctor. But I saw you with Joe...' The memory of the aftermath of that episode thundered in and I stopped talking.

'Technically I still am. I think that's why I got the job I've got now; Holly saw a way of having a doctor permanently on staff, and I'm cheap. But I don't practise. Not any more.' He took a deep, deep breath and threw another pebble. 'I was working on a geriatric ward when Covid broke out. I lost people, Seren. I lost too many people, patients who shouldn't have died.' Another pebble plopped into the water. 'We were firefighting as fast as we could but we couldn't find treatments that would work. We ran out of oxygen. People were dying, in isolation, afraid and alone and we were trying with everything we had but we couldn't save them.'

He stopped speaking. I could only see half his face, but the part I could see was wearing that expression that I'd noted a few times.

A kind of 'lost in the past' look. As though memories kept creeping up from a deep, dark place and ambushing him when he thought they were well tied down and hidden away.

'I had a breakdown. Was diagnosed with PTSD, but they needed me on the wards, we had to keep fighting and there weren't enough of us qualified to try new treatments, so I had to stay. And every day it got worse and we were losing. I was losing people I knew, people I had come to think of as friends; patients were dying all around us faster than we could move the bodies.'

He gave a small gasp, obviously seeing things he didn't want to remember.

'But surely it wasn't just you, Ned,' I said gently. 'Everybody in your profession must have been in the same boat. You mustn't blame yourself. It wasn't your own, personal failure.'

'But it *felt* as though it was!' An entire handful of pebbles pocked the water and sank, sucked into whirlpools as the water let them through and then swallowed them without trace. 'I should have been able to save them, Seren. More of them, anyway.'

I suddenly realised what he'd been faced with when Joe collapsed. The possible death of someone else he couldn't help. 'So you walked away from your job?'

'I didn't exactly *walk*.' A hollow laugh. 'I was carried out. It was death all round us and we were working flat out, couldn't take time off to recoup or think about what was happening. In the end – well, I failed everyone. Just shut down, right in the middle of the ward. Catatonic. Three days up in Psychiatric, medicated to the eyeballs, and then it was thought best if I left the hospital and went onto less stressful duties. Of which there were precisely none.'

'So you left London.'

The really painful part seemed to have passed now and Ned could look at me again. 'Yep. Sold up, to the extreme disappointment of my parents, who had been dining out on "our son, the doctor" for the previous ten years, and moved to the quietest place I could find, which was the North York Moors. Then eventually this job came up and I thought it might be a way to ease myself back in; helping older people but without being expected to be in the firing line. Until I was.'

'But Joe is fine. He'll be back bothering us by this time next week.'

Ned put a hand on my arm, unthinking. Just drawing my attention. 'But it made me realise that I still can't deal with the pressure. You saw how I – reacted.'

'Only *after* you'd helped him.'

A shrug. 'That's the training, I suppose. Force of habit. Deal with the emergency first and then worry about your feelings afterwards?'

'Oh, Ned.'

'So. Now you know. As far as my parents are concerned, I'm a complete failure. All that time and money spent on qualifying; all those exams, all that study, wasted. I'm thirty-seven and I'm repairing dishwashers and driving a minibus. They won't speak to me now, you know.'

'Well, mine are dead, so I win that round.'

He laughed, a sudden sound that sent some startled birds ricocheting up from nearby bushes. 'I deserved that, thank you.'

'I really meant it though; what's past is done. We can't do anything about it. And perhaps we shouldn't try.' I felt the warm weight of his hand on my arm. 'Did you always want to be a doctor?'

'I always wanted to help people. To do something good. My father was a doctor so he had, shall we say, "expectations" of me, and it just sort of went from there. Doctoring was what I saw happening on a day-to-day basis, so it was pretty much the only job I knew where I could achieve the results I wanted.'

There was a strange smell in the air. Something sweetish, that rose above the cool old-leaves smell of the river and the baked-beach scent of the sandy bank.

'You're not doing so badly with what you do now though.' I moved a little, turned so that I could see more of Ned's face. Still boyish, but maybe that was the scruffy hair and the shirt, because there was the weight of ages in the lines around his eyes and the set of his jaw.

'No. I like this job.' He met my eye. 'The perks are spectacular.'

The smell grew stronger and more noticeable.

'All those fresh-baked goods?' I was grinning now.

'Amongst other things.' He moved too now. 'Look, Seren, I don't want to make things awkward between us but – would you object if I kissed you?'

'If you're sure that you're not just being overcome with emotion and sentiment because you told me about your past.'

'Trust me, I have wanted to kiss you for weeks, this little talk has just been – well, circumstantial. Plus, you haven't run screaming from my revelations.'

'Why the hell would I do that?' My heart was drilling again, there was blood travelling under pressure to places that hadn't seen action for a very long time, and I was realising that I did, indeed, very much want Ned to kiss me.

'Because I'm a bit of a failure.' Ned moved sideways, the hand came off my arm and moved to push the hair away from my face. 'Finding out that someone has lost their entire past because they couldn't cope with the stress – it's not exactly the way to charm women, is it?'

'It's working on me,' I half whispered, and he laughed again, but quietly this time because his mouth was on mine. Softly and with a hint of hesitancy, he kissed me whilst his hand stayed cupping the side of my face.

He tasted of warmth. Nothing more specific, just a general sense of something welcoming and comfortable, like a good cup of tea, but with a hint of something fiery lying underneath. Earl Grey with chillies in. I put my arms up around the back of his neck and we were suddenly kissing with a power and a passion that made all my extremities tingle and my eyes close.

And then the smell became unignorable. Accompanying it came the unmistakable smell of wet Kez, and the dripping of a damp dog's coat. My eyes flew open.

'What the...? Oh, that is disgusting!'

I disentangled myself from the origami of limbs that Ned and I had become and we both stared at the dog, who was standing in front of us looking very proud of himself and waiting for praise, whilst staring at something limp, soggy and very definitely dead. From the smell of it, Kez hadn't been responsible for its demise, it had to have met its end at least a week ago. But he had brought it over and laid it carefully on Ned's leg.

Ned sighed and straightened away from me. 'Thanks, Kez. Keeping it real, well done.'

We looked at each other for a moment, lots of emotions battling for supremacy – embarrassment, lust, affection – but humour won out and we both started laughing. Well, we did once Ned had removed the deceased animal from his trousers and shoved it into a convenient hole in the bank so that Kez wouldn't just retrieve it and carry it like a trophy back to the car.

'I think he approves,' Ned said. He took my hand to pull me up, and then kept hold of it, linking his fingers through mine.

'He doesn't really get a say, though.' I happily accepted our joined hands. It was nice, as we started our walk back, to feel Ned's shoulder against mine, to occasionally meet his eye and smile a smile of hopeful futures and understanding. Kez raked the ground ahead as we went, the odd glance over his shoulder to make sure that we weren't legging it in a different direction was enough to keep him happy. 'Oh God, Andrew... Andrew is either going to be insufferably smug or... no, he's just going to be smug. In Andrew's book, absolutely everyone needs to be in a couple.'

'Are we "in a couple"?' Ned shook our joined hands. 'I mean, I'd like to be. I've wanted to be, ever since I first laid eyes on you in the hall, from behind a pile of cushions. But – well, if you don't mind me saying so, you seemed to have issues.'

'I don't have issues!' I was startled enough to come to a stop. 'Do I? No, I don't. No issues here. I've just been happy being on my own. Better happily alone than miserable with another person, as I keep pointing out to Andrew.'

'I promise to do my very best not to make you miserable with me,' Ned said earnestly. 'But you do have issues. Going out alone?'

'Only to places I don't know well,' I replied defensively. 'And that's not an "issue", that's just a personal preference.'

'But it limits your life. Anyway. Let's have dinner. A meal of any description, actually. To ease us into this "couple" thing, if that's what we are, and I feel the jury may still only be half in the room on that.'

I thought of the dating site. Of its assurance that I needed to 'get a life' in order to attract a man, and then I looked at Kez and wondered if, just maybe, they'd had a point. 'Dinner would be good. But not tonight. Let's pace ourselves a bit. Otherwise we might just do that whole "emotional confession, sex, arguments, break-up" in record time.'

There was a moment of silent walking, then Ned stopped. 'Is that what you think a relationship is?'

'I've been married. I know.'

'It doesn't have to be though. I've – OK, I've never got married but I've had a few goes at being with someone and they didn't all fit your somewhat regulated pattern. Plenty of people don't break up, for a start.'

'But yours all must have done. Unless you've got a girlfriend out there on the moors, and a few children that you haven't admitted to, and all this is just – extra.'

The thought that this might be the case; that I could be competing for Ned's attention against a gorgeous blonde and a bunch of mini-Neds running wild among the heather, was fairly quickly dismissed. That wasn't Ned.

'No. There's no secret family but my parents have been married for forty-three years, so I know things can work out in relationships. But of course we can take it slowly. I'm not demanding that we go back to your place, for example.'

This time, the thought was a lot darker and heavier, weighted with lust and dimmed by imaginary drawn curtains. The blonde wife and the children vanished, replaced by a bed and friction and sighing. 'Yes,' I said, and my voice came out hoarse and gritty as the sand.

'And we can't afford to let it get in the way of our work. So how about we concentrate on the open day first and think about "us" afterwards? Maybe do a bit more of this sort of thing in the interim?' He waved the hand not holding mine to indicate the running dog and the green overhang of woodland. Then he gave a short tug at my hand, which turned me to face him. 'We can afford to take our time,' he whispered, and this time his kiss was less introductory, more certain.

'I think that sounds like a good idea,' I replied eventually, when I could, and, with Kez impatiently leading the way back to the car and his dinner, we wandered back to civilisation, still hand in hand.

16

A couple of days later, Holly paid us a visit, gyrating her way into the kitchen as I pulled a set of experimental banana and walnut cakes from the oven.

'Disaster!' she announced her presence dramatically. 'We're going to have to call off the open day, Seren!'

I spun round and nearly dropped my tray. 'What? No! We can't! What about everyone coming and sending the message that we're successful and a valuable local resource?'

Holly shook her head, and most of the rest of her. Her elbows restlessly searched for somewhere to be and even her knees were in on the act today. 'It's dreadful. Truly dreadful. I don't know what to do, everyone's worked so hard and I've put the posters up and everything. We'll have to put an announcement in the paper – well, everyone will have seen the news, of course, but...'

'What are you on about?' I patted her and half pushed her onto a stool. Her constant motion was upsetting the buns. 'Here. Try one of these and I'll put the kettle on.'

'I *can't!*'

I'd never seen Holly really distressed before. She was normally the epitome of efficient management, ferociously organised and with a hundred sub-schemes up her sleeve. The failure of one element usually just brought out plan B, and we'd change direction but move as smoothly as a silicon baking sheet to the alternative.

'It's the brass band!' Holly was almost crying now. 'There was an accident last night, and their minibus overturned. Lots of injuries – thankfully nothing too dreadful, but broken limbs and concussions and I think someone bent their French horn.'

'Nasty. And?'

'Well, they're out of action for a month. Completely unable to play, even with reduced numbers. And they were the main draw for the open day! We're not going to get the numbers out just for a bake sale and a knitting stall, are we? People want entertainment, they want dancing and music and liveliness!'

The door to the hall opened and Harry put his head through. 'Is it time for tea yet, Seren? We're parched in here, love.'

There was the noise of vigorous agreement at his elbow.

'Just a minute, guys, I won't be long.'

'Better not!' That was Joe, calling through as he wasn't supposed to be walking around too much. 'I don't want to have to stage another collapse to get a cuppa and a cake!'

'That's blackmail, Joe,' Margaret said.

'Don't care.'

I thought of them all out there, massing around the tea table and arguing about puzzles or TV or whatever esoteric topic had been in the air today. The idea that we could be closed down and all this friendly rivalry and activity sent to the local care home lounge was just too awful to contemplate. There was nothing wrong with the care home, obviously, and the staff would do their best for our clients, but there was a world of difference between our independent and mostly autonomous group and those who were needing care. And I knew they'd miss my baking.

On top of which, where would I go?

Then I heard words I'd been dreading, ever since Holly had turned up, wafting through the hall and in to take her anxieties out on me. 'Oh, look, here's Kez!'

Kez had clearly had enough of lying upstairs and had let himself out to come down and greet his adoring fan club. I clattered pans and tried to cover the sounds in the other room. 'So, what are we going to do?' I asked, slightly louder than necessary.

Thankfully, Holly was too distrait to really be listening. 'I don't know, Seren. I really don't know. We need another attraction if we're not going to cancel. A headline act to bring people in; once they're here they'll buy stuff and have tea and all that sort of thing.'

'But the families will come anyway, won't they?'

Holly wobbled her head. 'They may. Or they may not. But we won't get the press coverage. Nobody's going to send a reporter and photographer to a table of cakes and some knitted goods, are they? We might just get a side paragraph in the *Gazette*, and I was hoping for a photo spread in *The Yorkshire Post*!'

Her words choked down into the beginnings of tears and she had to sip at her tea to stop them.

'Could we find a replacement band?' I prepared the tea things but didn't want to carry them through in case Holly followed me and saw Kez, so I sort of rattled them around on the tray a bit.

'With ten days to go? Even the local school bands and their choirs are off on foreign trips, all the local musicians are fully booked.' Holly took a deep breath. 'I tried as far away as Sheffield.'

'Oh dear.'

The door opened again. 'Do you need a hand carrying things through?' It was Ned. 'Only I'm afraid they might riot. There's been some border skirmishes – oh, hello, Holly.' I widened my eyes at him and nodded towards the hall. Ned pulled an acknowledging face and then said smoothly, 'I'll take it all through. You and Holly are clearly talking.'

Then he lifted the entire tray, stacked the buns on the top and whisked the whole thing out, kicking the door open with his foot as he went and giving me a gigantic wink that made me go rather hot.

Holly had remained on her stool throughout the process, which told me how upset she was. Normally she would have been charging through behind the cake plate, counting heads and talking about staff ratios and whether we could afford to replace the sofa or whether we should ask for donations. Now she had her chin on her hand and was staring rather bleakly at today's tea-towel selection spread over the airer and decorating the kitchen with Great British Trees. Her usually carefully set hairstyle, which curved around her face as if it were made of china, like a Dresden shepherdess's bob, looked raggedy, another obvious sign of her distress.

'What are we going to do, Seren?'

She was treating the unfortunate withdrawal of the Kirkby-moorside Brass Band with as much of a sense of defeat as though the Berlin Philharmonic had had to pull out of the Proms.

'I suppose we just have to have the open day without the band,' I said, opening a cupboard to check that I had the ingredients for tomorrow's pudding.

'But it won't be the *same*! It won't have the *draw*! And... and I've been telling the charity that we're guaranteed press coverage and a big crowd – I mean, the band really pulls them in, doesn't it? But now...' A waved hand indicated further unhappiness and she nibbled the icing off her bun thoughtlessly. 'It won't look good to the clients either,' she finished sadly.

'Everyone will understand. It was an accident, it's not like the band have pulled out on us to go and play for a more exciting cause in Helmsley or something, is it? We've not been usurped.'

'I should have had a back-up plan!' Now, to my discomfort, Holly got up off the stool. 'It shows a lack of coordinated planning, Seren,' she said sternly, as though the lack of coordinated planning had been my failure. 'A lack of a plan B is unforgivable. My own position may be at risk because I should have had something on standby to fill in in the case of...' Another miserable dropping-off of words, and she headed towards the door. 'I ought to put my head in and say hello at least. Let them down gently. Although they must already know about the band, they may not have put two and two together that it would result in putting the open day in jeopardy.'

Personally I thought she was taking the loss of the band rather harder than necessary, but I did see her point. All the posters had trumpeted, appropriately, the presence of the locally extremely well-regarded musicians and the fact that there would be dancing. Pulling the event back to tea and cake in a car park, with additional crafts, suddenly reeled us away from crowd-attracting Big Local Do to little more than the stalls that regularly set up along the marketplace to raise money for the school or swimming pool.

And Holly was right. We'd be lucky to get a sidebar mention in the weekly paper. No photographs, nobody from the big York papers. It was demotion, and a demotion we could do without.

'I might be able to come up with something,' I said, to prevent her from opening the door and discovering the dog, whom, I wholeheartedly hoped, Ned was hustling back up to the flat at this very minute.

It worked. Holly flung herself around just as she reached for the door handle. 'You might? Oh, Seren...' For a moment I was worried that she might leap across the kitchen and hug me. 'That would be wonderful! Do you know someone?'

Me? I'd got a social circle of three and a wider group of friends who were all in their eighties. Unless they all had very well-hidden talents that I knew nothing about, and publicity-pulling talents at that – I tried not to remember that Grace had once told us that she'd worked at the Windmill Theatre in London with no clothes on – I hadn't got anything.

'I might do,' I extemporised, hoping, desperately, that Andrew and Greg might have a classical musician or famous singer among their social group; one who was otherwise unengaged for the day a week on Saturday, and who could be persuaded to work for free. It was vanishingly unlikely, as most of their friends tended towards the design and graphic arts end of the scale, and I didn't think we'd get most of Pickering out to listen to a talk about The Return of Mid-Century Furniture and The Rise of Ercol. Not for very long, anyway.

'It would be – well, promotion may certainly be on the cards.' She didn't elaborate as to whether that promotion might be for me or for her. There wasn't really anywhere I could go in terms of career progression, unless they gave me an assistant to do the measuring and chopping, and I remembered how badly *that* had gone when we'd tried having work experience pupils in from the local school. One of the tea towels had been so badly stained I'd had to throw it away.

Then Holly's expression crumpled down from professional leader to worried worker. 'It really would be the saving of the day,' she went on. 'I would be so grateful, Seren.'

A little chirrup of 'grateful enough to overlook the fact that I seem to have acquired a dog?' went off in the back of my head. If I managed to pull this off, it would be very hard for Holly to say no to me for at least a fortnight, and I might manage to slip Kez under the radar while she was still lurching with gratitude.

'I am absolutely going to do my best,' I said, sounding

extremely heartfelt, because I was. If I could just find *someone*, *anyone* to do a 'turn' – be it a talk, a song or even just cutting a ribbon and eating a cake – to get us into the paper, my worries over Kez could be over.

I didn't ignore the fact that my saving the day would look good to Ned too.

BANANA AND WALNUT CAKE

I usually make this as a loaf, in a 2lb loaf tin, but it can also be made as individual cakes, in exactly the same way, just adjust the cooking times down to around 25 minutes. It is an excellent way to use up those bananas that are past the point of no return and are starting to collect fruit flies. You don't want them to be too disgusting, but just when you're thinking of throwing them out, make this cake instead.

Take 8 oz self-raising flour (sorry, this is one I can only do in imperial), 4 oz brown sugar, 4 oz butter, a couple of handfuls of sultanas (or you can leave these out if you hate them), and half a packet of crushed walnuts (you can also leave these out if you don't like them, but, quite frankly, if you do hate walnuts I doubt you've got this far in the recipe).

Rub the butter in the other ingredients, as though you were making scones, with your hands. If the butter is reasonably soft, this doesn't take long, and if you've used really dark sugar you get a lovely brown mixture, like breadcrumbs.

Then mash up two or three of your revolting bananas, until they are really pulpy. If the bananas are absolutely black this will take seconds. Mix in two large eggs and add to the mixture. You'll get a fairly loose, not-quite pourable batter. Pour or scrape or spoon (the texture depends on how many bananas you used and how large your eggs were) into a lined loaf tin and bake at 180 degrees C for around one and a half hours. It takes a bit of trial and error to learn exactly how long to cook it for, because, again, it depends on how many bananas were used. But, quite frankly, you can eat this cake when it's only half cooked and still soggy at the bottom. If you overcook it, let it get cold and serve in buttered slices. This is why I don't often make it as individual buns, it's harder to disguise the mistakes. But if you want to make it as buns, make the mixture, put into individual bun cases and cook for about twenty-five minutes. These are nicest served fresh, just cool, whereas the loaf keeps really well and even when it's gone a bit dry you can still butter it and serve as 'banana bread'.

17

TEN DAYS LATER

The last strains of the final song died away, at least, I thought they had. My ears were still vibrating. Even though we'd put the band right at the back of the car park, the windows had rattled so badly that I'd worried for the good china that I'd laid out for the tea stall. Even Silas, who was almost totally deaf and only came for a few weeks in the summer when his family went off to Italy and gave him 'pocket money' to drop in with us for his lunch and tea, had been tapping his toes. It had been that loud.

'That was a Rammstein song,' Margaret confided to me as she helped me bring another tray of cake out to replenish the stall. 'My grandson loves them. Plays it a lot.' She carefully centred the plate on the table. 'A lot,' she repeated, as though this was a severe bone of contention in the household.

'Aren't they great?' Joe, Jim and Tom had been at the front, Joe in his wheelchair, waving their arms and yelling along. 'I've not heard "Highway to Hell" done nearly so well for years.'

'And that Slipknot cover...' Tom gave me a grin. Perhaps my expression was betraying my astonishment, and I'd certainly had to reel my mouth closed several times. 'We're old, Seren,' he said. 'Not totally past it. I went to the odd punk gig, and heavy metal was all the thing when my kids were growing up, so you either learned to love it or you went deaf, those were the only alternatives.'

The band came over, gasping for cups of tea, and I introduced them to everyone. 'Seb, Dan, Jed, Ulrich, Tommo, Nate and Zac.'

There was a degree of hero worship in the air. Lena asked for an autograph, and John started talking guitars, as the rest of the open day began to seriously get started, having been held in heavy-metal stasis for the duration of the band's set. I had to admit, the music had drawn the crowds, probably, given the volume, from as far away as Leeds. After some frantic phone calls, and Andrew and Greg's intervention, plus the promise of a weekend-long D&D tournament with accommodation and food (Andrew had winced a bit at the accommodation part, but I'd cheerfully volunteered to cater for the entire event), Universal Heat Death had agreed to play our event.

Holly had been ecstatic that I'd managed to find a band to play at such short notice, but right now, she was standing against the geraniums, as though blasted there by volume, with a rather shocked look on her face.

'They were so...' her busy elbows searched for vocabulary '... *loud*,' she finished.

'But look at the crowd, Holly,' I pointed out. Universal Heat Death had brought their own fan club, decked out in band T-shirts and so many metal accoutrements that I wondered they could walk at all. Currently, the fan club was helping pour tea for our clients and eating furtive bits of cake when they thought no one was looking. They'd clearly alerted other fans to this impromptu appearance of the band, because we'd got people who'd come from Scarborough just to hear them play and who were now browsing the stall of handmade goods and buying huge quantities of my baking to fuel them on the – no doubt noisy – journey home. Our clients were humming riffs from the set, and there was a certain amount of shaking out of hair and straightening of backs going on.

'I reckon we should start a group,' John said, trying on Jed's metal gauntlets, but taking them off swiftly when they clearly proved too heavy for him to lift a tea plate with.

'Oh, yes,' Harry said. 'I used to play a bit of guitar when I was young.'

'I can play the drums,' announced Grace, surprising no one, but obviously giving Tom's imagination a good kicking. 'I used to play topless. It was very popular.'

I stood back a little, and Ned came to stand alongside me. He beamed happily at me.

'They were good, weren't they?' I asked.

'Sorry?' He carefully removed a pair of earplugs and put them in his pocket.

'I said, they were good.'

'Yep. And look at the crowd they pulled in.' He waved an arm. The car park was full of people. Not all of them heavy-metal fans, but all of them engaged in spending money, drinking tea and providing the photographer from the newspaper with an excellent backdrop. He'd even muttered something about this making the nationals, with the wonderful unexpectedness of the elderly dancing along to 'Down with the Sickness'. Watching Joe head-banging in his wheelchair to 'Ace of Spades' was certainly a sight that would stay with me for a while, whether it made the papers or not, and Greg had revealed that he knew all the words to 'Highway to Hell'. Universal Heat Death had stuck to classics of their genre, which had meant a large proportion of the crowd had, at least, known the odd lyric to sing along with, rather than playing some of the more obscure tracks from their oeuvre. I owed them not only that entire weekend's catering, but an enormous debt of thanks that I wasn't sure I could pay back just with meals. But national newspaper coverage, now... that would certainly be payment.

'There was some talk about getting *This Morning* out to do a bit on us,' Ned went on. 'Heavy-metal band meets picturesque elderly people – it's a grabber of a headline.'

I looked at him suspiciously. 'How do you know this? Bearing in mind you were wearing silicon noise-blockers through most of the set?'

He grinned at me and raised one eyebrow. 'I just might have phoned someone I was at med school with. He dropped out and went into TV production and he's currently working on *Loose Women*, but he knows people. He's over there, actually.' He pointed at a crowd who were mobbing Universal Heat Death in a way that was clearly gratifying for all concerned.

'Did he teleport?' I asked weakly.

'Called him last week. Told him your plan and he wanted to come and see for himself.'

John had got hold of Seb's guitar, which was covered in skulls and runes, and was trying out a couple of riffs. The feedback whined like the dogs of hell but everyone just laughed. I tried to imagine how this would have gone if we'd arranged it indoors as an 'activity', and whether the presence of a newspaper reporter, who was interviewing as though his life depended upon it, had made all the difference.

'So you called a TV producer up here when you didn't even know it would happen? I've been on the edge of my seat for this last week in case it wouldn't come off.' I looked at Ned. He had lost something of the darkness he'd held around him since he'd told me about his past. As though my knowing helped, somehow.

He put a casual arm around my shoulders. 'I had every faith in you pulling it together, Seren,' he said. 'Plus, I wanted it to be a success. You promised me dinner and – well, we said we'd see how things went after today, and I really didn't want today to be a miserable failure, just in case it boded ill for our future.'

Above us, the bunting he'd spent most of the last few days attaching to the outside of the hall flapped, and the geraniums lifted their heads in response. At the far side of the car park, Andrew was peering through the window of the antique shop, whilst Roger, standing beside him, pointed at things. I foresaw another car-stuffing session before today was out.

'I did, didn't I?'

'You did. Which reminds me, how about coming over to my place tomorrow? You can bring Kez. We could take him for a good walk up on the moor and, well, maybe we could cook something together?'

There was a whole host of implications in that offer. Seeing Ned's house, which I'd only heard about peripherally in passing. A lovely, slow walk with Kez, while we talked. Dinner. And then... well.

'I don't know where it is,' I said, with the implications weighing my words. I knew, and he knew, what they were.

'I'll give you directions.'

'Can't you come and fetch me?'

Now Ned looked at me. It was a long and steady look that carried a lot of weighty meaning. 'No,' he said quietly, and then, more robustly, 'there's a lot of cleaning I need to get on with before anyone else sets foot in the place. I *may* have somewhat neglected the dusting recently.'

Long, empty roads leading to places I didn't know. Trying to find my way home without knowing where I was starting from. Lost. Lost.

'I... don't know,' I said slowly and watched his face change. The dark look was creeping back, that expression that made him look as though something sat on his shoulder and periodically dug claws into his flesh.

'Oh. OK, it's fine. We'll do it another time.' He was trying to brush off the rejection, I could see it. Trying to see the offer as I saw it, and struggling to see the challenge it would be for me. He could understand my limitations, but not truly comprehend them.

'It's just that, well, I don't want to get lost on a hot day with Kez in the car.' I watched Grace sitting behind Ulrich's drum kit and giving it experimental taps. The noise of music had receded and been replaced by noisy chat and laughter. The 'knitted goods' stall was nearly empty and the cake stall had been replenished twice. Crowds stood around chatting, swinging bags weighted with crocheted baby blankets and iced buns, and people were queueing to have their photos taken with the band, who seemed to be accepting the mixed-age hero worship with admirable aplomb.

'No, I understand that.' Ned drew the arm around my shoulders a little tighter and I found I was being carefully marshalled back through the doors to the hall and into my kitchen, where it was cool and a lot quieter. Ned turned to face me and put both arms on my shoulders. 'I don't, actually, understand at all, Seren,' he said.

'Oh.'

'I thought... I *think* we've got something here. Something between us that I would like to be more.'

His eyes were fixed on mine. I could see the little flecks of lighter colours among the brown that gave them the hazel shade and it occurred to me that these were the only eyes I'd looked into for years. Except for Kez's, of course, and, whilst I'd admired the golden evenness of his lovely canine orbs, he'd usually been trying to bite my nose.

Ned wasn't trying to bite anything. His expression had crossed into sadness. 'Only we are going to struggle here, aren't we?' His voice had softened.

'It doesn't need to be an issue,' I almost whispered. 'I can work around it.'

He gave me a tight-mouthed smile. 'Seren, sweetheart.' He wiggled his arms. 'I know you can. But I don't think you should. There's something at the root of this fear of yours, something buried deep, and I'm a doctor, so that kind of thing really niggles at me, you know?'

I had a curious feeling at the top of my chest. At first I thought it may be indigestion, I hadn't been *totally* convinced about those cheesecake slabs, but after a moment examining my internal workings, I realised that it wasn't digestive issues. It was fear. 'I had therapy,' I said softly. 'Andrew paid for it. Years ago. They couldn't find anything.'

'Have you asked your brother, though? If he knows what may have caused this?'

'Well, like I said, he paid for therapy...'

'But what if he already *knows*? If the therapy was to help you live with some trauma rather than discover its cause?'

Ned was almost hugging me now. We'd had occasional physical contact, but not much more than a brush of hands, a quick kiss in passing, and this felt good, even if in a strange way. He was quizzing me about some fundamental part of my psychology, whilst holding me close. Maybe this was how it would always be? But then, would there be an *always*?

I looked out of the window. Andrew and Greg were sitting on a couple of the folding chairs now, holding paper plates that folded and flexed in the breeze, eating cake.

'Andrew wouldn't keep secrets like that from me though,' I said. I sounded a lot surer than I felt. Suddenly the kitchen didn't feel like my quiet retreat any more, it was dark and cold, whilst all the brightness and sound were outside.

'He might if he thought they would hurt you,' Ned almost whispered. 'I think you ought to talk to him. If I'm wrong – well, then maybe we think again. Maybe he genuinely doesn't know and therapy was *his* best guess as well, but if he does...'

I looked out again at my brother. Sandy-blond hair in a neat quiff, carefully dressed in beautifully toning clothes and wearing shoes so polished that the photographer was probably using them as a light source. Next to him, his husband, dark and bearded, big and gruff, made them look like an illustration of night and day. But they were laughing, not a care in the world, except, probably, whether whatever bit of furniture Roger had persuaded Andrew to buy would fit in the car. *Andrew wouldn't keep secrets from me. Would he?*

Ned's arms tightened, bringing me in closer against him. 'I think you need to do this,' he whispered into my hair.

My brother, who was out there, basking in the sun, with not a care in the world. He wouldn't have condemned me to living this little, restricted life if he could have talked to me and made it better, would he?

'Maybe I shouldn't rock the boat,' I said quietly. 'I can live with my restrictions. They don't affect me that much, after all.'

Now Ned stepped back and we fell out of the embrace. 'OK.' He sounded tired. 'But those restrictions – I mean, I'm very fond of you, it could even be more, but I've not had a lot of practice at all that but – your restricted life might affect *me*.'

He was averting his face from me now, staring at the carefully scrubbed tiled flooring. I knew it was carefully scrubbed because I had carefully scrubbed it last night, just in case any visitors found themselves wandering in. There was a vase of geraniums on the middle of the island – they had been the only flowers available, and they nodded their wide faces in a draught as Ned spoke.

'I've had quite a little life, you see,' Ned went on, still talking to the tiles. 'School, university, med school and then hospitals, and there was all the studying and shadowing my father to get experience. I've not really...' He looked up and out of the window now, at the people standing in the sun, chatting. 'I've not had time to look at the world. And I sort of hoped that we... I mean, we get time off, there are holidays and weekends and... plus, you know, my place might be a good location for a cookery school if you ever wanted to... I've got a friend out in Australia who's always on at me to visit,' he finished, with a certain lack of clarity. 'And I'd like you to see it all with me.'

Suddenly, in my head the world stretched. Beyond the moors, beyond the sea, it became a deep, wide place, filled with images that I'd only seen on postcards and tea towels. Iconic places, beautiful places, but places I didn't know. Places where I might get lost.

'But, you see,' Ned went on, taking my hand now and looking closely at my fingers as though examining me for scabies, 'I don't want to travel with someone who's scared all the time. I don't want to have to be with you every second of the day because you can't wander a Spanish street.' He let my hand fall. 'God, this is really hard to say, Seren, and I hope you take it the right way, but—' he took a deep breath '—I don't want *your* restrictions to have to become *my* restrictions, do you see?'

I drew back. 'That's not fair.'

'No. It's not. But it's also not fair on you, if you could get to the bottom of your fear. I'm not asking you to throw it off overnight, these things don't work like that. Believe me.' His face twisted now,

into a mask of the terror he'd shown that night Joe had collapsed.
'I know. But if you understand it, if you can see the root cause of it,
it can become easier to live with.' He turned right away from me
now, and began picking at a strip of loose sealant around the sink.
'I couldn't cope with being with anyone who might get ill, at first,'
he said slowly. 'I sat at home, in my room, medicated to the
eyeballs. I understand now that I can't save everyone. It was a hard
lesson, and hard learned, but once it got through to me – well, I
may never practise medicine again, but at least I can go outside.'

He looked up and the tight focus was back on his face again.
That laser stare that looked as though it wanted to burn all the bad
stuff out.

'But I *can* live with it,' I almost whispered. 'I'm fine.'

'But you won't come to my house. Not even for me, for Kez.'

'I…' I wavered. We weren't arguing, not exactly, but this was the
first time Ned and I had ever had a real difference of opinion. I
knew that I should be processing this. Andrew had always told me
that the best way to gauge how decent a man was was to tell him
no and see how he reacted – a good man would accept your decision and work around it, a bad one would push his own agenda.
Was that what Ned was doing here? Pushing his agenda?

Then the thought of Ned, fey, gentle Ned, pushing anything
almost made me laugh. His reasoning was sound. He was, in fact,
absolutely right. My ex-husband had railed against my inability to
go anywhere new alone too. It had made him feel, as he had put it,
'like your carer, and there's nothing wrong with you'.

'I could talk to Andrew,' I said slowly. 'I suppose.'

A look almost of relief crossed Ned's face. 'I don't want you to do
anything you don't want to,' he said, 'but I really think it could help.'

'I might just ask him if he knows why the therapy didn't work.
We never really talked about it.'

He nodded, slowly. 'It's difficult, I get that. Andrew is like a sibling and a parent all rolled into one. It's a complicated relationship.'

'You could say that.' I suddenly realised Ned was right. Andrew was more like a surrogate father than a brother. I regarded him with a degree of amused annoyance, as one would a parent who couldn't quite get to grips with the new model of mobile phone or how to work the smart TV. But wasn't that to be expected? After all, it had been Andrew who had seen me through primary-school parties, my first period, my first heartbreak – and it couldn't have been any easier for him than for me.

'We should get out there again.' I nodded towards the window, where a photographer with some big equipment had turned up. 'I think there may be a TikTok sensation in the making out there. Besides, I ought to put out some more cake, we've practically sold everything on the stall.'

Ned shrugged and half turned.

'But I will talk to him,' I went on, more quietly. 'I promise.'

Now he turned back and suddenly closed the distance between us, to wrap me in his arms again. 'And tomorrow?'

A house on the moor. But a house that might hold the promise of all the things I'd ever wanted...

'I'll message you.'

'I'll give you the directions.' He grinned now, and it was the easy, happy grin I was used to. 'Just in case.'

'Or we could do it another time.'

Now he nodded and it was strange how the simple action could look so accepting and understanding. 'You may need more time. That's fine, Seren.' His focused gaze was back on my face. 'It's fine. All I want is for you to talk about it.'

Then he turned, wove his way between the disarranged stools

and the spare furniture we'd stacked in the kitchen 'just in case', and was gone.

'Well,' I said to the tea towels. 'Looks like things just got...' but then I realised I was talking to damp linen and I didn't really know how to finish the sentence, so I shrugged to myself and took the rest of the baking outside.

18

The sun was beginning to fade. The shadows now hung over the car park as lopsided as the melted icing on the remaining buns that hadn't yet sold. The band had gone, heading back to York to an evening gig, which, Jed had told me, 'Won't be nearly as good as this one. We're like rock stars here.' Some of our clients had also left, their families taking them home with an air of slight reprobation, like scolded children still high on E numbers and System of a Down lyrics.

I waved them off and listened to the stragglers excitedly planning their band. We'd got John on lead guitar, Harry on second guitar, Grace on drums and Will preparing to learn to play his grandson's bass guitar. They'd negotiated with Roger to be able to use his big shed to practise in once a week and were now in the preparatory stages of persuading their families to let them buy the instruments.

Strange, I thought, how things got reversed. You spent childhood having to ask permission for things, then adulthood being autonomous, then advanced age seemed to bring you back around to being talked down to and not allowed to do things. But it was wonderful to see them so full of vigour and plans, for however long it might last.

Mimi hadn't come. I hoped she was all right, but then I had the thought that her family were probably in full swing with harvesting, so hadn't been able to spare the time. We should have sent the minibus out, but Ned had been needed to help with setting up and most people had come with their families. I wondered if she was sitting at home, by a window somewhere, gazing out silently at the view, and whether her family were worried about her.

'What a fabulous day, Seren, love.' Andrew popped up beside me. 'Terrific show and the banana cake was as good as ever. We're just off...'

'Andrew,' I said, still waving to a carful of happy, singing people, 'can I talk to you for a minute?'

'Of course, darling. If it's about money, I'll need to check in on the funds, if you're wanting to release a larger sum, for something big.' He gave me a little wink. 'Saw you and Ned canoodling earlier. That one's got "future husband" written all over him.'

'No.' I ignored my brother's light-hearted wind-up. 'It's more serious than that. I need to talk to you about why I can't go out. Why the therapy failed.'

All the amusement fell away from Andrew in that second. His normally open, boyish face took on an expression of clouded dread, as though this had been a moment he had been waiting for, but hoping never came. 'Ah,' he said. 'That.'

'If I'm going to have anything with Ned – and what the hell do you mean, "future husband"? We've barely started anything, I'm not committing myself in any way, you do understand that? – then I... *we*... need to get a handle on my fear.'

I looked at my brother. Just... Andrew, who had always been

there, tall and bluff and blond; sometimes confused by his little sister, sometimes amused and sometimes downright baffled, but always trying to keep me safe and well. Just Andrew. But now, looking at the frown that was pleating his eyebrows and the way he had hunched his shoulders, something he only did when he was facing bad news, I thought, *He knows.*

'Umm,' he said, and it was so unlike him to be lost for words that I almost laughed. 'Well, I...'

'We need to tidy up here first.' I felt sorry for him suddenly. He needed time to think, of course he did. 'Ned's going to stack the tables away until Monday when the playgroup want them back, so we just need to bring everything inside.'

'Yes. Yes, of course.' Andrew began to busy himself, seizing the black plastic bags we were using for rubbish and sweeping paper plates and cups into one to go into the recycling. 'Yes,' he muttered almost to himself. 'Of course.'

He was so obviously working on what he was going to say that I left him to it. I bustled our remaining clients into their respective cars, said goodbye to everyone else and collected the teapots and any spare china from the tea stall onto a tray. Ned, disassembling trestle tables, looked from Andrew to me and raised an eyebrow. A particularly vicious hinge snapped at his fingers and he winced, which made me pull a sympathetic face, and then return his quizzical expression with a small smile and a tiny nod, which made Ned grin, in between sucking his bruised fingers. 'Well done,' he mouthed, and winked, which made me feel warm, although that could also have been caused by the fact that I was holding three half-full teapots.

Holly, still looking slightly stunned by the unexpected nature of our sudden popularity, helped clear the car park and then headed off home, her bustling frame unnaturally quietened by the weight of heavy-metal music. Today, I thought as I waved to her vaguely whilst stripping tablecloths, was a day of seeing people differently. I would never have thought that Holly could be so out of her depth at an open day that was mostly hand-crafted goods and sticky buns. Universal Heat Death had clearly been her entry into a previously unsuspected and unimagined world. I hoped she wasn't going to suddenly take to piercings and leather armlets – her husband might come over and tell me off.

Finally, everyone except Ned, Andrew and Greg were gone. Ned and Greg were carrying the tables into Roger's shed to be stored until Monday, Andrew had fastidiously picked up every single piece of litter, paper and card around the place, and I'd straightened the kitchen, loaded the dishwasher and neatened the hall. From upstairs I could hear the occasional clonk of Kez jumping on and off the bed, probably most annoyed that I'd tied up the door handle to prevent him from making one of his sudden entries. I really didn't think that the guitar break in the middle of 'Killing in the Name' would be the ideal time for Holly to discover that I'd acquired a dog. She'd already been traumatised enough.

Without really saying anything between us, we all seemed to have agreed that the hall was the place to convene. Andrew and Greg sat together on the sofa while I brought through another tea tray, and Ned released Kez from his isolation unit upstairs to potter down and join us, spread-eagled on the carpet with eyebrows following every movement and nose alert for any dropped remains from the cake stall.

I looked at Andrew, his head bent close to Greg as they talked in low voices. *He knows,* I thought again. But what could he know? What could there possibly even *be* to know? My heart turned over in a moment of sickness and trepidation. I'd always just been Seren, that orphaned girl with her brother in charge, there had never been so much as a hint of old newspaper headlines about me – and, if there had been, my school compatriots would have been the first to tell me. There were no secrets when you were fifteen and might have looked in a funny way at someone's intended. So, no secret scandals. Just *something*, something in my past that I couldn't remember or didn't know, that had caused me to hate unknown spaces and the therapy, which had been quite expensive, I remembered, to fail.

Ned was sitting on a floor cushion, hands rumpling Kez's ears. I looked at the pair of them, the extended canine with his black paws occasionally stretching in pleasure at the sun and the attention of Ned, and Ned himself, with his hair awry. Looking like nothing more than Ned, our 'do everything' person, and yet being so much more. He glanced up and saw me looking at him, then gave a small smile that seemed to have some hidden depth in it. But then, wasn't that Ned all over? Hidden depths? When I'd first met him I'd thought it was hiding something bad, but now I knew that his depths contained terror and the fear of losing control of a situation and deaths that couldn't be avoided. Would anything he learned here about me make him see me in as different a light as I'd learned to see him?

My heart did the sickening turnover again.

I sat down next to Ned. 'Andrew,' I said. I had to repeat his name to get him to look at me. 'We need to talk.'

Andrew looked at Greg and I thought, *Greg knows too. Whatever it was, it was so bad that Andrew needed to talk about it to someone.* The base of my stomach solidified as though the tea I had drunk so copiously during the afternoon had contained cement.

At last Andrew took a deep breath. 'Seren,' he said and looked at the dog, sprawled out by his feet. 'Are you sure you really want to go into this?'

No! screamed my insides. *I'm happy here in my little life, not knowing!* But Ned leaned his shoulder against me, a quick pressure, and I looked sideways at him. He was carefully keeping his eyes on the dog.

I could say no. I could chicken out, walk away. Let Ned be no more than a friend, a work colleague, and stay as Seren in the hall, baking and tidying with my horizon no further away than the end of the marketplace. Worry about the future of the charity that paid me, and how I was going to break it to Holly that I shared my living space with a dog that was probably more intelligent than I was. No hobbies, no partner. *No future.*

'Yes. I need to know, Andy.' I used his childhood name and watched him react to the levelling. Only our parents had called him Andy. Aunt Sophie had always used his full name and it had become set in stone between us, but he'd been Andy, once.

Greg took his hand and muttered something in Polish. Andrew nodded and took another deep breath. 'It's... not good, love,' he said slowly.

'Well, I hardly thought something that has confined me to within two miles of my home and means that I don't like crowds or strange places was going to mean that I'd been plied with kittens and sweeties at a formative age,' I said, slightly tartly. All these meaningful glances and deep sighs were beginning to get to me.

Andrew smiled sheepishly. 'Yes, sorry.' I saw his grip on his husband's hand tighten. 'What *do* you know?'

'I'm not sure. About what?' Ned bumped my shoulder again. Fear, trepidation, were giving my voice a sharp edge. 'I'm sorry too, Andrew. This is – well, it's just weird, isn't it?'

'It's hardly an everyday conversation, you're right.' Another smile.

'You brought me up. You were always there, you were like Mum and Dad and brother all rolled into one and you did a good job. I mean, look at me.' I held out my hands. All three men looked, and there was an unflattering amount of silent blinking. 'I've got a job, I've got a home, I've got, heaven help me, a dog. I've got *qualifications*, I've got a life. And it could have gone so differently, but for you.'

Andrew wriggled, suddenly as embarrassed as a child hearing their good points picked out. We weren't ones for effusive gratitude, or much gratitude at all, really, and I had never properly thanked him for keeping me on the straight and narrow, which couldn't, at times, have been easy.

'You're my baby sister,' he said, looking at his knees. 'I couldn't let you... I couldn't let Sophie keep you. You would have turned out like her.'

'Sophie's all right.' Aunt Sophie, currently tanning herself to the consistency of a good handbag in Spain, couldn't possibly be the source of my fears. She'd told some pretty scary stories about what happened to girls who weren't 'good', but she hadn't scarred my psyche to any truly deep levels.

'She's a homophobic old...' A mutter in Polish again, that sounded like a warning, and Andrew stopped. 'No. That's not fair. I've always said I wouldn't let my experiences colour your memories. She looked after us both, after all, and she wasn't to you what she is to me.'

'Homophobic?' I was taken aback. 'Is she?'

'Darling, why do you think I don't take Greg whenever I visit her? Why do you think I put her out in Spain, well away from having to do family Christmases and parties and stuff? Why do you think she didn't come to our wedding?' Andrew's mouth twisted as though there were other, more bitter things he wanted to say, but he was keeping in check. 'She made my adolescence hell. But she was good to you. So—' he threw up his hands '—I reckon she's a repressed lesbian who can't bear to see anyone living the life she can't admit to herself that she wants, but that's just me and my amateur psychology.' He finished. His quiff had sunk a little now and was flopping down over one eye; he suddenly looked like the schoolboy Andrew that I didn't really remember, other than envying for his ability to climb out of his bedroom window. I suddenly realised *why* he'd been climbing out, and it hit me just under my lungs.

'Oh,' I said, on a little puff of outgoing air. 'I never knew.'

'So her views on politics, immigrants and the general state of the UK didn't give you a heads up?' Now his expression was sardonic. There was memory running behind his words, and the memory wasn't nice.

'You took me away when I was ten. She hadn't really had chance to give me much more than an outline view. Anyway, I was more interested in ponies and drawing back then. And we've only done little short visits over to see her, so I've only had her opinions on Spain, the Spanish and the impossibility of getting a good cup of tea.'

'Well, that's *why* I took you away and brought you up myself. I couldn't bear her to turn out a carbon copy of herself in you.'

My childhood memories were starting to rewrite themselves. I could *feel* it. Aunt Sophie asking Andrew where he thought he was going, criticising his clothes and his hair, generally being hard on him – I'd thought it had been because he was at that stage of growing up when he'd been 'difficult', argumentative and stroppy like just about every other teenage boy I knew. But this was only in retrospect. At the time, I'd been happily absorbed in glue and glitter and making pom-poms or watching cartoons on TV. My brother's fractious relationship with our guardian hadn't meant much to me.

'She never talked about Mum and Dad, did you notice that?' Andrew was watching me now, with an earnest, tight expression.

Ned went still and quiet, causing Kez to raise his head and wonder where the nice scratches had gone.

'I *did* used to ask,' I said. 'But she just said that it was too painful and she didn't want me to speak about them again. There was that one picture, remember? Of them, one Christmas? It used to be on the very top of the cabinet in the living room.'

That picture had fascinated me. My mother and father, much younger, before my birth or Andrew's, squeezed together in front of a Christmas tree, my mother showing off her engagement ring and Dad with his arm around her waist and a grin of pure happiness on his face. I had used to climb up and fetch that picture down when Sophie wasn't about, and stare into my mother's face, wondering if I looked like her and if I'd ever be as happy as she was on that day.

Andrew nodded. 'She found you looking at it and took it away.'

'Did she? I just remember that it was gone one day and I didn't dare ask her about it, because she hated me mentioning them so much.' I frowned as the edges of that memory tugged at something in my brain. 'Strange, really. I mean, Dad was her brother. I'd have thought she'd want to tell his children all about him, all about what he was like, and what they did growing up, but she never did. Never talked about them at all.'

'She used to shut us down when we tried.' There was a note in Andrew's voice now. A hint of a shake and a whisper in the words that told me this was the real crux of the matter. Something behind our aunt's intractable attitude that had been the crucible of my fears. Andrew was trying to lead me towards my own discovery.

'Yes. She did.' It was odd how memory returned, not as a smooth narrative but in lumps and heaps. An image, a conversation, an attitude. 'I've not really thought about it for years. It was just Aunt Sophie, just how she was. Food on the table, uniform bought, homework supervised, but not much actual emotional involvement.'

My brother swallowed hard and I realised then that his memory-narrative was very different from mine. 'Did you ever wonder? You never asked me...'

'I knew that they both died and you found them. Even when I was four, I knew not to talk about it or I'd upset you.'

'And Sophie told you that.' His voice was flat. Beside me, Ned shifted and Kez, ever hopeful, half sat up. They were all looking at me.

'If this is too painful...' Ned started, his voice gentle. I wanted to ask, *painful for who? Me or Andrew?* But I didn't.

'It needs to be said. Seren is right. It's not been fair, letting her go through life without a proper explanation. There are holes in what she knows.' Andrew didn't look at Ned though, I noticed, he kept his eyes on my face. Greg was looking at the floor, almost braced for impact. 'What *do* you know, love?'

'That Mum had been ill, we went to the park, when we came back you went into her room and she had died and Dad had had a heart attack when he found her.' I rattled the sentence off. It had been the mantra to my childhood, whenever anyone had asked why I lived with my aunt, why my brother was bringing me up. Schoolfriends, curious adults, teachers, they'd all had the same pat phrase. 'That's what you always told me.'

A cold dawn of thought. Andrew was watching me, waiting for something. 'Did... did you *lie* to me, Andrew?'

I saw Greg slide his arm around my brother, pre-emptive. Ned touched my leg, a light pressure, reassurance?

'Not a lie, love. Not really. Half-truths, maybe?'

The narrative was unwinding. Which part of what I knew wasn't true? 'Then you'd better tell me all of it,' I said quietly. 'Fill in those halves that I don't know.'

I saw Greg give a little nod, as though backing up Andrew's words. He must have known what had happened all along. Well, of course, Andrew had been carrying secrets, he'd have needed to tell them to someone, and it would have been Greg. A sting of bitterness rose from my throat. I'd always liked Greg, always thought he and Andrew made a wonderful couple, but maybe I'd been looking from the point of view of the sister who knew her brother. Suddenly, realising that Andrew had kept things from me made me see Greg differently too – these two men were almost strangers. Ned, perched beside me, was learning all these new things too – with a shock I found that I was thinking of Ned as the only person on my side in all of this.

I reached down and took his hand.

'You know Mum had been – ill, don't you?'

Now I nodded. It had been another part of the mantra. 'Mum was ill from practically the day I was born.'

Again, I'd never asked for specifics and I was beginning to see how Sophie's reaction to questions had squashed the will to ask – 'Oh, we don't talk about that, you don't need to know that, don't go asking things like that, it's upsetting.'

'Mum had been ill before. She had a brain tumour. She'd had it removed once, when I was, oh, about seven?' Andrew seemed lost in thought for a moment. 'Dad had to take time off work to look after me while she was in hospital and I remember her having her head all bandaged, but, hell, I was seven. I didn't really know much. Just that it wasn't completely successful. Oh.' He jerked his head up suddenly. 'I've just realised. It must have been about when they decided to try for another baby. I mean, I don't know what treatments she was on, but the operation – maybe that was so she could cut down on the drugs or something? Because they wanted another child? I've no idea, I'm no doctor and, like I said, I was too young to talk to about it.'

I was beginning to wish there had been more photographs. Andrew had kept one or two, mundane pictures of Mum and Dad feeding ducks or at parties, one of Mum with babe in arms that I'd always assumed to be Andrew. Sophie had overseen the clearing of the house, after all... she hadn't kept anything for us.

'So, when you were about two, the tumour was back and it began to...' He looked at Greg. Now I could see their relationship for what it must be, not just a fun pairing of two people who loved one another, but a deeper reliance. In each other they had someone to lean on when the going got tough, something I'd never had in my brief marriage. Someone to have your back.

Ned squeezed my fingers and carefully put an arm around me. It felt supportive. It felt *right*.

'Mum got a bit weird. You have to remember that I'm only about ten at this point. Old enough to notice things changing but not old enough to understand why. Dad just said that we had to be careful, and keep an eye on her because she might forget things or be a bit silly. That's actually what he said and I remember it because I didn't know adults could be silly so it made an impression. "Mum might do things that are a bit silly," he said. So I used to run home from school to see if she'd done anything "silly"; I think I half hoped that she'd do something really mad like paint the whole house gold or turn the garden into a swimming pool, but—' he came back from the distance he'd been looking down '—it wasn't that kind of silliness,' he finished. 'Obviously.'

'Do you know what type of tumour she had?' Ned asked, speaking for the first time.

'Ned's a doctor,' I explained when Andrew and Greg looked his way with questioning frowns.

'Was,' Ned corrected.

I didn't like to tell him that he talked about being a doctor in the present tense. He wasn't ready to think about all those implications yet.

'No. Fast-growing, malignant, I'm not sure. I was *ten*!' Andrew looked affronted and I almost laughed. 'I may have been told, but I couldn't even spell it, so it just...' He fluttered a hand to indicate the ephemeral nature of such things to a child. 'Anyway, Mum tried to carry on as normal, but she'd sometimes do weird stuff. And some of that weird stuff was going out for the day with a toddler when she wasn't supposed to.'

Now Andrew gave me a steady stare as though we were doing a crossword. It was a look I'd seen from Tom, doing *The Times* crossword with Joe, when one word remained to be filled in and Tom had worked it out. A kind of 'there's the clue, there are all the constituent parts, you just need to put things together and fill it in' look. An 'I don't want to have to help you here because you should be able to get it from that' look.

'She'd take me out and then... what? Do weird stuff?' I groped for the ends of the information, trying to tie them together to weave some kind of picture.

'Not so much weird stuff. She'd drive out to places like Whitby or sometimes out onto the moors to the river or so you could see the sheep – you really liked sheep when you were small, you kept trying to stroke them – and then she'd forget she'd taken you with her and come back on her own.'

Those words fell into a ringing silence. Apart from Kez panting as he lay in the warm sun, and the passing rumble of traffic, there was nothing, and the sentence fell through my brain and into my nerves. I twitched.

'She'd *leave me*?'

Ned's arm tightened. 'Hey,' he said gently. 'It wasn't her fault.'

Now he'd started, Andrew seemed to want to get the whole story out as fast as possible. 'Not often. Not all the time, just these few times, and you were always found and brought back really fast. Passers-by found you crying in a car park one time, and another time these two lovely ladies had taken you in and you were being fed ice cream and chocolate and watching videos when we picked you up. Nothing bad ever happened to you, we don't think. And then, of course, Dad took the car keys away because it wasn't safe, but Mum took you out on the bus instead and the drivers would have to remind her not to leave you on board – I think you got as far as Seamer once before they realised Mum had got off at Thornton without you.'

At two, two and a half, of course I had no memories of any of that. Or rather, I *did*. Empty roads, unspooling into wilderness. Lost.

'She didn't mean any of it. That's why we never told you; it wasn't Mum, it was the tumour. Her memory, her behaviour, she wasn't responsible for any of it.'

'But you should have told me! It would make sense!'

'When I was twelve,' Andrew ignored me and carried on speaking quickly, 'Dad sent us to the park for the afternoon. He gave me money to buy ice creams and told me to stay out as long as I could.'

My skin rose in gooseflesh. Ned's touch was suddenly too much and I stood up, with Kez rising to his paws alongside me. There was something in Andrew's tone now that I really didn't like.

'When we came back, he'd left me a letter, propped up on the sideboard in the hall. It was the first thing I saw when I came in, but I just picked it up and went off to tell them we were back. The door to the bedroom was open and it was dark in there, because the light hurt Mum's eyes, and I went in. I had the letter in my hand, I remember that, because I couldn't work out why Dad would write to me when he could have just told me.'

'Andrew,' I said, and my voice was a cracked, small thing. I heard Ned swallow.

'I only really found out later, when I talked to the ambulance people. Dad had given her sedatives and put a pillow over her face, then taken all the rest of her tablets. They were lying there on the bed, side by side. Hand in hand,' he added, looking at his fingers, wound around his husband's.

'The letter?' I had to clear my throat to get that out.

'It said just how much they loved both of us but Mum was suffering and he couldn't watch her "dwindle down and die". I remember that phrase too. I thought it was rather poetic, for Dad. And that he was sorry. Then he told me to call Aunt Sophie to deal with everything and to look after you, and some other stuff but that was by the by. I burned it. The letter,' he finished.

'Oh God,' I whispered.

'I really did want you to know.' There were tears in my brother's eyes now. 'I really wanted to tell you all this, years ago. But you seemed happy, you were doing stuff, you married that utter waste of space Hugh because you wanted to... and none of this came up. Until now,' he added and then eyeballed Ned as though this were all his fault.

I was looking out of the window, but not seeing the fragile falling blossoms of the flowers or the baked and cracked cement. All I could see was a small child, wandering an endless space, looking for her mummy.

No *wonder* I didn't like being alone in strange spaces and had a fear of getting lost. I had a moment of quiet pride that I'd actually turned out as well balanced as I was. After that kind of trauma I felt entitled to never have left the house again.

'I think you all ought to go now,' I said, and my voice sounded vague, far away. As though it too were still roaming a distant place. 'Kez and I have some thinking to do.'

Andrew scrambled to his feet from the saggy sofa, with almost indecent haste. 'Well, yes, of course, and we ought to get back, we've got a delivery due. Haven't we?'

Greg nodded but threw me a look of utter sympathy. 'You need to work things out. In your head,' he added, as though I might have been about to perform advanced mathematics.

Ned had clamped his hands between his knees. 'Are you sure you will be all right?'

'Yes. Probably. But I really do just need to go to bed and fail to sleep, I think.' I tried smiling at him but from the feel of my face and his slightly startled expression, it didn't really come over as a smile.

Andrew and Greg exited through the French windows, stepping down into the stifling air of the car park as though escaping from prison. I watched them cross to their car, heads bent together, clearly discussing things. Just as they were about to get into the car, Andrew turned and looked back towards the building, towards me. Head up, quiff slightly flattened but very much in place again, and I saw all the Andrews I knew overlaid on that one figure. Gay man, devoted brother, happily married husband, aesthetic art dealer, slightly fussy housekeeper, dreadful cook. And now, over the top of all of those, a man who'd kept secrets. He was still my brother, but he was someone else as well.

Behind me, Ned was packing up his things. As he went to leave, he pressed something into my hand, a folded piece of paper.

'What's this?' Kez tried to take it from my fingers. I assumed that he thought it was an extra-large piece of cake.

'Details. Directions to my house. I drew a map, sort of. It should get you there.' Ned looked away, out across the roofs of the town. 'If you want to try. And you already know my phone number, if you get – mislaid, call me. I'll come.' His hand came up, lingered for a second on my cheek. 'You've got sunburn coming,' he added prosaically. 'You need to put some cream on that.'

Then he was gone. An ethereal being, but not flying away into the sunset on a yarrow stem, rather driving off along the hot, dust-smelling tarmac, in an Audi.

'Come on,' I said to Kez, who was almost beside himself with excitement at all this movement. 'I think we both need a long, slow walk. But just around town. I'm not sure yet that knowing what I know is going to help me.'

19

I hadn't even known myself whether I would go to Ned's. There were implications in the visit, cooking together, maybe – well, maybe something else, which I wasn't quite sure that I could handle, on top of all the revelations of the day before. But a night spent trying to toss and turn whilst under a duvet weighted down by a considerable amount of collie told me that no amount of being alone and thinking was going to change anything. What had happened had happened. Andrew had done what he had done to protect both of us. He'd carried memories and knowledge that must have hurt him on a daily basis – knowing that I hated travel because I'd been left alone as a tiny child in strange places, and knowing that it would have coloured my view of my mother if I'd known that, must have been awful. Knowing that my father killed my mother out of love, and then himself out of – what? Not being able to live without her? Fear of consequences for what he'd done?

Poor Andrew had known all that. He'd known about Sophie too, and he'd rescued me from a lifetime of being told that homosexuality was wrong, that we had to police whom we fell in love with; a teenagehood that could have scarred me with its rigid policies. As, presumably, it had scarred him.

I wondered, for the first time, what my brother actually *felt*. One day I'd ask him. One day I'd find out how it had been to be a young gay man in a small market town where everyone knew your business and your guardian disapproved of who you were. What it had been like to pass through adolescence whilst living with bigotry and intolerance and the knowledge that your parents had been part of a murder-suicide pact.

He'd kept his secrets well, I had to give him that. There hadn't been so much as a mutter in my hearing, all the time through school, through my slightly odd behaviour around travel, nobody had uttered the words 'well, of course, given what happened...' or any hint that my parents' deaths had been anything other than tragically timed ill health.

And so, I had to give myself permission to feel stupid. To feel cheated and lied to. I'd learned that much through the therapy that hadn't worked – well, of course it hadn't, because I hadn't known about the root cause of my problem and Andrew had paid an exorbitant sum of money for me to talk to a very lovely and well-qualified mental-health practitioner for months, without the faintest idea of what I was talking about. It had ironed out a few niggles I'd had about feeling inferior regarding not wanting to go to university or study for a list of qualifications that school had decided would be appropriate, but instead going into cooking, and the feelings about the ending of my marriage. But that had all been by-products. None of those things had meant anything.

I wondered how long it would be before Andrew suggested more therapy. He really liked therapy, but then, I thought again, with what I knew now... he'd had years of Sophie. He'd probably needed that therapy. Maybe it had helped me in ways I couldn't see, but probably nothing that couldn't have been achieved by talking to friends. If I'd had any.

Then the sudden realisation that I found it hard to make friends because of Sophie, because of her attitudes to people that must have rubbed off on me, thundered in. The knowledge that I kept people at a distance because I'd been deserted by my parents at such a young age had always been there, the therapist had worked on that one with me, but now the new knowledge that Aunt Sophie – chilly, aloof Aunt Sophie who hadn't cuddled but had cleaned up after us, bought us clothes and food – had known that her brother had killed his wife and then himself. How had *she* felt about it all? I thought about phoning her and asking, but the knowledge that I'd get a sharp, 'What do you want to be thinking about that after all this time for? I don't want to talk about all that. Now, go and do your homework,' made me stop. I even giggled. Sophie was so engrained in my head with 'go and do...', with schoolwork and paying attention and 'not letting people down', that I could only think of her in the same way as I had when I'd been ten.

So that was how I came to be driving across the high moor, watching the known view dwindle in the mirror between the dog's ears, with my hands tight and sweaty on the steering wheel. *Nothing to be afraid of. You can just retrace your steps if you get lost.* The pale grey road stretching from visible border to invisible horizon, sturdy and settled and safe. I could do this. I'd recognise that bush there, and that tumbled pile of stone, which might have been a barn once. And there, that bleak finger of signpost that looked as though it might have grown there at the crossroads, pointing its way down to a hidden dale, I'd know that too.

As long as the road was straight, I was fine. But Ned's place, it turned out, didn't lie on the single road that crossed the moor. There were junctions. Turns I needed to take. The first wasn't too bad, a right-hand turn onto a small lane that sank its way down into the moorland as though the weight of all the centuries of passing traffic had depressed it into its surroundings. As soon as the bracken hung over the roof of the car and I could no longer see where I'd come from, my hands started to slip on the wheel and I began to feel sick. I had thought it would help, knowing *why*. But it turned out that trying to override my inner two-year-old was harder than I'd imagined, and when I reached another junction, where the road ran alongside a narrow beck and its peaty-brown waters, I had to pull over onto the side of the road.

'This is stupid,' I said to Kez, who was contemplating a lovely run up the grassy slope that blocked my view of the sky. 'I'm *not* lost. I'm really not.'

Then I put my head down on my arms and cried. I cried for the toddler, left confused and afraid by her mother. I cried for Ned and his helplessness in the face of a pandemic that killed his patients. I even cried for Andrew, though I couldn't come close to knowing how things had been for him growing up. But most of all I cried for me *now* – for the little life I was living, constrained and reduced by my fear, which was being compounded by my attempts to overcome it.

There was a tap at my window. I raised my head, horribly aware that my face was a streaky mass of snot and swelling and I was probably blocking a tractor and fifteen tourist vehicles from carrying on their blithe and unafraid way into the depths of the moor.

It was Ned.

'I hoped you'd try,' he said, when I wound down my window. 'So I've been patrolling this bit of road for the last two hours. I'm knackered. Let's go and have a cup of tea.'

He opened the driver's door and I fell out into his arms, a snivelling, wretched mass. I stammered a few apologies into his shoulder, and he gave a short laugh.

'Seren, if anyone knows about PTSD and traumatic events preventing you from living your life, it's me.' His voice was in my hair. 'You got this far.'

I took a huge breath and raised my head. 'We'd better let Kez out,' I said, and even to my ears my voice sounded pathetic. 'Otherwise we're here under false pretences.'

'Yes.' Ned didn't move. He just let me finish crying. Once I'd largely stopped, and sniffing had taken the place of actual sobbing, he loosened his hold a little. 'Let's go inside. We can take the dog for his walk later. He can roam around the garden in the meantime.'

We let Kez out, much to his delight, and then Ned took my hand and led me along an ivy-covered wall that bounded the road, to a gate. 'This is my place.'

I stared at the wall, the gate, and my car, which was about ten metres away. 'But... it looks like miles on the map you drew!'

'Yeah, well, I'm not much good at scale.'

'If I'd known I was nearly here, I wouldn't...'

'But maybe it's best that you didn't.' Ned opened the gate, which led into a walled garden; lawns ran smoothly down to a huge oak tree at the end and various flowers and fruits studded the walls. The house itself was an impressively monolithic feature beyond a beautifully laid patio, decorated with a white painted bench and several planted tubs.

'This is gorgeous.' I stared. 'I mean – really lovely.' I remembered that I'd thought he lived in his car, and made a vow to myself never to tell him that.

'I sold my place in London.' Ned seemed to be enjoying my

amazement. 'I don't know if you know much about property prices, but...'

Kez saw a squirrel and hastened off to raid the oak tree for more. I turned a circle. The high walls encircled the whole garden, except for the gap where the gate had let us in, and the house formed the fourth side of the square; the sun angled through the oak leaves and fell in shifting patches on the grass. Birds sang and I could hear the beck gurgling to itself as though it too were amused at my reaction.

'Let's have that cup of tea and then take the dog out,' Ned said. He was still holding my hand.

While the kettle boiled we toured the house, which had six en suite bedrooms and had once been used as an exclusive small hotel. The kitchen was top-notch, large and professional, everything else was small and old-fashioned: thick walls and sash windows, low ceilings and beams. Then we took Kez out, back along the road to make sure my car was still there and hadn't been stolen by rabbits, which Ned assured me were the only regular travellers along that stretch. Up and out onto the vast stretch of purple moorland, where we climbed to the highest point on the rump of slope that faced towards the grey twinkling that was the sea, and watched Kez roll in disgusting things.

We didn't speak much. Somehow we didn't seem to need to. I just drank in the wild beauty of the place and Ned smiled quietly to himself, and then we went back to the house, where I spent a very happy hour poking around the incredible kitchen.

'Is the range multifuel?'

'Yep. Bottled gas though, we're a long way from civilisation here.'

'It's got a built-in bain-marie!'

'Oh, is *that* what that is?' Ned sounded relieved. 'I thought I was supposed to be doing something with it. I just use it to heat beans.'

'Remind me to say something similar about my internal organs at some point.' I raised my head from the shining steel and chrome and grinned at him. Although the inside of my head was a mass of confused thoughts and imaginings, somehow seeing this slightly unconventional and rather scruffy man leaning against a marble worktop and enjoying the sight of me discovering his high-tech cooking apparatus made it all feel rather less complicated. 'Why though?' I suddenly stopped as we were walking between the kitchen and the 'pantry' – which turned out to be a stone-flagged cold room that had apparently once been the dairy. 'Why sell up in London and buy this? Isn't it a bit... much? When you could have bought a little flat in York?'

Ned shrugged, holding the pantry door open and running a hand along the slate shelves that lined the room. This place would have made an *Ideal Home* spread, given a few more cushions and an interesting paint job. 'I wasn't really thinking,' he said slowly. 'I had half-hearted ideas of opening a B & B and getting staff in, but – it's too far from anywhere for people to want to work and there's not enough space to accommodate them. But it's ideal for cooking courses. Small ones, obviously, I don't think we'd get Mary Berry up the drive.'

'Mary Berry?' I was puzzled.

He shrugged again. 'She's the only cook I know. Well, her and Delia Smith. And now, you.'

The cool slate-and-granite air of the pantry room suddenly felt a lot warmer. 'I, er. Ned...'

He let go of the door, which closed and shut us into the small, grey stone room. It now looked very much like the cell I'd suspected him of escaping. A tiny, high window let a north light peek weedily onto the topmost shelving. 'I know. It's too soon for anything like that, obviously. I just wanted you to know that – well, that I'd thought about it. About *you*.'

A huge stone slab that had probably been used to roll butter gave me a convenient place to perch and look at him. I could have been scared, shut here in a tiny room miles from anywhere with a man, but Ned had that air of capable randomness that felt familiar now. 'I think about you too,' I said.

'Well, it's a start.' I had wondered if he'd kiss me, but he didn't. He just looked at me with a slight quirk to his mouth that I hoped was a smile. 'We can't leave the guys yet, after all. *Someone* has to be around to hear John play the opening bars to "Stairway to Heaven" fifty million times and to apologise to the neighbours. This is just —' he waved a hand at the glory that was the house '—for later.'

A future that I had never dared contemplate suddenly poked its way from the darkest corners of my mind into the forefront, like a screwed-up and discarded piece of paper unfolding to reveal wonderful plans written on it in glorious colours.

I could see the house accommodating students. People travelling to this beautiful corner of the moors to learn to bake, then spending evenings sitting out in the gardens with chilled wine, eating the results of their labours. Me, in chef's whites, organisation plans and recipes tacked up on the oak cupboard doors and the pantry full of rows of produce. And Ned, fixing things. No, that wasn't right.

'What would you do?' I asked. 'I mean, if this hypothetical cookery school ever comes off?' I cocked my head at him. 'You aren't going to be happy mowing lawns and screwing chairs back together forever, are you? You're too restless and it would be a waste. You're not a handyman, for all you pretend so hard. I saw you with Joe. You're a doctor underneath and you always will be.'

Outside the pantry, Kez whined and a black paw appeared in the gap under the door. We both ignored it.

Ned turned and pretended to wipe some dust off the back of a shelf with his sleeve. 'PTSD,' he said carefully. 'It doesn't just go away. It sits like... like shingles, away in the back of everything, waiting for that raw moment when you wonder "am I right?" And then, bam, there it is roaring back in to infect everything you do, every thought you have. When you think it's all over, it won't let you go. You're going to find the same, I'm afraid. Well, you did, back there.' A jerk of his head in the vague direction of where I'd left my car. 'Just wanting to be better doesn't always make it so, and it's no way to live.'

'Oh, Ned.'

'You saw me with Joe, yes. I can still doctor, in the moment, in an emergency all the training comes in, but – you also saw afterwards.' Now he crossed the small bit of flagged floor that had lain between us. 'I can't go through that every time,' he said quietly. 'It's too much.'

I looked into his brown eyes, saw the ages of pain that lay tucked away behind them. 'Then what will you do?' I slid a hand onto his arm. 'You need to have something.'

He smelled clean. Of air and water and light. As though he'd come built by nature. 'There will be something for me. Hell, maybe I can make a go of the photography. I sold half a dozen pictures yesterday on the handicrafts stall, maybe there's a future for me in that. There's an old stable round the front I could convert into a darkroom, maybe make my own frames. There will be something,' he repeated. 'Things that don't involve people dying in front of me.'

'But you will always be a doctor, underneath.'

'Oh, yes.' He touched my hair now. Almost wonderingly, he pushed his fingers through the wind-tangled mass and smiled to himself. 'It might come in useful. You know, poisoning, choking, dreadful stabbings with kitchen implements.'

'We'll be running a cookery school, not a murder mystery.' I smiled too.

'And I know you think it's a waste of an education. My parents do too, and they haven't stopped reminding me, but I don't think I was ever really cut out for the medical world. I'm too...' He was looking right into my eyes now. I wondered if he was trying to see my truth, to see whether I thought of him as soft, or damaged, too beta-male to be anything other than background.

'Too confused, maybe,' I said. 'Too burned out.' This quiet, edge-of-the-moors location, with its big fireplaces and low ceilings, seemed so much more 'Ned' than any medical surroundings. He was gentle, he was calm and quiet, moving through the world causing as little fuss as possible. Almost not wanting to be seen. There would be a lot to unpack about his upbringing, I suspected, but we'd get there. We would definitely get there, in time. 'You need to be here. You need this.' I waved the hand that wasn't on his arm.

'Maybe something a *little* more comfortable than a larder.'

'You know what I mean.'

Now he *was* kissing me. We moved out of the pantry, still kissing, and up the stairs to Ned's bedroom, with a dispirited collie padding at our heels. In the doorway, we stopped.

'Is this all right?' Ned whispered. 'Are you sure? Because I don't want this to be just – a thing.'

'I don't think it could be "just a thing",' I whispered back. 'The guys wouldn't let it be. I think they've got us married in their heads already anyway – I'm sure Margaret is discreetly working on an embroidered tablecloth for my "bottom drawer".'

'I still need to hear you say it.'

Outside swifts screamed as they dived past the window.

'Just shut the door.'

'There's no neighbours, you know.' Ned smiled, his eyes

mischievous again now. He'd swung away from the traumatised doctor and back to the fey.

'No, but there's a collie who will take any opportunity to climb in bed with us.'

Ned slid the door shut with his foot. 'Sorry, Kez.'

The dog and his resigned expression sloped off down the landing as the door closed. 'He's probably going to drink out of one of the toilets now, in revenge,' I said.

'Well, there's a thought to kill the mood.'

But it didn't.

The sun slowly moved around to shine obliquely in through the window, the swifts shrieked their way off elsewhere and eventually there was nothing but warm air and a wood pigeon doing its best to imitate an owl in the branches of the oak tree.

* * *

I stretched lazily on the linen sheets and stared up at the beams. Beside me, Ned was using me as a living anatomical chart, running his fingers along my ribcage as though checking for damage, and then down to my hip bones. He'd kept his watch on, the dark strap incongruous against his skin.

'Is that so you can take my pulse?' I put my hand on his wrist.

'Ha! No. Force of habit, I think. There are no clocks in this place and I keep putting my phone down and forgetting where I left it. Hence...' He wiggled his wrist.

'So it's not you keeping an eye on the time whilst we're having sex because you're waiting for the football to start?'

He scrabbled to a sitting position. 'No! Good Lord, woman, your ex was a piece of work, wasn't he?'

'Sorry.'

'Anyway, I'd just set an alarm. There may not be any clocks, but there's a lot of Alexa.' He smiled and there was a new relaxation about his face. A new nakedness that had nothing to do with our current unclothed status, or maybe it did. Maybe this, our moving the relationship to a different level, made him drop a guard he wasn't even aware of.

'Shut up.' I stretched again. This wonderful room, with the bare floors sanded to an oak-boarded perfection, minimal furniture and the huge old bed, invited laziness and bed-picnics and all day-lovemaking. The man with me invited pretty much the same, with his limbs lightly tanned and dusted with hair and his knowledge of the female body. 'We ought to get up.'

'Ought we?' He raised his eyebrows.

'Yes. Kez needs feeding, and another walk. And I'm hungry too.'

From outside the door there was the thumping sound of a wagged tail of agreement.

'Has he been out there listening to us this whole time, do you think?' Ned looked startled.

'Probably. But it's all right, he won't tell. Anyway, he probably found himself another bed to lie on and you'll go into one of the other rooms and find a collie-shaped dent and lots of hair. He's only making his presence felt now because it's dinner time.' I elbowed my way to sitting. A pillow-mass behind me like a fleet of clouds reminded me that Ned had bought hotel-quality bedding for all the rooms, which also accounted for our reluctance to get up.

'Right. Another quick stroll by the stream, and then we'll make something to eat.' Ned stopped himself. 'No. *I* will make us something to eat. You cook all the time, you won't want to do it on your day off.'

And, just like that, I fell in love with Ned. I'd liked him up until now, but even the competent distraction of sex had only added lust to the liking. But his thoughtfulness about not expecting me to cook tipped the whole list over into love. It would take time, of course, there would be many more conversations, and his parents were going to be a tough act to get over, but – yes. We'd got something here.

20

It was Monday and I was back in my own kitchen, turning biscuits out onto a wire tray to cool whilst listening to the sounds of guitars being tuned in the hall. Everyone capable, it seemed, was wanting to recreate the sounds of Universal Heat Death, or maybe just the sounds of their youth.

Ned wandered over, put his chin on my shoulder for a second, stole a biscuit and went back into the hall to help with setting up amps. The newly-formed band was about to have its first practice session, and they'd decided to have it where everyone could listen, so a few of the more sensitive souls had relocated to folding chairs in the car park, where they were exchanging magazines and discussing the hot weather. Ned had just taken them out a tray of soft drinks.

I looked at my biscuits. Pretty good, although I said so myself, crisp around the edges and soft in the centres, no challenge to older teeth but still with a satisfying crunch. Teaching people to do this, people who'd always believed that they couldn't cook, people who'd survived on microwave meals and takeaways, would be tough but fun. Future-me would enjoy it. But that was for then, for forward planning and making arrangements and setting up. For a future that I knew Ned and I could forge together. But right now, the future held preparing seventeen lunches, washing some cushion covers and booking someone to come and look at the leaky roof before winter.

For now these people needed us. One day we'd be ruled financially unviable, and that day was inching ever closer. There would be incremental moves made away from the hall – the odd day spent exploring the lounge at the care home, maybe attending open days there, and then, first closing us on Mondays, then having us only open three days a week, with the home providing its snacks and teas to take the sting out of no longer being able to spend all day in the hall. And then... and then. Budgets and the council's desire to sell our building for housing would win out, as we always knew it would. But hopefully, by then, we'd have the kitchen up and running and I'd use weekends to start teaching – and Ned and I would have a future.

I just hoped our current clients wouldn't see that day. Listening to the laughter and feedback whine from the hall, the banter and light arguing so much part of my day, I couldn't really imagine it stopping. For now, the reimagining of Universal Heat Death was providing such entertainment and occupation that it had given everyone a new lease of life.

I took the biscuits through and put them on the table and the band instantly broke off from fiddling with instruments and herded around the baked goods.

'If we're good enough, my lad says we could play a gig for them, up at the works.' John had his guitar slung around his neck, where it swung and got in the way of the biscuit-eating, but marked him as 'with the band', a role he was relishing.

'My granddaughter works at the Co-op,' Grace said, tapping her electronic drum kit experimentally. It had taken some persuasion to get her to use it, but transporting a full drum kit to and from the hall every week was not on her family's agenda, so she'd caved in and now had a wonderful set of pads that plugged into a computer. It could also, her granddaughter had admitted to me with some relief, be used with headphones, so the entire household didn't have to listen to the nightly practice. 'She said they'll let us play outside for a couple of weekends, to raise some money.' She tapped again. 'As long as I promise to keep my vest on.' She gave me a grin and waggled her eyebrows and Tom had to go for a little sit down outside.

To my surprise, Mimi wasn't sitting in her usual chair by the window. She had started out the day there, having inched her way from the minibus with Ned's help, recommencing her silent stare across the car park. But as the others had arrived and unloaded the guitars, double bass and drum kit, I'd noticed her casting the odd glance away from the less than riveting view. And now, here she was, standing leaning on her stick and looking at John and his guitar with an engagement that she'd previously only shown when stroking Kez.

'Would you like a biscuit, Mimi?' I thought I'd give it another try.

I wasn't just surprised, I was astonished enough to lower the plate when she said, 'No. Thank you.'

Accented English, French or German, I thought.

'How about a cup of tea?' I asked, sounding a little weak because she'd taken the wind out of my sails by actually replying.

'A tea, I think.' She moved a few painful steps forward, towards John. 'Thank you.'

I looked across the room at Ned, who was screwing something into the back of something else. He met my eye and smiled. Unsurprised, but then it was quite hard to surprise Ned, with his even temperament that gave no hint of the power and passion, of the thoughts and stresses that raged underneath. Maybe he'd learned that 'nothing fazes me' expression at medical school, I thought. Apart from his breakdown in the kitchen, after the Joe incident, and a few, less tearful outbursts when we were in bed, Ned had 'unflummoxed' off to a T.

I poured Mimi a tea and left the pot on the table and by the time I got the cup and saucer to her, she was talking to John, about the band.

'Are you going to play? For people?' she asked.

John was as unruffled by Mimi's new-found desire to communicate as Ned seemed to be. 'Well, yes. If we can persuade, bully and blackmail people into letting us. We won't necessarily want paying,' he said, looking thoughtfully at Harry, who was holding his newly borrowed guitar upside down. 'Although it might be nice,' he added. 'Bit extra on the pension. Show these young types that we're not all washed up just because we're older.'

Margaret and Lena were fluttering around, helping to hold things and generally demonstrating that age was no barrier to a band attracting hangers-on. 'There are always places wanting music,' Lena said. 'Lots of opportunities for live bands, at the pubs and so on.'

'Well, first things first,' John put in. 'We need to practise. Get ourselves together. And get Harry to learn how to hold that bloody thing properly.' He leaned over and turned Harry's guitar the right way up. 'Maybe next summer. For fetes and flower shows and stuff.'

'And outside the Co-op,' Grace threw in.

'You will need costume,' Mimi said. She spoke assertively, as one who is used to being listened to, her accent sounding very exotic among the Yorkshire that was prevalent here. 'For cohesion, you know. T-shirts or some jackets that will all match.'

'Well. Er, yes, I suppose we will.' Will, trailing biscuit crumbs and a bass guitar, leaned over. 'To make us look like a proper band, not just a bunch of old geezers who wandered in off the street.'

'I will design.' There was no brooking that tone. Mimi had spoken. 'It was my job, you see. Before...' She looked down at a twisted hand resting on her stick. 'Before I retired,' she finished. 'I will design on a computer, but someone else must do the sewing. I cannot sew now.' Another look at her arthritic fingers.

I helped her walk back across the room to her customary chair, carrying her teacup for her.

'You must have found retirement difficult,' I said. I wanted to keep her talking and didn't want her to lapse back into her silent world of geraniums and concrete.

'I have been useless.' She spoke very matter-of-factly. 'When my husband died, my family brought me over here to live with them. I cannot help with the house, I cannot help with the animals. I must sit always. The children do not need me, they are too old. My grandson and his wife, they are kind, but they are very busy. So they send me here.' She waved her teacup to indicate the hall. 'Where I am useless.'

My heart ached for her. Uprooted and brought to England, with no role to play.

'I designed costumes for the big shows, you see.' Mimi laid her cup back on its saucer, carefully removing her tangled fingers from the handle. 'And for the musicians. I made clothes for Abba.' She nodded in fond recognition. 'Also for Michel Sardou.' A small nod. 'You will not know him, I think. He's very famous in France.'

'You're French?'

Another graceful nod. 'Here, I am nothing. I cannot always follow the talking – the accents, you know. I cannot move. I cannot sew. I am not needed.'

'Oh, Mimi.' I wanted to touch her, to reassure her that she was very much needed, but there was a ramrod straightness to her, a glint in her eye that told me that such sympathy was not required.

'But if they wish, I will design a uniform – *non, pas de uniforme* – a *costume* for the band. I can do this.' Another glint in the eye. 'It is my job.'

'Oh, my goodness.' It was all I could say.

'I will enjoy it, I think.' Mimi smiled now. 'Oh, and your cooking? It is very good. Almost as good as the French.' The smile was a definite grin now.

'Seren! Holly's here!' Margaret rattled her cup in my direction. 'She's in the kitchen.'

I left Mimi to her tea, and to John, who had shuffled his way over to consult with her. Of all of our clients, John had the least broad Yorkshire accent, so I hoped she'd be able to understand him. I'd never thought of it before. But then, we hadn't known Mimi was French before, couldn't make allowances for her, so maybe we weren't totally to blame.

'Seren!' Holly had a gleam about her as she perched herself on one of the kitchen stools. 'Oh, it's been amazing!'

'Has it?' I hitched myself up alongside her and pushed the plate of biscuits-that-hadn't-turned-out-quite-so-well towards her. 'It's been pretty amazing here too, actually.' I was thinking about Ned, about his offer to use his house as a cookery school, about his slender, slightly bronzed body in those linen sheets and his careful gentleness. But she didn't need to know any of that, of course.

'Things have gone viral on the YouTube!' Holly always behaved as though current technology were a flash in the pan and people would soon see the error of their ways and go back to three TV channels and writing letters. 'The band you got to play and our clients dancing! It's all over the TikTok thing.' She looked around vaguely, as though TikTok might be manifesting through the walls.

'The newspaper and TV people got hold of it, then?' These

biscuits could use a touch of salt, perhaps. Just something to lift the flavour a little.

'Oh, yes! And John – *is* it John? – yes, John taking that young man's guitar and starting to play.'

'Oh, social media is going to *love* the band they are setting up, then,' I said, hoping that social media was ready for them and that the exposure wouldn't encourage Grace to take her clothes off.

'Are they? Oh, yes, then, I suppose it will. We got into *The Guardian*, you know. This morning. I'm out to buy copies so we can put cuttings in frames. People want to come and talk to us and we may even get some TV coverage.'

Behind us, Ned came into the kitchen, with his sleeves rolled up and a screwdriver jutting from his shirt pocket. 'Hello, Holly. Hey, Seren.' He gave me a brief kiss that sent Holly's eyebrows up into the fringe of her careful bob. 'What are we talking about?'

'The guys have gone viral.' I moved over on the stool so he could prop himself alongside me.

'And it's all thanks to Seren and her quick thinking.' Holly was clearly employing some pretty quick thinking of her own – her eyebrows had come back down and she was behaving as though her handyman and housekeeper were usually all over one another. 'So I came to say thank you.' She turned back to me. 'If you hadn't got Universal Heat Death to play for the open day, it would have been a disaster.'

'Not quite, it would just have been a tea stall and some handicrafts, that's all,' I said.

'I sold loads of photographs.' Ned pinched a piece of my biscuit. I had to say that I thought he was maybe overdoing the 'Look! We're a Couple!' just a touch, but it was fine. Quite nice, in fact, to feel his body alongside mine, as though it belonged there.

From beyond, in the hall, there was a chord struck and then a good deal of feedback whine. 'Damn. Thought I'd got those speakers set up right.' Ned stood up again. 'I'd better go and adjust them before people start banging on the walls.'

Holly and I watched him go. 'You and Ned,' Holly said, after the door had closed on a burst of laughter.

'Yes.'

'Ah.'

'And I've got a dog.' I thought now, whilst in Holly's good books, might be as good a time as any. 'In the flat.'

'Oh.' Holly took another biscuit. 'Is it a big one?'

'Quite a big one, yes.'

'That black and white one? That everyone said was Ned's dog? In the hall, the other day?'

'Yes. Sorry,' I added.

Holly shrugged. 'Everyone seems to love him.'

'He's a very good dog.'

There was so much we weren't saying aloud, but that was leaking through in our body language. My worry, her slight concern, my apologies, her decision that it didn't, after all, matter that much. We'd known one another a long time, Holly and I. Plus, I *had* saved the entire open day from failure and got us onto TikTok.

'We won't worry about that, then,' Holly said finally. Then, 'Are they really going to start a band?'

'I'm very much afraid that they are, yes.'

Another, louder note, and then someone, predictably enough, played the opening bars to 'Stairway to Heaven'.

'But they won't be doing it in the hall. Roger's letting them have his shed to practise.'

Both Holly and I looked across the car park to Roger's shed, and our eyes met as we privately and silently agreed that the distance might not be sufficient, but it was better than nothing.

Better than them practising in the hall, if the number of people currently sitting outside was anything to go by.

Holly bustled for a moment, moving around the kitchen and touching things: the tea towels – Castles of Wales again today – my line of mixing bowls, the jars of ingredients carefully displayed on the shelf in case of spot inspections from the food safety people. Then she stopped and spoke without looking at me.

'It's all going to be all right, isn't it, Seren?'

I thought about what I now knew about my parents. About all those secrets Andrew had been keeping from me, and about Ned and his past. Then I thought, unexpectedly, about Mimi. About the new band, rapidly coming together in the hall. New futures. New interests. Things always moving forwards. And I thought about Ned, lovely, straightforward Ned and the way he'd held me in that oak-scented bedroom filled with light.

'Do you know, Holly, I think it will be?' I said, and ate another biscuit.

A VERY EASY BUT VERY FLASH CAKE

For When You Have To Knock Out A Showstopper Cake For An Open Day (or birthday or even a wedding) At Short Notice

Firstly you will need three Victoria sponge tins. As long as they are the same size, it doesn't matter what size that is. Grease and flour these, and you can bottom-line them too, if it makes you feel better.

Now you make an ENORMOUS amount of sponge-cake mix. For the size of the tins I use (and sorry, this is in ounces, because I can only cook this cake in ounces too, no idea why...) 12 oz butter, 12 oz flour, 12 oz sugar and six eggs. Make sure that the butter is soft (you can, of course, use margarine or any other cooking spread of your choice, I just prefer butter) before you put it in the bowl, and sieve your flour, but apart from that just chuck it all in together. I know this is non-tradi-tional, but Delia Smith says it's OK, and if it's all right with Delia, then it must be all right.

Now mix. If you've got a food mixer or hand blender this is easy. If not, you are going to develop biceps. Mix as though your very life depends upon it (which it may, depending on whom the cake is for). Once it's all blended and looks like a cake mix should, take 1/3 of the mixture out of the bowl and put it in another bowl. Stir into this 1/3, a tablespoonful of cocoa powder. (If you want to make this cake precisely, then you should really make this mixture separately, lower the amount of flour you put in by 1 oz and use 1 oz of cocoa powder instead, but we are in a hurry here!) DO NOT USE DRINKING CHOCO-LATE! It must be cocoa powder and the darkest you can find. It's more for the colour than the flavour though, so don't worry if you've only got the cheap stuff. But I cannot emphasise enough, NOT DRINKING CHOCOLATE.

To the other 2/3 of the mixture, add about half a teaspoon of vanilla extract/essence/bean paste, whatever you've got. If you haven't got any, don't worry.

Now put these mixtures into the three tins. The chocolatey one goes in one tin, the other mix is split between the other two. Shove them in an oven at 180 degrees C and cook. Timings will depend on the size of your tins, but keep an eye on the colour and you will be also able to smell when they are nearly done. Check by pressing very gently on the top of the middle of the sponges. When the mark your finger makes springs back up and doesn't stay indented, your cakes are done.

Take them out and let them cool. Wire trays are great for this, especially if you need to hurry things along, and if you need to cover them, a clean tea towel works well.

Whilst your cakes are COOKING (not cooling, unless you have plenty of time), make the fillings.

You need roughly, again, depending on the size of your tins and how much filling you like, about five 100g bars (I know I'm mixing metric and imperial here, but it doesn't matter) of white chocolate (preferably not cooking chocolate, although cheap eating chocolate is fine) and two 100g bars of dark chocolate, about 175g of butter and a carton of double cream. If you can lay your hands on any raspberries or strawberries, now is the time, too.

Melt the chocolates, separately, in bowls. Now you can do this the old-fashioned way, over hot water, but I do it in the microwave. Break the chocolate up into bits, add half the butter and cream into each, and zap for about 10 seconds at a time, then stir. The white chocolate bowl will probably melt faster, but you NEED TO KEEP WATCHING. Don't be tempted to shove it in for 30 seconds while you go for a wee, the chocolate will sense your absence and burn or go solid. If either of these things happen, then you have to throw it away and nobody wants to throw chocolate away, do they?

So, in and out of the microwave until the chocolate has melted and the contents of your two bowls (the dark chocolate and the white) look like sauce. Now, put them in the fridge until your cakes have cooled. This bit is an imprecise science, because you want your chocolate to still be spreadable when the cakes are cold enough to be spread on, although if your chocolate sets too solid to spread when you need it to, another ten second zap in the microwave will usually get it loose enough. If you over-zap and it goes runny, you have to put it back in the fridge again until it's the right consistency.

Right. Now get your cake plate and put one of the vanilla sponges onto it. If the cake is very puffy you may need to level the top off with a sharp knife, otherwise your stack will be unstable (it's all right, you are allowed to eat those offcuts). Onto the top of this, spread half of your white chocolate icing (it's actually a ganache, but let's not get fancy here). If the icing starts to drag the cake and pull crumbs off, it's too hard. Give it a quick zap until it behaves better, but not too much or it will just slide off the cake. It needs to be the consistency of softish butter. So, a nice even coating of this white chocolate goes on and then you fetch your dark chocolate sponge. Stick that, with any necessary and appropriate trimming, on top of the white icing. Spread your dark chocolate icing carefully on top of this one (be careful, as the cake will be liable to slide off the icing underneath it. You can ice it first and THEN put it on if you think its structural integrity will allow it to be lifted up once iced. Mine never will, so I ice in situ). Then put the top vanilla sponge on and use up the last of the white chocolate icing on the top of it. Fancy bakers make extra icing and put it round the sides, but we are talking basic cake here and it can be tricky to get it even round the sides without crumbs.

So here you have your three-tiered cake. Now you can decorate as you wish. I tend to the easy end of the spectrum by dipping either strawberries or raspberries in dark chocolate (melted on its own in the microwave), letting the chocolate set and then putting the fruit on the top of the cake, but if you feel like the risk you can dribble melted dark chocolate over the top of the cake with a spoon, or put edible flowers on, or pretty much anything you like. The contrast of the vanilla sponge and white ganache with the dark sponge and dark chocolate ganache gives that extra 'wow' factor when you cut the cake and everyone sees the layers too.

To be honest, it's cake and chocolate. You really don't need to worry too much what it looks like, and if it turns out to be a little disappointing on the plate, pre-cut slices and serve them on individual plates, where it looks tidier, but just as WOW (and if it looks really weird, put a dab of thick cream over the worst bits). Then stand back and practise your 'it was nothing, really, only took me a few minutes' face, and take the praise. You will get plenty.

MORE FROM JANE LOVERING

We hope you enjoyed reading *The Recipe for Happiness*. If you did, please leave a review.

If you'd like to gift a copy, this book is also available as an ebook, large print, hardback, digital audio download and audiobook CD.

Sign up to Jane Lovering's mailing list for news, competitions and updates on future books.

https://bit.ly/JaneLoveringNews

Explore more funny and warm-hearted reads from Jane Lovering.

ABOUT THE AUTHOR

Jane Lovering is the bestselling and award-winning romantic comedy writer who won the RNA Contemporary Romantic Novel Award in 2023 with *A Cottage Full of Secrets*. She lives in Yorkshire and has a cat and a bonkers terrier, as well as five children who have now left home.

Visit Jane's website: www.janelovering.co.uk

Follow Jane on social media:

facebook.com/Jane-Lovering-Author-106404969412833

twitter.com/janelovering

bookbub.com/authors/jane-lovering

Boldwood

Boldwood Books is an award-winning fiction publishing company seeking out the best stories from around the world.

Find out more at www.boldwoodbooks.com

Join our reader community for brilliant books, competitions and offers!

Follow us

@BoldwoodBooks

@BookandTonic

Sign up to our weekly deals newsletter

https://bit.ly/BoldwoodBNewsletter

Printed in June 2023
by Rotomail Italia S.p.A., Vignate (MI) - Italy